Praise for
WHAT I HAD BEFORE I HAD YOU

"Gorgeously crafted, Cornwell's tale shimmers and shimmies with nimble dialogue and poignantly flawed characters. . . . Grafting magical thinking onto gimlet-eyed acceptance, Cornwell's debut novel enchants."

—*Kirkus Reviews*

"Sarah Cornwell's debut novel meshes past and present, mothers and children, and magic and memory to give readers the kind of book they can be glad exists."

—*Daily Candy*

"Captivating. . . . Depth of insight, dreamy prose, and an engrossing story line mark this wonderful debut."

—*Publishers Weekly* (starred review)

"Sarah Cornwell has a brilliant eye for the telling detail and a wonderfully original way of embodying family history. I was captivated by her memorable characters and the perfectly paced revelations of their surprising relationships."

—Andrea Barrett,
author of *Archangel* and *The Voyage of the Narwhal*

"The subtle workings of past trauma on present-day lives underscore Sarah Cornwell's psychological page-turner."

—Vogue.com

"Cornwell's first novel is an authentic and artful coming-of-age story that is uniquely multigenerational. In lyrical language, she renders a turbulent adolescence that is achingly believable and a heartfelt tribute to the struggles of mental illness. Readers are kept on their toes as Olivia's story, by turns endearing and suspenseful, unfolds and the search for Daniel drags on. With great attention to detail and a smooth flow between past and present, this emotionally charged narrative is as memorable as it is compelling."

—*Booklist* (starred review)

"An engaging debut. . . . Well-paced, with enough tension to be absorbing, *What I Had Before I Had You* is replete with lyrical turns of phrase and spot-on details."

—*New Jersey Monthly*

"Sarah Cornwell's first novel is as unnerving and authoritative as Hilary Mantel's *Beyond Black*. This is a beautifully written book, bold and wounding. Read it and you will never look at the Jersey Shore in quite the same way again."

—James Magnuson, author of *Famous Writers I Have Known*

"Only a few writers can genuinely capture that stormy period between childhood and adulthood, and Sarah Cornwell is one of them. Her narrator, Olivia, is a dangerous teenager, and she becomes a fascinating and troubled adult. *What I Had Before I Had You* conjures up many nights in the life of the younger Olivia and one night in the life of the older. The result is an exhilarating, hurtling, unstoppable ride for the reader."

—Margot Livesey, author of *The Flight of Gemma Hardy*

"Cornwell's debut novel is equal parts page-turner and dreamy meditation on the nature of mental illness. Set in the continuous present tense, its characters challenge the reader to establish what is 'real' about real life, and what is 'imaginary' about the oh-so-important imaginary life. An important exploration of the deepest philosophical inquiries into the nature of existence, family, and love. I highly recommend it." —Antonya Nelson, author of *Bound*

"[Cornwell] handles the delicate subject of mental illness and the realities of living with a mood disorder with compassion and grace, providing a new lens through which to explore questions regarding the burden of inheritance, parent-child dynamics, and what it truly means to come of age. Cornwell has previously garnered awards for her screenwriting and short fiction, but if this thoughtful and powerful debut is anything to go by, it won't be long before she starts racking them up for her novels as well."

—*BookPage*

"Cornwell's debut is a dreamy trip to the past with one foot planted in the present. Readers will enjoy trying to figure out the puzzle of Olivia's past, while desperately hoping she finds her missing son. This haunting tale of a childhood distorted by trauma, myth, and devotion will stay with readers long after they've turned the last page."

—*Romantic Times*

"If reading literary fiction truly increases one's emotional intelligence (as a recent study suggests), this lively debut novel by Sarah Cornwell has much to contribute. . . . The novel involves deft plot twists and last-minute revelations that add to the suspense." —*Dallas Morning News*

WHAT I HAD

Before I Had You

. . . .

A NOVEL

SARAH
CORNWELL

HARPER ● PERENNIAL

NEW YORK ● LONDON ● TORONTO ● SYDNEY ● NEW DELHI ● AUCKLAND

HARPER PERENNIAL

A hardcover edition of this book was published in 2014 by
HarperCollins Publishers.

HarperCollins books may be purchased for educational,
business, or sales promotional use. For information please
e-mail the Special Markets Department at SPsales@
harpercollins.com.

FIRST HARPER PERENNIAL EDITION PUBLISHED 2014.

Designed by Fritz Metsch

Library of Congress Cataloging-in-Publication Data has
been applied for.

ISBN 978-0-06-223785-9 (pbk.)

14 15 16 17 18   OV/RRD   10 9 8 7 6 5 4 3 2 1

What I Had Before I Had You

I

. . . .

THE FIRST TIME I see my sisters, I am fifteen years old. It is June, and the ocean is just warm enough for swimming. I am floating on my back out past the farthest buoy. If I turn my head, I can see the beach, glutted with tourists, rising above and dipping below each wave swell. The world appears and vanishes, is and isn't, is and isn't. Sometimes the lifeguard is sitting, and sometimes he is standing up on his white wooden tower, shading his eyes. The closest swimmers are some forty yards off, a few old ladies doing the crawl, their crepe-paper elbows rising and falling. A wave breaks against my face, and I sputter under the water, come up coughing.

Yards away from me bob two pale redheaded girls. For a moment, we watch one another. Our shoulders work as we tread water out of rhythm. They are so familiar. They look like someone I once knew and have forgotten. Their noses are narrow, and their mouths turn down at the corners. Their cheekbones make high planes that hold the sun. At first I think they are identical, but then I see that they are not—that one is made of sharper angles, and the other has a slight pouty overbite. Their eyes are green, and though their hair is dark with water, I can see that it is my mother's hair.

"Sorry, we didn't see you," calls the sharp-angled girl. Her voice is a buttery alto. "Courtney was splashing me."

"That's okay," I say. I kick harder to keep my head above water. I know they are my sisters with a sureness of intuition that I have never felt but have heard my mother describe all my life, like the sureness of the ground to a falling thing. This is it: my first vision, my birthright.

Courtney turns to her sister, and they are caught up in each other. "Race me?" They dive and disappear, and though I watch for them, I do not see them again that day.

THIS IS WHAT I think of as I lane-weave up the Garden State Parkway in a rented convertible: my sisters in the water that first time. Heat blurs the horizon, where cars become indistinct and then vanish. Ahead, too far to see: Ocean Vista. I am expecting this fate for us, too; when we get close enough, we will flicker and fade. By the time we arrive, we could be totally invisible.

Carrie is rhythmically kneeing my seat back to the beat of whatever she's listening to on her iPod. Beside me in the front seat, Daniel sits with his two small hands twined together in his lap, index fingers pressing acupressure points on his inner wrists to stave off carsickness. His father taught him this, and Daniel believes in it so firmly that it works. His eyes are closed, and he looks like a little yogi. I chose the convertible from the rental-car menu because I thought it would be fun, but the kids complained until I put the top up—Carrie afraid of messing up her hair, Daniel afraid he would somehow get sucked out of the car.

"It's impossible to get sucked out," I tell him. "Gravity holds you in your seat. Otherwise you'd be floating right now, and you're not, right?"

"No," he says, unconvinced.

Carrie whispers to him, "That's 'cause the top is up." I try to catch her eye in the rearview mirror. She is wearing giant tortoiseshell sunglasses. She is supposed to help me. Carrie is discovering her power, now that it's just the three of us, and I don't like the devilish tilt of her mouth in the rearview. Who is this spiteful sunglassed person?

I have promised the kids a trip to the beach before we continue up to New York, part of a larger campaign of fun detours and ice cream for breakfast with which I am trying to buy their complicity. I thought I might score points by showing them where I grew up, as if sole custody means that I owe them more explanation, more background, more proof of myself. I thought: We'll buy a box of taffy, we'll chase the waves. It's something I can give them so easily. But now, as we near Ocean Vista, I am starting to feel squeamish. That sound, tires on asphalt. The slack gum-chewing boy who pumped our last tank of gas. The white globes of dandelions in the tall grass. I can almost see myself, a wild, skinny kid, sepia-tinged, running alongside our car behind the guardrail through the untended highway scrub.

We are traveling light, having failed to pack all kinds of

necessary things: Carrie's mouth guard, my reading glasses, Daniel's favorite dinosaur. These things will be waiting for us at the Seventy-third Street house in a moving pod, but for now, we miss them acutely; we let them stand in for other things. In Austin we kept a henhouse and two cats. The cats are being schlepped up to New York by a pet transportation company, but the hens have been left to individual and varied fates. We named them for old Hollywood actresses: Betty Grable, Rita Hayworth, Jayne Mansfield. I wonder which Sam has sold and which eaten.

"Are we going to see your house?" Daniel asks.

"No," I tell him. "They tore it down. It's a Wendy's now."

"What about your school?"

"Nope, that's gone, too." This time I'm lying. I think of the stone turrets, the uniformed girls lining up on the lawn for fire drills, the shrill, doughy teachers.

"What if Dad tears down my room now that I'm gone?" Daniel asks me. I know he doesn't really believe this will happen; he just wants me to confirm for the millionth time the fixed nature of the world. He is worried, lately, by the concept of solipsism, though he wouldn't know to call it that. That the whole world dissolves when he closes his eyes.

"Your father would never do that. Where would you sleep when you go back to visit?"

I drive. I drift. Suddenly, seamlessly, I am in the passenger seat and my mother is at the wheel. We are driving home from New York in the rain, at night. The highway is blank and slick. We have been to the Broadway production of *Annie*, and now it is late and I am tired and thoughtful, and she has made me wear itchy tights, which I am plucking at with my thumb and forefinger. I have just asked her Daniel's question, or some variation, and she is feeding me the same line.

"No," she says. "That house is gone. There was a fire."

I can't tell what she is thinking about: poker-faced, her eyes trained on the road, her thick auburn hair twisted and tied at the nape of her neck. The past, I feel in this moment, is something that parents dangle in front of their children, something hoarded and valuable that we can never touch. They pretend to share, pulling out the old albums at Christmastime, but under their breath, they are saying, *This is what I had before I had you.*

"Burned out, boarded up."

I WAS MY mother's only living child. She told me that when the twins were stillborn, they were so pretty the nurses cried. They were like china dolls, she said, not the froggy fetuses you see in pictures. Little perfect girls: four perfect hands, teeth like grains of salt. Before they were taken away, she held them in her hands, and she said she could feel their goodness and their love, and she knew they would never leave her. The nurses couldn't understand her stoicism, but then, she said, the nurses were limited thinkers. Death was a black door at the end of a long hospital corridor, which they left, obediently, closed.

A year later, I was fished out premature, head down, heels up, screaming at the brightness of the outside world.

My mother told me when I was old enough to listen that my sisters had become the stars in the sky and the shadows of bumblebees on grass; that I had two infant ghosts following me through life and I would never be alone.

We lived off the Garden State Parkway on the inland edge of Ocean Vista, where semitrucks roared by in the early morning. When I was a child, sometimes my mother took me out to see the car wrecks, and we held hands while paramedics lifted the living and the dead onto gurneys. I remember the dangling of hands from gurney edges, gnarled and smooth and white and black and small and large and one with a ruby ring the size of a june bug on the index finger.

"You see, Olivia?" My mother's voice traveled down to me from above. "Death isn't so serious." The mangled metal smoked and the policemen shook their heads, hats in their hands. I remember the tentative heat of a May morning and the circling of a gull, lost too far inland. I can see the small rusted-through place in the car door that had landed on the asphalt near where we stood, the circle of wine-red rust and the dark of the pavement through it, like the pupil of an eye. I had a sense, even then, of the difference between my mother's sight and mine. She looked out over the parkway into the trees, watching the flight of a soul, while I toed the debris and thought about lunch.

My mother's name was Myla Reed. She was a psychic and very beautiful. Men and women—but mostly men—came to our house to hear her read the tarot or trace the future in their palms. When I was home, I would bring her clients tea and sugar wafers before she took them into her study. Then

I would run outside to look at their cars and decide whether or not I liked them by the stuff on the passenger seat or, if the car was unlocked, by the stuff in the glove compartment. A few of her clients were from Ocean Vista and a very few were tourists, but most were from unknown inland towns and sought her out for her remoteness and discretion as well as her renown. When clients left, we discussed them—if their hair was real, if they were flatulent or otherwise hilarious, if the questions they asked revealed loneliness or chaos, spleen or secrets.

We were so much alone together that my memories of childhood are almost entirely of my mother and the ways she animated our house: the folk songs she sang while she dried the dishes, the fuzzy rings her wineglasses left on all surfaces, books left open to their cracked spines. We were never bored, unless it was our pleasure to be bored. We went on adventures: spy missions, animal rescues, picketing campaigns for environmental groups, random acts of kindness. On Saturdays we parked by the boardwalk and sat in the Atlantic surf, eating pizza gritty with sand. She said she could hear the talk underneath talk, and when I was very young, I trusted that my thoughts were laid out for her to read like a played hand of cards. As I grew, I found that I was wrong— that I could hold my thoughts away from her, and this discovery made me bolder but lonelier, too.

I TAKE DANIEL and Carrie straight to the beach. We have our bathing suits on under our clothes; all day we have been slightly uncomfortable. I drive the last few blocks into town, and it feels like twenty years scissored away. The businesses have changed—the pizza parlors no longer Sal's but Al's, chain restaurants and gas stations where there used to be homes. But the fundamental structure of the streets and intersections has remained and recalls to me my bike swiveling beneath my slighter weight, a turn here, a jump there over those ancient tree roots. The people, too, are unchanged: feathery-haired women reaching out with fists full of sunscreen for their tomato-red, indifferent husbands; little girls running on cracked sidewalks with neon toenails and knotty hair; leaning, watchful men outside the bars. I suspect that these are, in fact, the same people I remember, eternally damned to haunt the coast of New Jersey.

Daniel and I wait for Carrie outside the public restrooms on the boardwalk, leaning against the whitewashed wall, feeling the bright burn of the paint on our backs. The beach is smaller than I remembered. Gulls fight in the air. My bathing suit is a somber black one-piece, widow swimwear. I see a group of teenagers hanging on the boardwalk fence, spiked and gelled and pierced, with hard expressions, and I feel an impulse to join them.

"We're going to miss it. She always makes us miss things." Daniel unsticks himself from the wall and starts to pace, lionish, with great pouncing steps. He is very small for a nine-year-old, my little fish, my lima bean. He can fit in a standard packing box. I can't tell yet if this pouncing thing is fun or serious, but I would like to head it off either way, so I dig a root beer out of my beach bag. It's pill time, anyway.

"You want a soda?" I ask. He shakes his head and

continues to pounce. "We can't miss it, Daniel fish. The beach is always there."

"How do *you* know?"

A good question. "Tell you what," I say. "Any beach time we lose, we'll make up tomorrow. What do you think?"

Daniel belly-screams, doubling over from pure vocal force, and then catches his breath in quick shallow gasps. An old couple turns to look at us as they pass. I hand him his root beer, and he throws it on the ground. I pick it back up and wait for the fizz to subside. I see him hooked by this, the bubbles burning away, so I set the bottle on the boards, and he squats to watch. Then I open it and he drinks. I dig his pills out of my purse and hand him one; he holds it in his palm until I've found my own. We count *one two three* and gulp them down, handing the soda back and forth.

"Is root beer beer?" he asks me.

"No."

"Dad let me have beer." He looks at me expectantly, but he has told me this three or four times in the last few days, and I am not shocked. He means a sip. Daniel wants me to be more outwardly angry; he doesn't understand why we are getting this divorce, and how could he? It would be a lie to say it has nothing to do with him, and Daniel can always tell when we are lying. Carrie trudges back from the ladies' room, still wearing her headphones. She is wearing a pink-and-black striped bikini, and her shoulder blades are like sharp wings.

"Carrie!" I saw the pink-and-black halter ties poking out of her T-shirt earlier, but I assumed they belonged to a one-piece. She knows I can't enforce the rules right now.

"What, it's all I brought," she says, and then focuses on something beyond me. "Mom?" she says. "Daniel."

My son is sitting on a bench five feet away, already deep in conversation with a sunken-cheeked man wearing a salmon-colored undershirt and jeans so caked in filth that I can't tell if they are blue or black. Daniel's face is rapt, his mouth pinched with listening.

I call out, "Daniel? Come on, let's swim." I approach, and the salmon man appraises me. They are two together and I am one alone. Daniel says, "Mom, Mom, Mom! This is Mr. Carpenter. Can I go on his boat?" The man's hands, resting on his thighs, shake with delirium tremens.

"We don't have time for that, Daniel fish. Come on." I hold out my hand to my son. His lip quivers.

"We have time, you said we can borrow time from to-morrow."

"We don't talk to strangers."

"Yes, we—" he starts, and I grab his hand. Daniel goes limp so that when I pull on his hand, his whole body slides from the bench onto the boards, and he lands hard on his shoulder. I hate this trick. On the ground, he begins to rage. He rolls onto a dropped paper plate soaked through with grease. He grabs my ankle, and I feel one of his fingernails pull a line through my skin. "I want to go on a boat! I've never been on a boat, he said we could go on his boat and I want to!"

I crouch over him and pin his right bicep with my knee. Let this be a short one. I am still holding on to his other wrist. I try to rub his back with my free hand as he jerks around. "Stop it," I say sharply. How many times have I been gentle and enduring? Carrie has moved a safe distance away and stands scowling, shading her eyes with her hands, trying to blend in to the gathering crowd. "Daniel fish, my love, find your calm thought. Find your quiet room and go inside."

"I hate you!" he yells. "I want to be dead. I want to be dead and not have any more thoughts."

"Let's go swimming," I say.

He writhes and shrieks. People watch. I know what they are thinking. Why am I holding him down like this? *They* would be gentler or more firm; *their* children don't act like this. I pull him to his feet and yank him along with me. He hacks out his sobs. People step back to let us pass, and I hate them all.

I lead Daniel out onto the beach, where the sand is still painfully hot at four in the afternoon. Overhead, the sun is glancing bright like a coin. Daniel's fingers twitch in my palm. Carrie trails after us, kicking the sand. Daniel and I step out of our shoes and run until the surf slaps at our shins. When we are deep enough, I let go of him and dive, and I open my eyes underwater just long enough to see his white legs through the green salt murk, like two lily stalks. He is still crying up there in the air.

Sam has eaten my hens. Carrie is growing up mean. Daniel says he wants to die. If I trace things back to their roots, in every case I find myself to blame: the unfaithful wife, the cold mother, the poor role model, the flawed chromosome.

I would like to burrow into the sand like a worm and sleep. I would like to close my eyes and emerge from the ocean young and blameless. I could just bike back home and go inside and find my mother singing in the kitchen, slicing avocados with a shining knife. My mother's hair is flame and her skin is paper. She cuts the fruit cleanly and it falls apart, the perfect pit rolling out like a glass eye that looks at me. I would like her to say that she forgives me, but even in my imagination, I can't make her speak.

WHEN MY MOTHER died, I came home for one night, and I was so angry I could barely bring myself to look at anything. We scattered her ashes in the ocean. I have since considered the entire Atlantic a sort of gravesite and my daughterly duty done by vacationing in Corpus Christi or Nags Head, lying out on sand dampened by some family molecule. Twenty years have passed, and I have not set foot in New Jersey once. I don't know what made me think I could do it today casually, without consequence. For the truth is, here is the locus of my guilt. I left my mother here when she was sick and sad and alone. When I was fifteen, someone lowered a rope into my well, and I climbed it and pulled it up after me. I like to think that if my mother had waited two or three more years than she did, I would have grown up enough to come home to her. But I can't be sure.

For the longest time, I've found ways not to dwell in my guilt, but now I am here, I am failed, I am fatigued past help. I am floating in my old piece of ocean, holding my breath so as to avoid the present for as long as possible. Memory reaches for me with seaweed fingers, lifts me dripping out of the ocean, and sets me down on the seat of my old green bike to pedal back into that terrible summer, the last summer of my childhood.

. . . . .

2

E VEN BEFORE I saw my sisters in the ocean, the summer of 1987 promised misery. My freshman year of
high school had just ended, and I was free of Burling Academy, the all-girls' twelve-grade school that cost my mother
half of each paycheck from her checkout job at the grocery
store. All year we repeated Latin conjugations and drew
scatter plot graphs. We wore green polyester pencil skirts
and white shirts with stranglehold collars. This year, girls
began to wear their belt buckles on the side if they were single or to the front if they were going steady. I stopped wearing mine altogether. I grew five inches during my freshman
year of high school, but little else changed. I was a strange,
overbold girl with a notorious mother. I was fast and strong,
and nobody would accept my challenges in capture the flag;
they knew I'd just pull them over the line and march them
to jail. When we were shown movies in class, I laughed out
loud at moments that made the other girls cry, and I cried
sometimes in math when we talked about infinity.

I did not have friends, though I knew which group to sit

with at lunch: the fat girls and the nerds, girls without subtlety, who accepted my strangeness the same way they accepted each other's silence or halitosis. I didn't mind; I had
no desire to sit with the twiggy blondes or the A students.
I measured each girl in my class against my mother and
found none of them worth my time. This year I had begun
to admire, from the corner of my eye, the older girls I saw
sneaking away through the athletic fields at lunch, their ears
pierced all the way up through the cartilage, their manner
sulky and sly. They always seemed to have somewhere better to be than where they were. In the hallways, they spat
gum on my backpack and tripped me just as they did all the
freshmen. They didn't notice me at all. At three-twenty, I
would flee the dull prison of the school day and pedal hard
for home, where my mother waited with quiche hot from
the oven and our evening's adventure planned.

Summers have always been respite from the school
year, but this summer, the things I used to love have become unbearable; I nurse a global feeling of poor fit. My
clothing itches and pulls, and all things become shadow
cousins of themselves: songs slide off-key, the sand is too
hot, the ocean a rude blue, mean with undertow. The sun
scorches the part in my hair. I have appetite only for citrus
and cold tea.

I BIKE HOME from the beach, and if I close my eyes, I can
still see my sisters' faces on the inside of my eyelids. I swing
by the grocery store to cash in on our employee discount. I
collect tanning oil, grapefruits, iced tea, and two boxes of

frozen SuperPretzels, and spill them on the moving belt. My mother disappeared again just as the school year ended, and I am set loose on the long empty days to swim, to wander and photograph the tourists, to pity myself and my—at fifteen, I am sure of it—uniquely boring life, to watch sitcom reruns and drink endless sodas until my teeth rot out of my head and she *has* to come home to get me to the dentist.

"What's the matter?" asks the checkout clerk as she scans my things. In the hours since I saw my sisters in the ocean, I have thought of nothing else. I feel as if I have lost the grip of my feet on the floor and am floating ever so slightly through a stage set. This thought makes me giggle, and the clerk appraises me over her glasses. She is too old to be a checkout clerk. She is like a withered leaf with eyes. My mother told me once that this woman lives with her developmentally delayed adult daughter, and thinking about that kind of bondage sets me on edge.

"Spit it out, hon." I don't spit it out, so she sighs. "Is your mom coming in tomorrow? She's going to catch hell."

"I think so," I say. "I'll ask her. But I think probably." When my mother disappears, the rule is to play along. She started disappearing when I was in elementary school, and I still don't know where she goes. Sometimes she is gone for a few days, a week, two weeks. When she comes back, it is always with dark undereye circles and strange gifts. "This made me think of you!" she'll say, handing me a box of dinosaur marzipan candies or an alpaca poncho or a book about walking tours of the pine barrens. She usually says she's been in New York with friends. If I ask her what friends, where in New York, doing what, she will grow cold and brisk and turn from me. These are things we do not share, even with each other: how I learned to cook for myself at eight years old, how I forged her signatures on utility checks and school forms, how I sensed who I could ask to help me in an emergency and who must never, ever know that my mother performed these vanishing acts, and would report us to the county.

I bike home with my groceries in the crate behind my seat. My route takes me through the backyards of a row of vacation homes, and the summer people startle from their plastic chaise longues, flip their hamburgers into the grass as I hurtle past, building up speed for the patch of poison oak where I hold my legs up and coast the last twenty yards out of town before turning up the parkway drainage ditch toward home.

Our house is a yellow box with a flat tar-paper roof accessible by ladder, on which we grow strawberries and herbs in pots and often eat meals cross-legged on old bedsheets. All around the house's perimeter, my mother has planted tomato and pepper plants too shallowly and then mounded the soil around them to compensate. This rectangular burr of dirt gives the house an air of having been dropped from above. Our front door faces out to a little gravel street which is never plowed in winter and always mud in summer, and the rear of the house is naked to the parkway save for twenty feet of scrub forest in which tourist children who didn't know they had to go before they got in the car squat nervously to pee.

Blanche, our dog of the moment, accosts me as I chain up my bike by the back door, and thoroughly licks my shins. Like all our dogs, Blanche appeared at the back door in winter, a starving, sniveling sycophant. She is mostly golden retriever. She grew red and glossy and fat in weeks, so we surmise that she must have had many such adoptions and abandonments. She is Blanche for Blanche DuBois; she has always depended on the kindness of strangers.

In the cluttered kitchen, I pour her a bowl of kibble while my SuperPretzel rotates in the microwave. I open a cabinet and hang on the pulls, staring hard at the shelf of baby food. Before now, my sisters have always presented themselves as infants. Two high chairs complete the square of our kitchen table, where my mother makes offerings of creamed corn and Gerber spinach. Every week she buys diapers, and every week she throws out last week's diapers, spoons the expired baby food into the disposal. My sisters consume less than living babies would, which she admits is lucky for us.

It is my job to clean the nursery each Sunday, a pink and dim and changeless place. Sometimes I catch a glimpse of my mother watching me covertly from a doorway down the hall, smiling at the communion of her daughters. It was hard for me to understand at the age of four or five, when I became conscious of my own growth and change, why my sisters did not grow, too. I couldn't see them, but that didn't stop me from believing. I figured that my mother's ability to see my sisters came from the same place where adults learn adult things, like how to keep track of time or how to fall asleep when you are very excited. As I grew older, I found a comfortable place between believing and not-believing for my sisters, the same place I kept God and Sasquatch. I listened to the neighbors' whispers, and I agreed with them that my mother was gently crazy but a decent cook and a rare beauty.

JAMES SHOWS UP with a pizza I don't want. I eat a piece anyway, for show, though my stomach roils as if there is a wasp pinballing around in there. I feel the slow bloom of this new misgiving: that I am crazy, or gifted, or both. That I'll turn out just like my mother.

James is the most constant of my mother's companions. When she disappears, he shows up like this, with food, with extra lightbulbs. He has a bristly brown beard, from the center of which his pink, wormy lips protrude obscenely, and a heavy head that draws him forward when he walks. He speaks slowly, hatching each word in his mouth, which makes me wild with impatience. I like to flick paper balls at his forehead while he sleeps in the Barcalounger and watch him twitch. I haven't realized yet how kind he is to us.

"What's it going to be, kiddo?" he asks me, tearing paper-towel squares to cover his lap. The pizza drips oil, the way we both like it. My mother would towel it off. I flip through channels and settle on a *Star Trek* marathon. I am in the mood for the neat resolution of intergalactic crisis. In the blue glow of the TV screen, James's face is a comfort right now, his eye-crinkles and even his awful smacking lips. These are the times when I can feel the heft of our bond: We are the left behind. We are in the same boat.

"I'm tired of this," I say after an hour.

He offers the remote.

"No, of *this*." I gesture expansively.

He shrugs. "I don't think it'll be a long one." James knows where my mother goes, and he knows that I would like to find out. But in this one area, he is as strong as she is against my questioning.

I watch TV with half my brain and worry with the other half until it is one A.M. and James is snoring beneath his greasy paper towels, and I am wider awake than I have known I could be, thinking of my sisters. The porpoise curves of their shoulders as they dove. I am too wide awake to be in the house, and almost without thinking, I am out the door and on my bike, pedaling back out through the woods into the drainage ditch and along the highway toward town. Cars are nothing but headlights swooping past me, and I swerve around a deer carcass, its neck twisted, its shining dark eye. I feel compelled. I feel something new waking up.

OCEAN VISTA IS another place at night. The parkway glistens like a river. I can see the grass growing and the sand shifting, layering, wearing away. Everything yearns for itself. Everyone holds secrets in their mouths. Groups of people stumble from neon-lit bars out into parking lots, the men loud and sweaty in button-down shirts too unbuttoned, the women with flagging curls, holding their shoes in their hands. A group of boys beat a smaller boy in the shadows behind the carwash. Vision throbs in my temples. I photograph a woman sleeping on a bench under a red blanket, but I do not wake her.

My camera is heavy around my neck and bruises my collarbone when I ride over broken cement. I turn onto the boardwalk and ride past the dark hulk of the Emerald Hotel. The moon is full, and I can hear the waves blocks from the boardwalk. I feel calmer out here. I feel kin to the moon, full of moonly wisdom. Now I want it to be true: I am a visionary, too. A mystic with eyes for another world. My mother will be proud of me. She will teach me everything.

I feel sure that something is going to happen tonight, so I am not surprised when it does. I have hidden my bike in the spidery driftwood beneath the boardwalk, and I am standing in the surf, throwing rocks at the ocean. Gulls take off up the dim beach. And I see them again: my sisters. They materialize from the darkness into the halo beneath a street lamp, heads together, whispering, and then pass again into the dark. I recognize them utterly; my blood calls to theirs. Later, I will come to know this certainty sensation as my enemy, but now it is thrilling. My sisters are walking quickly, destination-bound. I throw my last rock and follow them.

They lead me along the boardwalk a ways and turn down the stairs to the rides, which are planted in a sunken concrete lot. We pass the sign, spray-painted in silver bubble letters, proclaiming FUN LAND. The closest street lamps have burned out and it is unfathomably dark, but I have been here a million times. There is a swinging pirate ship and a rotochamber, which spins fast enough to stick you to the walls when the floor drops out; if you practice, you can turn sideways and spit on a target feet away. There is a Ferris wheel for couples on dates. There are some kiddie rides— bobbing plastic dolphins with silver handlebars stuck through their brains, the Jamaican Bobsled, the Haunted Ruins. And there is one white wooden roller coaster, the Ocean Spirit. The tracks rise a hundred feet above the boardwalk on a flaking cross-braced timber frame. When the coaster cars click up to the summit, the whole structure shudders and hacks like something feverish.

My sisters walk to the back of the lot and slip through a snipped place in the chain-link fence. A few other forms duck in after them. A small crowd whispers at the foot of the Ocean Spirit, where, against the white timber lattice, I can make out a wiry, dark-haired boy climbing hand over hand. The jagged tree-root ends of the chain-link scrape the asphalt as I duck through. I move from shadow to shadow until I am close. I recognize girls from my school, older girls, leaning up against boys and sprawled on the ground, hands over their mouths to keep from laughing, eyes wide and glassy to the star-backed roller coaster. I know a few by sight and reputation—the gum spitters, the hallway trip- pers, metal-faced stoner girls with nothing to lose—and beside them, Kandy Williams, all bleached blond and black leather. Notorious.

My sisters sit leaning back to back near some ratty boys they seem to know. Courtney lights a cigarette. I want to take her picture, but I don't have enough light. The tip of her cigarette glows orange in the dark. And climbing, that's Jake Ireland, with the beautiful hands. He is wearing jeans and an army vest that keeps snagging on nails and tearing audibly. I see that he has on bike gloves, and I feel relieved for his hands. Jake was in a summer craft workshop at the public high school with me two years earlier, and once he walked me to the nurse when I cut my thumb on the band saw, leaving scarlet pennies of blood to mark our path on the school's linoleum floors. He held my wrist up to stop the bleeding, his thumb in the cup of my palm.

A guy with long blond hair starts heckling him; I thought he was a girl until he spoke. "Chicken! Bwak, bwak bwak." Jake's climbing has slowed. He cranes to peer down at us, and I can sense the fear in him, the tightening of muscles. He is only about forty feet up, but he struggles to hand-walk up the diagonal boards to the joints. His body hangs, dead weight. I wonder if he's thought about how to get down. I look at the pattern of boards and work out how I would do it, how I'd wrap my legs around and swing myself up. Everyone has silver flasks, but nobody is drinking.

Then Jake falls. He glances off a beam and drops five feet. He catches hold of a joint and hangs there. My gasp blends into the general noise, but one of my sisters—the taller, sharper one—turns and sees me. Then everyone is running to Jake, holding up arms, and he drops himself down from board to board to the concrete and grins, ashy, some weird kind of hero. He lies on the ground and drinks, and so does everyone. It gets loud, kids punchy with relief and adrenaline and whatever else they're taking in. Some boys monkey around on the low boards of the roller coaster, showing each other the right way to do it, doing it wrong. My sisters watch them. I move forward, magnetized. I have no plan.

Courtney climbs up the concrete base and tries to hand-walk up to the first joint but drops flat-footed. "Ow," she says. "Laura, you try."

Laura.

"Don't hurt your pretty feet," says a ratty boy, and lifts off Courtney's sandal to massage the sole of her foot. My sisters seem so corporeal. And yet, who hasn't heard stories of ghosts passing among the living—girls in outdated dresses who ask for rides home from dances and get out at the graveyard. The long-dead boy sitting at the top of the hotel stairs bouncing his rubber ball. Right now, in the hallucinatory darkness under the roller coaster, my sisters seem equal parts real and unreal. I tell myself I am not afraid of them. I step forward and say, "You have to wrap your legs around."

Laura turns her elegant face to me, tiger-striped by the shadows of the boards. She says, "So you do it." She looks at me steadily, and I am sure that she knows who I am. This is a test.

I am standing by another concrete base, farther from the crowd, and the structure rises above me, stretching into the dark world. In a moment I am up and climbing, flip-flops kicked off. I use my legs to inch up the boards, and at the joint, I swing into a massive pull-up. I swing my camera to my back and wear the foam strap like a choker. My sisters are watching, and I am proud to have their eyes on me. I am torque, I am strength. I am almost to where Jake fell when the rest of the crowd notices me.

"Who is that?" someone asks, and they are all on their feet, looking up. I hear a girl from my biology class say the word "biology." When I look down, I can see Laura and Courtney standing still and serious, watching me. Pleasure thrills down my spine; I can do what all these boys cannot. I climb. I can look down at the dark huddle of kids below me without fear, without imagining drop or impact, and that makes it easy. I trust in my arms and legs. Quite suddenly, I reach the top. Kids will tell me later that it took forty-five minutes. I stand on the wooden track, curling my toes into the metal grooves where the coaster anchors to the wood, imagining how I must look from the ground: a starless area of sky in the shape of a girl. I feel a whole-body quiver of joy.

Hoots and cheers rise from the ground. I think the noise will draw police, but from up here, I can see that the streets are dark for a mile. I lift my camera to my eye and take a few shots of the view and the drop to prove that I was here. From this angle, the lattice of boards below me looks unfurled, like a swaying length of lace. I shimmy and swing my way back down. I feel dizzy as my toes touch the concrete, not because of the heights but because everyone is looking at me. My sisters are gone. They led me here, to do this. They wanted me to be here.

The upperclassmen slap my back and ask my name. "Olivia." They say it like they are going to say it again. They say, "Wow, fucking rad, were you scared?" I flash a smile and say nope. Someone gives me swigs from a flask, something hot and toxic that I will try to find for years afterward but never will.

Kandy Williams steps out of the crowd and smooths my hair behind my ears with her long black-lacquered fingernails. "You'd look good with bangs," she says, chewing her lip thoughtfully. "So, what are you, a virgin?" One of the older girls claps her hands and bends over, laughing silently. I stumble backward a step and wish I hadn't. I don't speak this language yet. Kandy's face blooms with pleasure. "You are!"

A girl with dark curls and pale, finely cratered skin punches Kandy on the arm and tells me, "She's just fucking with you, she does this to everyone. I'm Pam. You go to Burling, right?"

"Yeah." Pam is looking at me kindly, and there is something to the glances of the kids watching, like they have seen this before. Something almost jealous about the girls. Jealousy means you're getting something good.

Kandy points at me. "You. The Emerald. Eleven. Friday."

"A.M.?" I ask, and they laugh.

LATER I TRY to sleep, but I am too excited. It infuriates me that my mother should choose this particular moment to be gone. I have things I need to ask her. If I am going to see ghosts, I need to know the rules. She will be so happy, and so proud, to welcome me into my gift. I can hardly wait to tell her. There is her pink bathrobe on its hook; there is her Joni Mitchell in the record player. The shower drain is full of her hair.

My mother's genius runs on a schedule. She keeps a chart labeled *Divine Energies* and amends it constantly, adding color-coded lines of rise and fall: *tides, zodiac, holy days*. Where the lines converge at the top of the grid, her psychic convictions run strongest. The overall effect is a kind of braided sine wave, the troughs corresponding to her lowest times. Then, I'll find her in the nursery, staring at the crib, knuckles white on the wooden frame. "Where are they?" she'll ask me. I'll make her coffee and sit with her watching TV until she falls asleep, and then I'll take her sandals off, lift her ankles onto the couch, and leave her.

She is always adding new factors to the chart, trying to make her patterns of mood into an exact science. When she is most powerful, she doesn't sleep at all. Gardens bloom in the backyard, stacks of library books appear and disappear on the end tables. Clients come in droves. Sometimes the cycles are slow—a few months here and there—and sometimes they are breakneck quick. A week. A day. This is not to say I haven't watched her fake a reading a million times. But when she is right—when she feels that shuddering rush of future—she is really right. Once she told a man he should never travel by air, and when he flew anyway, he died immediately of deep vein thrombosis. I have seen her diagnose illnesses that did not show through symptom: tumors, brain irregularities. And throughout the seventies, she had recurring nightmares that made no sense until the

Jonestown massacre, and then she described things about Jim Jones and his adherents that she could not have known and which have since been proved true.

I never doubted my mother's authority over the world. But when I reached the questioning age of eight or nine and began to come up against the brick wall of her certainty, I realized that I would always be wrong by default. She was right about Jim Jones, so she must also be right about how best to knot fishing line and how to train a dog. She must know the most perfect way to peel an apple; there was no room for any innovation of mine. I could never cast a deciding vote in our house; all our decisions came from above, transmitted to my mother by God or by instinct. Though I practiced for months, she wouldn't let me sing in my fourth-grade winter concert; she was sure something terrible would happen. I heard no such reports in school the next day, but perhaps my absence prevented some tragedy. I had to trust her intuition. There was no alternative.

IT IS ONLY Wednesday, and I don't know what to do with myself. Without my mother telling me what to do, I bolt around, making messes. I spend a lot of time on the board-walk, dreading ghosts, hoping for ghosts. I spot James at a seafood restaurant with his real family, two little boys with cocktail sauce on their chins, one crying. A wife with short hair and spider veins creeping up her white thighs. They are seated in a chicken-wire-enclosed patio area. I stroll back and forth outside, making myself obvious, clasping my hands behind my back, until James goes inside. The wife eyes me critically.

James and I rendezvous on the other side of the restaurant.

"You can't do that." I think he might really be angry this time. "You know you can't do that. You look terrible. Have you eaten? Do you need groceries?"

"*You* look terrible."

"Is there something that you need?" he asks me, scanning the restaurant parking lot fearfully. There is. I need to tell someone.

"I saw my sisters," I venture.

"Olivia—"

"And they're grown up. I mean my age, or a little older maybe. Their names are Laura and Courtney. I talked to them."

"Slow down," he says, maddeningly slowly. He pockets his hands. "Have you been sleeping?" he asks me. "Have you taken a shower?"

"James," I say, trying to draw his focus in with my hands, slicing the air with my fingers like he is a plane I am directing down the runway of focus, "I can see them."

"How do you know they're your sisters? Did you ask them?"

"No."

"Maybe you should make sure before you get yourself worked up," James says, backing away. "I'll come by this weekend, okay? You go home and hit the hay." He turns and hurries back toward the restaurant. I stand, considering. When I pass the restaurant patio on my way out, James is trying to get the little boys to stop crying. The wife's cardigan is draped over her empty seat.

I SEE MY sisters for a third time. Blanche pulls and whines at the end of her leash. I am hanging out with my favorite of the boardwalk junkies, Stan the Deserter, who is full-steam-ahead ranting about Reagan to anyone who will listen. Sometimes I take photos for him and develop them for free, photos of him with upside-down flags and X'ed-out photos of generals, and he sets them up all around him and sits here waiting for audiences. Today he is talking again about the boy he killed, a twelve-year-old Lebanese boy with, he says, the face of Jesus Christ, who follows him everywhere, ten feet behind.

I am here also because we are at the best spot on the boardwalk, the corner by the central ramp, where everyone passes through on their way to where they're going. I create my sisters again and again in other girls' auburn hair, other girls' lanky stance or sandy limbs. Each disappointment strings my nerves tighter. I clutch my camera. My mother will come back eventually, and when she does, I need to have proof of what I have seen. How sad it is, I have begun to think, that she can't see how her daughters have grown.

Stan packs up at four, and I still haven't seen them. The sky is white and swollen with rain. The boardwalk has cleared out in anticipation. I walk Blanche down past the southernmost stretch, heading out for the dismal private beaches, where the rich people swim so rarely that they don't note the occasional dog pile, and I let her run free. Just when I have despaired of finding my sisters, there they are.

They are fighting in the depression just beyond the last turnstile, where feet have trampled the sand and cigarette butts hard as concrete. Their shorts and T-shirts are filthy. They pull each other's hair and grind their heels into each other's stomachs, pound each other down into the sand. It looks more like animal play than like a real fight. They grapple and fall.

I crouch behind a stand of beach grass in the lee of a sheltering dune, and I take pictures. The click of the shutter sounds so loud in my head that I worry my sisters might startle, but they don't. I look around for some other witness, someone to tap on the shoulder and ask that craziest of questions, "Can you see them, too?" But there is nobody.

I make myself stand and approach them. I am going to ask them who they are. My breath comes shallow, my armpits damp. I'm afraid, though I don't know why I should be, and I'm embarrassed. Now I know what I didn't know then, that the most frightening possibility was the one I hoped for: that they should say yes, we are indeed your sisters, we are following you through life and you will never be alone. It is safer to live with the possibility that you are wrong than the certainty that you are crazy.

Blanche sees my intention and enthusiastically preempts me, bounding into my sisters' fight. They shriek with confusion and come apart, legs and arms flailing, dog everywhere, joyful and unwelcome. They see me. Laura says something to Courtney, something that I can't hear. They scramble to their feet, sand sheeting from their clothes. They look at me and then turn and run away.

I'm too surprised to give chase. As they tear off into the distance, I see that they would have outrun me anyway. They are lithe as cheetahs. Blanche trots back to me, pleased with herself. I rub her velvet ears and sit down and cry a little bit; nobody can hear me out here, and it is all too much.

JAMES GAVE ME my camera on my tenth birthday, and I will never need another. It's an old boxy Olympus, unbreakable. Even my mother couldn't have predicted how I would neglect the Casio keyboard she gave me that year, forget to wear the little silver locket, but spend weeks upon weeks buried in photography books. This little black-and-silver box presented a way to make the world my own. I was riveted.

Over the years, I have converted our basement into a darkroom. I steal the expensive chemicals from the darkroom at my school, where the stained counters and battered old cameras-to-lend indicate that it has seen more popular days. I crave privacy, especially from the art teacher and her terrible critique wall. The photo club kids have to pin up their work for public ridicule, and they would ruin my plain-truth pictures with their technical speak: composition, cropping, balance. I like the solitude of my dirt-walled basement, where I set up a counter made of a door I found in a trash heap and screwed a low-wattage red bulb into the naked fixture that swings from the ceiling whenever my mother slams the oven door above me.

I buy cheap black-and-white film and crack it out of its plastic shell by feel in the dark, wind it on reels, and plunge it into chemical baths. I watch with reverence as scenes take shape in my tray of developer, first the high-contrast areas and then the mid-values. My photos tell me the truth; when I photograph something, I have proof of it. I have secured most of Ocean Vista in this way: the toddlers leashed to the boardwalk fence, the deep-creased faces of the very old men who sit on benches doing nothing for hours, the cellulite-heavy women who stretch out to dry like caught fish. In a photograph, a person is either present or absent but never in between, and you can stare for as long as you like. In real life, people move so fast it's hard to see their lights and darks.

I develop the film of my sisters with held breath. I had taken most of a roll before I found them fighting in the sand. I have heard conflicting things—that ghosts show up on film as streaky orbs of light and that ghosts don't show up in pictures at all. I clip the film to my strung-up clothesline and stand watching. Slowly, from the eye-ache of a blank, emerge the unmistakable bodies of my sisters, their hands flung out to hit, the spray of sand like a curtain. Their hair is snarled and appears bright white against the black negative sand. Their faces are full of ire and play. They rest taut in midair or curled into the ground. Their hands grip each other's arms, ankles, hair. My sisters are real.

3

. . . . .

SWIMMING CALMS DANIEL down. I spread my palm beneath his small soft chest so he can stretch his limbs out and be Superman. Carrie lies on her stomach on a towel and reads a book about, as I understand it, werewolf doctors. By day they perform open-heart surgeries; by night they ravage the recovery ward.

Daniel hasn't given up entirely on crying, but now he must keep his mouth shut if he doesn't want to swallow salt water, which he hates, and that physical necessity has mellowed his anger. There is new scientific evidence along these lines that smiling makes you happier. Sometimes I try it when I'm alone at home, grinning at the dark windows.

We wade out of the water, and I towel Daniel off with his big blue pelican towel, then burrito-wrap him. Carrie flips onto her back. "So I guess these aren't working, either," she says. She means Daniel's new meds. I dig a plastic bucket out of our beach bag and get Daniel started on a castle so I can talk to Carrie covertly, in an attitude of sunbathing.

I lie on my back and turn my face to hers. Her skin is

flawless. She has grown tall early, and sprouted delicate tea-cup breasts, but she hasn't started in on the greasy or gangly qualities of adolescence. She has my mother's auburn hair instead of my common brown. She is a beautiful tall child, a nymph. Men look her over before they notice me at her side, and then they look away. I am nervous for her and also, I admit, jealous. The rule is supposed to be no bikinis until she turns sixteen.

"No, they're not working," I say to her. "But we have an appointment with the guy in New York on Tuesday."

Carrie groans. "If I don't kill him by then."

"Don't talk about killing. He picks stuff up from you."

"Whatever." I can see beneath her enormous sunglasses that her eyes are closed.

The kids wanted to stay with their father, but he preferred that they come with me, *at least for now*. He meant that until Daniel is returned to an even keel, he is my responsibility, because the gene that makes Daniel bipolar is from my genome and not his. Then he added that he thought we should keep the kids together, and in this he revealed himself. Carrie would love a break from Daniel, and Daniel wouldn't mind my undivided attention. It is Sam who wanted a break, not just from me and Daniel but from Carrie, too. From all of us.

Of course, the kids don't know any of this. All they know is that I'm the divorcer and Sam the divorcee, so they think that I'm the one refusing them a choice, dragging them away to a colorless Yankee life while their father weeps for them, all alone in our wonderful tumbledown ranch house in Austin. I loved that house. I can't bring myself to tell the kids that their father doesn't want them, and this makes me a little proud. It seems like the high road. Already, I bet he is not alone.

Daniel has moved off a bit down the beach, absorbed in the construction of a long winding ridge of sand. The light has cooled, and the beach crowd is thinning out. We should get to Kandy's; I didn't call to tell her we'd be late. I stuff the sunblock and the water bottle back into the beach bag and stand to shake out my towel.

Daniel runs up to me, panting, clutching the bucket, which he has filled with shells. "Mom," he says, "I made a monster, and it came alive!"

"Cool!" I say. "Do you want to take those shells with us or leave them on the beach?"

"Listen!" he shouts. "I made a monster, like a long dragon monster, and when I put in the eyes, it *blinked*. And then it crawled into the ocean, and look, it's gone." It's true that the long ridge of sand he was building is no longer there. The tide has come in quickly.

"Did you make him legs?"

"Her. Yes."

"That explains it."

Carrie sits up. "He's thinking of that sea-turtle movie." She's right. Daniel is thinking of an IMAX nature documentary we saw a few months ago, about the life cycle of the sea turtle. We stared up at the domed screen, and when the baby sea turtles first trundled down the beach and were lifted on the outgoing tide, Daniel reached out for my hand in the dark.

"No! It's not from a movie, I saw it! I'm not lying!" His face contorts miserably; his eyes search me for faith. "You don't believe me."

"I believe you."

"No, you don't," he says. "I can see in your head you don't."

I shouldn't be surprised that he is so volatile today. He is uprooted, kidnapped, betrayed. His schedules are off. He has been battling carsickness all day. I probably let him have too much sugar. Shouldn't I be better at this? My own disorder is so slow-cycling by comparison, and so easily managed, that I sometimes forget what it used to feel like. His diagnosis is early-onset bipolar, and comes with a whole host of new and surprising troubles. Psychotic symptoms. Night terrors. Rapid cycling: a demon pulling levers inside my boy, winding him up tight, letting him spin out, and then jamming him up again. No rest for either of us, not one day of rest.

Carrie grabs the bucket from him and starts going through the shells, picking out the pretty ones. "I saw it, too," she says, and looks at me sidelong. Though we're supposed to be flexible with Daniel, nobody has told us to lie.

"Carrie. Pick up your towel. Let's go."

"No, I totally saw it," says Carrie, her eyes mock-wide, and now I see that this is an act of aggression. "It walked down the beach and floated away. There it is! A giant fucking dragon Daniel made!" She points at the horizon, where the light is a purple gray, pressing down on the smoggy, striated neon-orange band above the farthest ocean. In the water, nothing but motorboats.

"Yeah," breathes Daniel, and looks joyfully back at us, lagging, before he reads his sister's sarcasm. Before his symptoms began to manifest, he adored Carrie, but she recoiled from him the fastest and most completely of anyone. Now it has been so long since she invited him into a game or took his hand to cross the street that I wonder if he even remembers what that sisterly guardianship felt like. I take this moment to grab the bucket from Carrie and thrust it into the bag, along with our sodden towels. Daniel glowers but puts his shoes on, first the left and then the right, in his normal methodical way. I think, as we head back to the turnstile, that for once, whatever her intention, Carrie may have helped me. Ha! I think, as if we are opponents.

The boardwalk is changed in that familiar twilight way: the day people vanished and the night people materializing, stepping out from doorways. It's only seven, but some of these women must be hookers, in all that mesh. Is it possible that Ocean Vista has gone even further downhill than it had when I was a kid? The promises of night in this town feel attractive in a way they shouldn't, not to me, not anymore. It's too easy to imagine myself younger, childless, unencumbered. I need to get out of here. A group of girls around Carrie's age passes us, licking ice-cream cones and laughing. Carrie looks at them hungrily. "Are we coming back out here tonight?" she asks.

We are not, but I don't want Carrie to see how urgently I

need to leave this place, or she will fight me just to fight me. I hurry us across the boards. "I think we'll see what Kandy and her kids are up for."

"She has kids? This fucking sucks."

"Watch it," I tell her, and immediately regret this approach. Carrie didn't curse at all before this year. It's not the words themselves that I disapprove of, but her tiresome need for emphasis.

We pass a storefront selling Italian sausages and pizza by the slice, with a white pasteboard menu sign. Daniel is transfixed by the grill cook, who throws a shower of onion onto the hot black griddle. From the corner of my eye, I see a bench where I sat with my mother countless times, right at the top of the boardwalk ramp. I can picture her there, knitting, her legs thrust out and crossed at the ankle, her lips in their resting smile. I can feel the press of her calf against my shoulder as I play with a plastic truck on the boards. It hurts impossibly much to feel the warmth of her skin and then recall myself to the present and know that she died, and that I left her long before.

I realize I am standing still.

I turn to Daniel, but he is not where I expect him to be. I thought he was at my elbow, watching the man at the grill. I look up and down the boardwalk. The tall iron street lamps blink on helpfully. Vacationers throng past. I force my eyes into a slower panoramic sweep; maybe I am not being thorough. Mothers bend down to their children. Small black birds land skittering across the boards. I look for the salmon man, but I don't see him. Daniel is nowhere.

"Carrie?" I say. "Do you see your brother?"

She is texting. I rip the phone out of her hands, and she makes an affronted face. "What the fuck? He's—Oh."

We both yell his name a few times, but I can feel it: He is hiding somewhere, he doesn't want to be found. People follow us with their eyes as they walk past. Although we are evidently having a problem, it doesn't concern them.

Please not this. I have managed, I have corralled, I have done passably to convey my children from Texas to New York, from one life to the next, despite everything. Not this, not *here*. I look at the cell phone in my palm and see that I am gripping it white-knuckled. Carrie's half-composed text says this: *on rd w freakshow miss u will—*

"Is that what you call your brother?" I snap at her. She stares at me with a rabbitty fear. "Freakshow? Do you think that is helpful? Who the hell is Will?"

"No, Mom, *will*, like, will call you soon. I was texting Alana."

I thrust Carrie's phone in the beach bag. Alana. It will be good for Carrie to find new friends in New York, less princessy. I should send her to wilderness camp or something. Drop her off unwilling and pick her up improved.

"Should we split up?" Carrie offers weakly. "To look for him?"

"No. You stick by me." We walk down the boardwalk, close to the storefronts, scanning the crowds for Daniel, his lime-green swim trunks, his gray T-shirt, his thick brown ‸urls. Of course I would lose him here; this is where I lose ‸le. My past is leaching into my present, and even in the midst of this panic, I feel a sensation of walking a few steps behind myself.

Carrie is dawdling. What is she doing, doesn't she care? "Come on," I snap at her. She stands up, and I see she was tying her shoelace.

"Shouldn't we call the police?" she asks.

"Maybe. No. Not yet." Just the thought of having to deal with the police. And how stupid I would feel if, as I suspect, Daniel is crouched behind a bench watching us. We didn't believe him, and now we are being punished. He will come back when he feels we have received his message. But there was that salmon man with the boat.

I cup my hands over my mouth and yell, "Daniel, we're sorry!" A few passing faces turn to us, puzzled. Daniels, maybe, but not our Daniel. Carrie slumps at my side, almost as tall as I am, her narrow shoulders round, her chest caved in. "Daniel," she calls halfheartedly, and it is her voice that gives me a moment of terrific clarity—my daughter calling out for my son who is lost.

My son is lost. *I've lost my son.* When I grant my thoughts this directness, I feel as if I've woken up straitjacketed—that helpless, constricted terror.

The sun has ignited the orange chemical glow where the ocean meets the sky and soon there will descend a moonless dark. Sequins on a dress passing by. Little boys who are not mine licking cotton candy off their palms. If anyone can find Daniel here, it should be me. I once knew every pier, every crawl space, every alley. And it is my fault; I am the one who brought us here. Unless this is my

mother's work, and I a dangling marionette she manipu-
lates from some high, dark balcony. Imagine: She has stolen Daniel from me to keep me here, searching, forever.
This is my punishment. She wants me to know what it is
to lose a child. I swallow this thought and feel ashamed.
I've been in Ocean Vista for hours only, and already I am
trying to blame her for what is wrong with me.

Carrie and I start by retracing our steps back out to the
beach, where the tide has continued to rise. She jogs to the
far pilings. I watch her slim running form in the twilight,
her tangled hair switching back and forth with her gait.
She comes back red-faced and shakes her head. We crouch
in the beach grass to look into the sinister, bottle-strewn
space beneath the boardwalk. The shadows extend indefi-
nitely over mud putrid with dropped rotting things, a dead,
spread-winged gull, twisted shapes of old windbreakers and
wet cardboard, somebody's bed. "Daniel!" we shout, and
the wet space absorbs the sound so quickly that I start for-
getting whether I've called out at all.

When we have exhausted the dark spaces, we remount
the boardwalk and stand blinking under the street lamps.
Where would I go, if I were Daniel? He would know only
the options visible from this spot, unless he chose to wander,
but that would be unlike him. He is purposeful and decisive.
Behind us, the searched beach. Ahead, a strip of storefronts:
restaurants, novelty shops, candy shops, bars, pizzerias,
arcades. Ocean Vista proper is visible through the alleys
nd down the big central boardwalk ramp: aluminum-
 buildings looking gray in the fading light, dark trees,

parked cars. Over the boardwalk shops, I can see the Ferris wheel and the new spiky spinning rides. The Ocean Spirit is gone, replaced by a metal roller coaster with corkscrew loop-the-loops. I wonder how it went—a death and a lawsuit or a simple collapse. The whole thing tumbling down like Popsicle sticks.

"Let's check the shops," I say to Carrie, and we dash madly from one to the next, making little bells ring as we shove open doors, elbowing to the front of order lines to ask, *Have you seen a little boy?* We agree to each take every other, so I find myself alone in an arcade, angling at little boys of Daniel's build, rapt little faces lit blue and red by the flashing screens, before I realize that this is *my* arcade. My ears ring with beeping and gunfire and boys yelling in triumph and defeat. Here is the same old Asteroids machine, vintage now, the original operating instructions worn away by a million greasy hands and replaced by a taped-on laminated card. The lights strobe over me, and they don't go away when I close my eyes. The noise pounds from inside my skull. My mother says, "Olivia, five more minutes." Kandy laughs and leans on the machine, sticks her ass out.

I run out into the light and smack into Carrie. We stand, scanning, thinking. Where would I have chosen to hide? I am eight, I am twelve, I am fifteen. I storm the streets with my friends. We know everyone, we know everything. Blanche runs at my heel, my sisters appear and disappear on all the benches, smiling, egging me on. The town opens up to me, the buildings hinging into cross section.

I look north. Beyond the rides is the old town—the

naked concrete foundations, the empty littered lots, and, still decaying in peace, the Emerald Hotel. Through the loops and arcs of the metal coaster, the Emerald seems to loom. I see Jake leaning over me, I see Kandy laid out on a chaise, her hair like a sun. Some of the Emerald's windows are boarded up, and some gape dark. The building calls out sadly, it invites me. I take Carrie's hand and pull her north toward the end of the boardwalk. I half-recognize that this is a strange decision; I am now making strange decisions.

As we approach the Emerald, I look at my daughter side-long and feel curious. How unlikely it is that this person came out of my body, how unlikely that I bore a son who is now missing. How did all this time slip past me? Who put me in charge? Here, with the ocean in my ears, it seems more reasonable to think that I am the one who is missing, making my way boldly through the dark town, accepting my first invitation into the rule-breaking world.

4

· · · · ·

FRIDAY NIGHT. THE Emerald Hotel is condemned, full of asbestos and rats. Whoever owns the building long ago stopped taping up the cracks in the windows and scrubbing the graffiti off the brick walls. I have never been inside. Everyone said it might collapse at any moment, and I was a practical child. Now, though, I feel invited to transform: I am a real teenager, a devil-may-care trespasser. So let the building collapse.

The Emerald is a relic of our town's optimistic beginnings, built for a more elegant crowd than ever graced its faded, gilt-stenciled hallways. Ocean Vista was a fishing town until the early twenties, when it caught the eye of a young speculator just back from a summer on the French Riviera. He bought most of the town dirt-cheap, tore down the fisheries, and built luxurious seaside medical clinics and hotels on the European model, as well as the original boardwalk, which rotted through and was replaced long ago. His enthusiasm was just promising to pay off when the country was plunged into the Great Depression, and nobody could afford that kind of luxury. People went instead to Coney Island or Ocean City, where hot dogs and beer were cheap, and rooms could be rented by the hour. Our town benefactor went into enormous debt and disappeared. Most of his buildings stood empty until condemned, and many of the condemned, like the Emerald, still wait in financial limbo for demolition. Around them, the town grew into the thing it is now: not an American Riviera but a tasteless playground for the middle class. Most people who live in Ocean Vista work in the service industries, as nail techs, store clerks, waiters. There is a certain respect between year-rounders that does not extend to the summer people. We live in this ruin, we know the secrets, we hold the keys.

The windows are dark as I make my way through the littered crabgrass field at the rear of the hotel. I picture betrayal: empty rooms, a thick-armed groundskeeper, "gullible" written on the ceiling. I find a stairwell leading down to a basement door that stands slightly ajar. At the bottom of the stairs, wet leaves swim in muck, plastering themselves to my feet inside my sandals. Moving through the dark basement toward a fuzzy area of light, I hear noises above me—a crash and laughter, faint music cut by the slam of a door. I climb stairs, trailing my fingertips across the green-and-gilt diamonds of the wallpaper, mold blooming from the cracks. The chairs on the landings are mildewed and mouse-nested, and the brass of the lamp sconces is mottled green.

I follow the sounds up to the top floor and gather myself for a moment before I push open the double doors marked *Honeymoon Suite*. Inside, rooms full of kids and music—the

Smiths—games of cards going on, one girl down to her bra. Gas lanterns hiss on tables and in corners. The walls glisten with paint, gunked on so thick in some places that plastic soldiers and the front halves of My Little Ponies hold fast, as if they are jumping through. The ratty boys are here, hitting a Hacky Sack back and forth with tennis rackets over a sofa where two short-haired kids of indeterminate gender are making out. This exists? Everyone else has been doing this while I festered in my little house, playing Monopoly with Mom? I pick my way through. "Get off my foot," says someone on the ground, and snaps a leg up behind my knee so I buckle and go down.

From this closer vantage point, I notice that the floor is entirely tiled over with dirt-blackened circles of chewed gum. When I turn my head, I can see between ankles and chair legs to the corner of the room, where the colors remain undirtied: cinnamon red, ice blue, wintergreen. I snap a photo. Then there is running and laughter, and Pam is lifting me up. She smiles at me, tucks her frizzy curls behind her ears, and leads me over to a couch in the bedroom where Kandy reclines like Marie Antoinette. She is talking to, or at, Jake, who sits on the floor with his hands laced together over his knees. He acknowledges me only with a cool glance. I wonder if he is ashamed to have been outclimbed.

"Told you," Pam says to Kandy, who sticks out her tongue.

"What?" I scan the room for my sisters. The relief I felt when I developed the pictures has dissipated. The photographs prove *something*, but what? That others can see them, too? People see the face of Jesus in a piece of toast. All day I have been vacillating between faith that these are my ghostly sisters presenting themselves to me, and terror that I believe this, that I have taken photographs of girls I know are dead.

Kandy rolls her head toward me. "I didn't think you'd come. But Pam had this, like, deep feeling that you were meant to chill with us."

"Look, I already did you." Pam points to a mural that stretches across the wall where a bed once stood, the light shadow of a carved wooden headboard preserved in a black paint outline. The mural is a landscape from a dream, full of halfway logic, buildings rising from lakes that double as the eyes of a huge fish, a volcano erupting, lava spilling down a mountainside toward an impervious hovering town. Parts of the painting are clumsy and other parts exquisite. I look where Pam is pointing, at the edge of the hovering town, and there I am, rendered excellently, a tiny figure standing on top of a tiny white roller coaster, my hair dark blue and flying out wild.

"Like it?" Pam asks. She can't know how well her welcome fits me. To be included, not only invited but *included* in this way, in an image. I am bowled over by this gift. Maybe it's through Pam, but I know it comes from my sisters. The room is warm from bodies and lanterns, and I am in the picture. Kandy widens her eyes at me from the couch. "Do. You. Like. It."

"It's amazing," I say, and Pam rocks back on her heels, pleased. She points herself out, right by the corner, wearing a suit of armor, holding out a gigantic paintbrush like a sword. "And Kandy," she says, giggling, "is there." She points toward the ceiling, where a tiny Kandy sits Indian-style in a cloud, draped in gold, with many snakey arms and an elephant's trunk. "She wanted to be a goddess."

"Fuck you, Pam," says Kandy lovingly, with the intonation of "thank you." She flicks her gaze back to me. "You're the ninety-first on the wall, baby doll. But most of these kids are gone now." She swings her leg down to tickle Jake's side with her toes, red-vinyl polish on her toenails. "Show her Jake." Jake watches as Pam pulls me across the room to the other side of the mural. Paint Jake is flying, arms out to his sides, over the ocean.

Kandy picks up a beer from the floor and swills it. "See, you can climb, but he can fly." She smiles at me for a long moment and then scrambles down from the couch, lighting candles on the floor. "We're going to have a séance," she says. "For the new girl." Through the window, I can see the lights of boats far out on the water.

Pam sits down, tugging me down next to her. "So, your mom? Is she a fake? It's okay if she is. Most of them are."

"No, she's not fake," I say. "But she's crazy." The word hangs in the air. I am bragging, intuiting that these kids will be impressed, but once I say it out loud, it feels dirty. I've never called her that before.

Kandy groans. "Everybody's crazy. Crazy how?"

I think of my mother staring into an empty crib. I think of the three crisscrossed ballet-slipper ornaments that hang in our front hall, and my sisters' faces bobbing above the shifting surface of the ocean. "She's a pathological liar," I lie. "And she thinks that time travelers are controlling the government."

"No. Way," Kandy says. "That's pure gold. You better get the address of your next of kin, 'cause when that shit blows, it's gonna be messy." She mimes a lobotomy with her index finger. "Join hands," she says, grabbing for Jake and Pam. "Who has a question?"

Pam giggles. "I don't think that's how a séance works."

The ratty boys are talking in the next room. They were with my sisters. I could ask them questions.

"Whatever," said Kandy. "Shut up." The Talking Heads' "Psycho Killer" is playing, and some kids are dancing.

Jake stands up, gives his shoulders a little shake as if to get free of something, and wanders off. When he is out of view, Kandy flops back onto the floor and yells, "GOD!" Pam hands me a warm beer that tastes like pumpernickel bread. I drink it fast and take another.

How many of my mother's rules am I breaking? I settle on about half. The rules have never been enumerated, but I know them very well, since, as the only living child, I have nobody else to mitigate my mother's scrutiny of my every act. My sisters are perfectly obedient. They do not make mistakes, and they do not change. They are an impossible ideal beside which I appear to flail. I am supposed to be strong and brave and self-sufficient. I am supposed to live unencumbered by the shackles of social conformity. This is freedom. I am not to associate with, befriend, or desire persons of the male gender (this one is deeply implied, if not stated outright). I am not to stay out after ten, because that's when such persons roam New Jersey, ruining women. I am not to dress provocatively or try to look older than I am. I am not to use substances that could make me a desirable or limber rape subject.

Further, I am not to neglect the nursery or the carpets, to let pretzel crumbs embed themselves in the weave of the sofa cover or soap scum snake across the bathroom tile. When I was ten, my mother turned off the vacuum cleaner one day and let it smack to the floor. "I'm done," she said, and went to bed midafternoon. A month later, the kitchen table gluey with old cheese gratings, the bathtub brown with grit, I checked the divine-energies chart to see how long it would be before she swung back up. The chart showed colored lines climbing from a point weeks earlier; it was just a hopeful guess, like a weather report on the news. The house was wrecked enough that even I could see that a stray teacher or social worker would be justified in making an officious phone call.

I remember the bounce of the screen door that day when I came home to find her slumped on the rank kitchen table, her head pillowed by a smooshed Kleenex box, a brown mouse nosing at crumbs by her toes. Her eyes were round and glassy, like the eyes of a doll. She didn't move when I laid my hand on her shoulder or when I said her name. I put my face up close to hers and sang a little; sometimes this brought her up from what she called a deep-thinking state. *The water is wide, I cannot get o'er. And neither have I wings to fly* . . . The house cringed at my small flat voice, accustomed as it was to her room-filling alto. I thought maybe she was dead, but a spoon in front of her lips fogged and fogged, so I called 911 and watched men in uniforms like spacesuits carry her away on a stretcher. I told them that my daddy would be home soon, and they believed me and let me be.

When they were gone, I went to the closet and pulled out the dusty vacuum cleaner. I slapped a Beatles album onto the record player and taught myself how to clean the house. As I worked, a bitterness hatched in my stomach. For the first time, I thought of girls I knew from school who threw fits when given the wrong doll for Christmas, who complained about having to make their own beds, and I felt jealous of them, where before I had felt only scorn. A few days later, my mother blustered back in, as usual, with bags of groceries, and made no comment on the immaculate surfaces or the soft, clean carpet. It embarrassed her to need my help, especially at times like these, and so she never thanked me.

I AM DRUNK. It is wonderful. I feel like a brand-new Olivia, life of the party, mystic powerhouse, lit from the inside. The sky is gray and purple, and I have no idea what time it is. One of the ratty boys is looking bored on a sofa. I walk over to him.

"Do you remember," I ask him, "last week at the Ocean Spirit, those girls you were hanging out with, Laura and Courtney?"

He shrugs and assesses my chest. "No."

"You were talking to Courtney by the roller coaster, and you told her she had pretty feet. Remember?"

"Lot of girls have pretty feet," he says, and breaks into a grin. "I bet you have pretty feet." He dives for my sneakers, trying to unlace them. I shuffle to get free, but he clamps on to my ankles, and for the second time tonight, I fall. We tangle awkwardly on the floor.

"I'm serious." I try to catch my breath. "Do you remember her? Do you know her?"

"Babe," he says, "there's no other girl in my heart but you, babe."

And he kisses me. I am not ready for it. It is my first kiss, and how terrible. His tongue is chill as lunch meat. Kandy howls somewhere behind me. His hand is on my back under my T-shirt—how did he get it there?—and I feel the muscles in his lips, the hard-on against my leg, the vacuum of his beery mouth on mine. I push hard at his chest, but the suction holds, so I use my hand to shove his face off of mine. My hand is stress-fisted, though, so really, I punch him in the face, mid-kiss. He curses as he falls away.

The laughter of the kids around us is uproarious. Pam says I am fucking *nuts,* as if this is a fantastic thing. I'm surprised again by what impresses my new friends. The ratty boy slumps on the floor, holding the back of his hand to his nosebleed.

"Please try to remember," I say, and he scowls up at me like he wants to bitch me out, but like he is afraid of me, too.

I walk home in the chalky dawn, drunk and pleased with

myself and blissfully distracted. I am a teenager now. I am
armed with new weapons. I fall into bed and sleep at last.

I SWIM UP toward the surface of my dream and hear the
song before I realize what it means: *Sweet William on his
deathbed lay for the love of Bar'bry Allen. So slowly, slowly, she
got up, and slowly she drew nigh him, and the only words to him
did say, young man, I think you're dyin'.* My mother is home. I
calculate quickly: It was nine days.

I'm still wearing the clothes of the night before: cutoffs
and a white T-shirt brittle with beer stains. I stink. I leap up
and dig my cotton flowered pajamas from a pile on the floor,
hop on one foot as I whip shorts off and boxers on. I slip the
dirty clothes between my dresser and the wall. My room is
painted peach and furnished haphazardly—my bed is dark
wood and my dresser is pink laminate, meant for a little
girl; a brown oval shag rug swallows dropped earrings. I
spray myself with drugstore papaya body spray and hope it's
strong enough.

She's not in the kitchen, but something smells rich and
salty and makes me hungry like I haven't been in weeks.
An enormous lasagna is browning in the oven, cheese bub-
bling on Pyrex. My mother is out back, hosing gunk from
the grooves of a tomato-paste can. The world rights itself.
She stands with one bare foot up on the tilted porch, in a
black sundress with gold buttons up the front, her red hair
burning up in the sunlight. Her freckles and moles in all the
familiar places, the old friendly jut of her shoulder blades

as she bends over her task. Seeing her there is like a good breath of air after an underwater hour.

She spots me blinking in the doorway and drops the running hose.

"Olivia! My tiny bunny rabbit, I am home!" She comes at me full-force, grabbing my cheeks and kissing around her pinching fingers. I pretend to mind; this is an old game. I laugh and groan and wriggle free.

"I can see that," I say, and sit down on the edge of the porch, dangling my feet in the grass, as she picks up the hose.

"So. You made some new friends." She wants me to believe that this is a psychic intuition, but I know better: She looked in on me while I was sleeping, before my costume change. It doesn't matter; I have more important things to talk about. The pressure of the visions on the inside of my mind is too much to bear a moment longer.

"Mom. I started seeing my sisters. I saw them three times. Out on the beach. But they were older, like my age."

My mother hoses fiercely at an already clean can. "That's impossible."

"I'll show you."

I dash inside and down to the basement to grab my photos. When I come back up, my mother is spooning baby food into cups at the kitchen counter. I slap the prints down in front of her. "Their names are Laura and Courtney," I say.

She inhales sharply, and I think I've got her with the names. Are they the ones she chose? She's never called them by name. I watch her face for pride, but she is impassive.

"No," she says. "I don't know them."

She is using her absolute tone of voice, and I am baffled. Why is this moment so cold and so flat and so far from what I had envisioned? Could it be pure selfishness—that she wants to remain my sisters' only ambassador? She places a cup on each high chair tray, in the circular indentations, and turns away to the silverware drawer.

"I *know* they are my sisters. Like you know things."

She places two tiny spoons in the cups. "You think you're coming into your gift."

"I don't know. Maybe."

She puts a hand to my forehead as if I am sick and draws my face up to hers, our same-green eyes very close. "I don't see it in you," she says. "I would see it."

"But I *know* them."

"That's impossible. Your sisters are right here." She gestures at the air beside us.

The narrowness of her logic oppresses me. It was easy to play along with her visions when I had none of my own. Now I feel a rising disgust. She is utterly convinced of her own point of view, like the explorers who staked their lives on the flatness of the earth, who stared at a globe and said, *Impossible.*

"Impossible because *I* saw them, not you," I say.

"You're mistaken. Let it go." She pulls her hair off her face, and I see that her fingernails are clipped and bitten bare. "Shall we go swimming, you and I?"

The force of my fury surprises me. I always imagined that the day I inherited her gift would be a great day, a threshold between an ordinary childhood and an extraordinary future. And now she has ruined it. I am not mistaken; I felt that blood thrum of recognition, I knew those girls in a way I trust like my body's will to breathe. If my mother is right and I am wrong, it means that I am not simply *mistaken* but that I can trust nothing I see or feel, that my intuition itself is broken. She must know this, yet there she stands, sweetly smiling.

I grab the toaster from the counter and throw it on the floor. It does not break, and we both regard it for a moment before I flee the house. As I mount my bike, I can see her through the screen door, kneeling to take the lasagna out of the oven. I think of the plastic-wrapped portion I'll find in the fridge later, and I resolve not to eat a bite.

THE EMERALD CROWD absorbs me completely. I slip out my bedroom window after my mother's curfew and back in at dawn, and I am gone again after breakfast. With these kids, there is none of the noodling around about who calls whom first, who sits next to whom. We are like hive insects, congregating, swarming, dispersing. Kandy is the queen; if she says you're in, you're in. We generate so much noise, in every sense of the word, that I can barely hear the anxious whine of my own mind. We sprawl on the beach, we party in the honeymoon suite, we see who can pocket the most candy at Rite Aid. I wait for my sisters to join us again.

Pam wears Doc Martens spattered with paint and suspenders over rumpled T-shirts that she screen-prints herself: ducks with radio antennae, vases of flowers with baby-head centers, a diver poised on a water tower. Being at Pam's house is like being inside a sitcom: Something wacky is bound to happen, but everyone will band together to put things right, and the episode will end with a good one-liner and everything back to normal. Pam's parents, Lynnette and Doug, do crosswords in the mornings and kiss in front of their kids. The first time I go over there, I watch Lynnette chase Doug across the house with a flyswatter, laughing, and she won't tell us why. She is a pharmacist. Pam writes herself prescriptions for Dexedrine or Percocet on her mom's Rx pad. To fill them, we drive to other towns in Pam's hand-me-down Honda wagon. Pam's brother, Drake, is taking a year off before college to *find himself.* There are photos of family kayaking trips on the mantel.

Kandy's has the feel of a flophouse, but all the stubbly guys draped over the couches playing Action Fighter on their SEGA, studying the contents of the fridge, and yelling at one another for clogging the toilet or drinking the last soda—these are her brothers. Her mom is born-again, and her dad just sleeps.

I AM HANGING at one of our spots (*our* spots, now) on the benches in front of our favorite boardwalk arcade. Kandy is watching Jake play Asteroids in the dimness, leaning her forearms on the lip of the game control board, sticking her ass out. Out on the bright boardwalk, the boys are kicking around a Hacky Sack, and the girls are talking. It seems that we are seeing who can talk the loudest. Pam and I are draped over the boardwalk fence, our legs laced between the rails. Pam throws her head back to watch a flock of gulls wing overhead. "You're going to get pooped on in the eye," I tell her, and she wails with laughter. Over on the beach, jocks pile up, diving after a volleyball. And then I catch a glimpse of tangled auburn. My body snaps alert.

But receding down the boardwalk are two strangers, with hair not so thick nor so red as my sisters'. One of them scowls back at me. Pam looks at me curiously. "Who's that?"

"Nothing," I tell her. "Nobody." Panic, in these moments. I feel myself rising and falling like an old helium balloon, and I think that if I don't ground myself now, I will float up to join my mother, high above reason, trailing a snipped string. But I don't know how, and so, because I am trying so hard not to think of them, my sisters are always there, hovering at the edges of my vision.

JAMES IS NOT my mother's only boyfriend. There is Riley, an electrician with enormous forearms who brings me Charleston Chews and, even in the summer, asks me that most inane of questions, "How's school?" There is Terry, who says he works in the import-export business, whatever that means. He brings me books of photographs—Ansel Adams or Man Ray or E. J. Bellocq—and nervously adjusts his long black ponytail. Right now there is another, a French guy who wants us to call him Rocko. He doesn't have to bring me anything, I assume because he is so good-looking. The boyfriends don't bother me; I know my mother will never open our door to a man, not really. They are good for presents and trips but not forever.

My mother doesn't know who my father is. When she was younger, she worked for a madam in New York City and opened her legs to countless men. She doesn't have to tell me not to mention this period of her life to other people, though I am not shocked—I am impressed, even, a little. She never hid it from me, though I understood better as I grew. At some point, she told me, God decided it was time for her to be a mother, and He willed a pinprick hole into her diaphragm. Who knows how long it was before she noticed, how many sperm—of every kind and color—swam through that little tear into the world of my uncertain parentage? I don't envy my friends their fathers. At Pam's house, the bathroom sink is full of disgusting beard shavings; when she wants to go on an overnight, she has to get permission twice.

My mother taught me about sex before I can remember, about the circular journey of the egg and the way the sperm muscle in to fight for position. She said sex is only a tiny flea in the fur of love, which is a magnificent tiger, but that love, like a tiger, will kill you fast. When I asked her if she'd ever been in love, she said no and that she was glad. I didn't particularly believe her, but when she spoke with such finality, there was no way to needle her into saying more. Her past, as always, a locked vault.

Tonight she is out to dinner with Rocko, which tends to occupy her for three or four hours, so when Kandy and Pam show up at my back door with a joint, a bag of fun-size candy bars, and *Back to the Future* on rental, I let them in. "Are you alone?" asks Kandy, craning to see past me into the kitchen. They clatter inside, and I see the house along with them, as if for the first time: the white high chairs and the empty Gerber jars on the table, spilled apple juice sticky on one of the trays. I notice that I have been derelict in my duties—a perilous tower of dirty dishes in the sink, paper water-ice lids everywhere with their lemony crust, heels of bread wadded in countless Pepperidge Farm bags. Pam takes in the tacked-up pictures of horses from last year's *Mustangs of the Sierra* calendar. The kitchen's blue paint is cracked at all the ceiling corners, and beside the refrigerator sit boxes upon boxes of my mother's favorite five-dollar cabernet.

"Score," says Pam, pulling out a bottle. "Opener?"

Kandy traces the back of a high chair with her finger as she studies the room. I feel a nauseous, nervy thrill: My new friends have stumbled into the secret center of my life, and they have no idea what they're looking at. "You have siblings?" Kandy asks.

I scrabble through the drawer of loose utensils for a corkscrew, planning to pretend I forgot that the wine bottles are screw-top, buying myself a moment to think. The impulse to lie is very strong. Yes, I had toddler brothers, but they died yesterday. I'm doing fine, thanks. No, the chairs are for my little cousins who visit sometimes from Trenton. Actually, our house has been rented for a movie set. But why should I lie? As far as my friends know, I am the kind of crazy where I punch boys in the face and climb roller coasters. Fun crazy, not sad crazy. I can tell them about my mother's phantom baby rituals without implicating myself at all. I can tell them I am whoever I want to be, and then *be* that way.

"Oh, wow," says Pam, and I turn to see that she is standing in the open doorway of the nursery. In contrast to the kitchen, I kept the nursery immaculate during my mother's absence. I can't pretend I did this only for her. The bars of the cribs gleam with Lysol lemon. I even ground my fists into the pillows to make the appearance of recent sleepers.

Pam looks at me critically. "Are they out? With your mom?"

"No," I say. "I'm an only child. I told you, she's crazy." It's easier to say it this time. I feel how much further I can go in this direction, and it is exciting. I am not her tiny bunny rabbit. "She had stillborn twins before I was born. She says she can see their ghosts."

"And she believes it?" prompts Pam, opening the diaper closet. "She really sees them?"

"Oh, yeah."

"That's so fucked up," says Kandy, and sighs happily. "So you want to watch the movie?"

Kandy and Pam look a little let down at the ordinariness of the rest of the house: wooden coffee table, cream chenille couch, some pictures on the walls, ceramic swan candleholders, scattered issues of *National Geographic* (my mother subscribes for me, for the pictures). Our curtains are made from old pink and gold saris, and Pam reaches behind the couch to touch them. Kandy says everything is *nice*. "Nice spider plant! Oh, nice place mats."

We have gotten through all the chocolate and most of

the movie—Michael J. Fox is hanging one-handed from the clock tower—when a key turns in the lock. I grab our wineglasses and throw them out the window behind us, followed by the bottle, and the tinkling shatter is masked perfectly by the loud creak of the front door. Pam and Kandy stare at me with puffed cheeks, containing their amused shrieks—again, I shock and surprise!—as my mother steps inside.

"Hi, girls," she says casually, as if this is not the first time she has come home to anyone in the house but me and James. She turns and whispers out the door, which tells me that Rocko is standing just outside, and then she comes in alone and drops her purse on the floor. "Nice to meet you. I've heard so much about you!"

This is not literally true. Since she denied my visions, I have begun to lie more and more about whom I see and what I do when I'm outside the house. Part of this is logistical; I am breaking rules and must not let on. But part of it is an amplified need for secrecy itself.

Outside, the wine soaks into the earth, and a tomato plant starts feeling dizzy. The movie's epilogue unfurls, but my mother sits on the floor opposite the sofa, drawing focus. "Four is the right number for hearts," she says, and she deals us in. "What are you girls up to this summer?"

"Nothing," says Pam, "just chilling, swimming, hanging out with everybody."

"Everybody?"

"Friends from Burling," I'm quick to add, to paint an inoffensive all-female tableau.

"Tell me about yourselves," she says to them, and nods

along to their heavily censored descriptions of their homes, their families, their interests. As they talk, my friends turn toward my mother like plants to sun. The appearance of her deep listening is so inviting, so polished. She is a professional. When Kandy says, "If I don't find my soul mate by the time I'm thirty, I think I'll fucking shoot myself," and my mother laughs musically, a smile of acceptance on her lips, I know she is playing for the win. There is nothing about this statement that, if I said it, wouldn't send her into a desperate lecture. The concept of a soul mate. The selfishness of suicide. I can see the devious clockwork beneath this friendly normal-mom act.

Pam pipes up, "Mrs. Olivia?"

"Myla."

"Can you tell our fortunes?"

"Sure."

Kandy hoots with a monkeylike excitement. I roll my eyes and excuse myself to the bathroom, where I hunch on the toilet, half-listening to my mother's opening ritual. I dawdle. I pinch the baby-fat ring around my belly. The floor creaks. She is going to the sideboard to pull out a deck of tarot cards—probably the standard Rider deck, but the hippie-dippie Morgan's deck if she thinks that Pam would be impressed. She will hand Pam the deck so her question can pass through her fingertips into the vinyl coating of the cards and on into the spirit world, where ghost babies float above us and everyone's just-dead fathers wait patiently to forgive them, granted my mother has been paid forty dollars up front.

When I come back, I see that she is using the Rider deck. I used to play the role of the seeker when my mother practiced. We would lie on our bellies on the loose-looped green carpet, and I would ask ridiculous questions (*Will you buy me a pony? Will there be root beer flavor at the water ice place this week?*), and she would give me wildly inaccurate readings just to practice her facial expressions and her pacing. She noted the implications of the cards with an inclination of her head, a sympathetic wrinkling of her brow, or a curl of the lip. This is her forte, the buildup of tension—the moment when her client watches her face with perfect attention for a smile or a tic that might mean she knows what will happen to him tomorrow or the next day, that she knows how to satisfy his most secret longings. We would play our roles as seriously as possible until we couldn't keep it together, and then we would fling ourselves on the carpet and whole-body laugh.

I used to love watching her read, but now the performance seems showy and false. "You have come through a rough time, but you are very strong," she is telling Pam. "You are in love with a dark-haired person."

"What was the question?" I ask.

Nobody answers me. Pam stands up and hoists her backpack on. "I gotta get home."

Kandy whines: "But it's my turn!" Pam is the only one with a driver's license, so Kandy trails out after her, looking wistfully back toward my mother. My mother is calm and radiant, waving my friends off with a condescension they don't pick up on, pitying their valuation of love. I know how she must see them—innocents baring their jugulars to the pacing tiger. *So young*, I imagine her saying, and shaking her head.

Later, when I can't sleep, I pick the glass shards out of the dirt by flashlight, bleeding from a cut fingertip, and over the next few days, tomatoes ripen furiously and in record numbers. Is it the tannins? The iron from my blood? We roast them and braise them and slice them fresh into salads. We eat them whole, like peaches.

5

* * * * *

CARRIE AND I walk until we are in the shadow of the Emerald. A roll of toilet paper rots in a gray puddle. I lead us around to the back and down the stairwell to the basement door. I know just how to jiggle the handle.

Carrie grabs my arm. "This is crazy," she says. "This building is, like, falling down."

There's still light to see by. I check myself; I should capitalize on Carrie's prudence. She could fall through a rotten floor. "You stay outside," I tell her. "I'll be quick." I hand her the beach bag.

"Why would he even come here?"

"It's just a hunch."

"It's just crazy," she mutters, sitting down on the steps to wait.

I push the door open. The basement is completely dark. I step inside, and it is just like the first time. Back through the square of the door, I can see Carrie sitting with her elbows on her knees, but the farther I move inside, the smaller she becomes until I can hardly see her at all. The staircase is darker than I remember. My feet bump into the first step. I imagine wild-eyed, murderous men waking in the dark.

I ascend by feel, and as my eyes adjust, I can make out more and more: the sconces on the walls, the depth of the landings. I call out, "Daniel?" My voice rings to the top of the building and bounces back down. There is a creak above me. At each landing, I call for him, and always the creaking is from a higher floor, until I am at the top, passing between the burned-out studs of what was once the door to the honeymoon suite.

I emerge into wind. The walls are partial, jagged lath and cinder that comes away in my hand. One whole wall is gone, the suite open to the ocean. I could just step out into nothing. This was the wall with the big window, the one we all climbed out of. I danced here, in this spot. And over there, that was the wall with the mural. I feel each step with my toes before I shift my weight. I call, "Daniel?"

Something bursts out of the darkness, and I shout. It hits my ankles and glances away. Pale furry hindquarters disappear around a corner. Then the cat creeps back in, staying low, to look at me. He is all bones. The last time I stood here, I would have trapped him in a milk crate and taken him home.

In my childhood, there were always animals: stinky lovelorn dogs and pregnant cats to birth in our laundry room and broken-legged mice that we kept in shoe boxes full of moss. I never had a stuffed animal, because my mother thought that real ones deserved our care. They were free to come and go, and not a few of them ended up as grease on the parkway, cats especially. We buried front halves and back halves of things so many times that I learned to love generally and with measure. The animals were not allowed in the nursery. That rule was strict. After all, reasoned my mother, cats have been known to smother infants, and even the sweetest dog, when provoked, will bite.

For a few years when I was very young, we had an old parrot called the Admiral who spouted nautical phrases like "Thar she blows" and "Come about," sending us into belly-aching fits of laughter. My mother inherited the Admiral after the death of a client, his secret nautical enthusiasms outed by his bird. The Admiral ate Cheerios from my bowl and rode on my shoulder, to the oohing and ahhing of the neighbor kids. When he flew off, I waited days and days in hopes that he would come back, that he loved me more than he loved the endless sky. When it was finally clear that he was gone forever, I wailed for hours, and my mother held me on her lap and stroked my hot face with her fingers and told me that the only sure thing was her and me, and the rest of the world could do you wrong, and this was how it felt.

SAM ASKED IF I loved the man I was sleeping with—the one he found out about—and I couldn't answer. People talk about love in a binary that makes no sense to me. Check a box, yes or no. The man in question worked at a bike store, and I loved finding grease marks where he had thought-lessly rubbed the back of his neck as he worked. I loved his square golden jaw and the delight he could take in the stupidest things—YouTube videos of cats, songs he liked coming on the radio, things like that. But he is not someone I could miss. Sam, on the other hand . . . At night, slumber-headed, I am still careful not to tug the covers too far to my side. I find myself picturing vacations we planned but never executed, and he is still there, in the morning at hotels, shaving his incorrigible thick black facial hair, or on the slopes, stacking Daniel's skis on top of his own and showing him how to take the curves, or leaning over Carrie's shoulder and pointing at whales surfacing in some tropical bay. So many years of his lemon-and-coffee scent, his neat-freakery, his three forgetful trips back inside before each workday. It didn't occur to me that I could lose those things, or even that they were things I'd mind losing.

When I met Sam, we were both twenty-six. He was a sous-chef at a restaurant out of my price range and I was, momentarily, a vegan. I tasted butter in my mashed pota-toes, and he came out of the kitchen to apologize, bowing over me and my date, standing his fingertips on the edge of the table. It was his sincerity that caught me. In later years, we would make mashed potatoes yellow with butter and laugh that we met thanks to one of my briefest enthusiasms. No matter how steady and stable I am, with my pills and my set bedtime and my one-glass-of-wine rule, I will always be given to enthusiasms. I know to examine them for source and relevance, and Sam used to help me do that. My enthu-siasm for keeping chickens, for instance, we examined and agreed would be reasonable and educational for the kids. My enthusiasm for wooden boat building we examined, found expensive and unlikely, and mutually discarded. Though I would have come to that conclusion on my own.

I think now that Sam liked being the sane one, the supporter, that maybe it was *why* we worked for so long. My mild and occasional unsteadiness, my monthly check-ins with my psychiatrist—these things made him feel whole. There are times when my disorder gets wise to the chemicals I'm feeding it, and shape-shifts, resurges, bubbles up. I feel that heating-up feeling, a disproportionate joy, or a sour downward slide, and if I don't recognize it myself, Sam sees it in the patterns of my behavior, and I go to my psychiatrist for an adjustment of my meds. I don't always go gently, but I go. It can take a few weeks to figure out the new dosage or the new drug, and during those weeks, I am my own prisoner. I give Sam my credit cards and do my best to be honest with him about my thoughts. In some ways, Sam has been my mood chart; now I will have to work harder for such self-knowledge. Maybe I will keep a written chart again, like my mother's.

The kids never picked up on my shifting moods until last time, and then it was only Daniel who understood. Carrie construed my sudden temper entirely as response to her cutting a half-day of school with her friends. She didn't even use the time well; she went to someone's basement and watched TV. I let her misinterpret me. I probably should have been angrier, anyway.

But Daniel seemed to know. For a week I slept only for minutes at a time. I spent the nights reading fat paperbacks that had belonged to my mother, some with her inane marginalia (*Shocking! How sad. Delightful*). I wonder if she came back to these moments when she needed a kick, as I did now. One night Daniel tripped sleepy-headed from his room to curl against me in my armchair in the yellow lamp glow. "You can't sleep," he said.

"No."

We made cookies and did a thousand-piece puzzle. We met each night like this, furtive as burglars, and neither of us mentioned it to Sam or Carrie. I faced the mornings feeling charged, absent my counterweights. At work, I reorganized our administrative systems so well and so lustily that the vice principal ordered early voting for employee of the month and stuck a star sticker to my shirt.

When I picked Daniel up from the babysitter's house, he watched me. "Did you eat Froot Loops?" he asked me accusingly. This was our question for inexplicable happiness, an old family joke.

We drove to the park instead of home and lay eating Swedish Fish from my purse and watching the sun move through the layering leaves, until some tattooed, shirtless young hippies passed close by and I was struck friendly. We learned to play their drums and that two of them were brothers from Alaska and had never before left home. I let them paint sticky henna on Daniel's back. The characters, they said, spelled wisdom. This seemed excellent.

Sam found us in the twilight, having spotted the car. He busted into our fairy circle in a polo shirt, clean-shaven, intolerable, jangling his keys in his pocket. I was prepared to stand my ground without quite knowing why.

"Mom ate Froot Loops," said Daniel.

"I know she did." Sam gestured toward the parking lot. "Come on, let's go."

"Why?" asked Daniel.

"Yeah, *why*?" I echoed, only half joking.

"Because it's eight. I'm hungry." Sam was trying to be politic and not to cite the cause of his worry in front of our new friends, but the hippies latched on.

"Woman, bake me a pie," they chorused.

Daniel stood up and padded over to his father. Sam leaned down and Daniel whispered in his ear. The two of them went up to the car. In half an hour, I felt ready and found them throwing a football in the parking lot.

"What did he say to you?" I asked Sam.

"He said I should leave you alone and you'd come up in half an hour."

We looked at Daniel, who was throwing the football straight up in the air and diving to catch it. The henna on his back caked terra cotta and flaking, his chest white, almost blue in this waning light. Like a child from some science-fiction tribe. "How does he do it," he was saying. "He is the most amazing football player in the whole entire history of the world. The people cheer."

In this way Sam would rescue me. But what works with a wife doesn't work with a son. In my rarest and worst moments, people would catch Sam's eye sympathetically. Once

I would not be dissuaded from diving into a pond to try to touch the ducks. People stood with Sam on the shore, watching the ducks scatter, watching me slog back euphoric and covered with guano. They saw his patience and the glint in my eye, and they thought, Here is a good and patient man, to stand by such a woman. But if Daniel did the same thing, they would assume something else altogether: Here is a father with no control over his son. This father's laxity has put his son at risk. This child is not getting what he needs. Sam did not feel responsible for my behavior, but he did feel responsible for Daniel's, and that made all the difference.

We started to split the first time Sam walked away from one of Daniel's rages. We were trying to seat ourselves ten minutes into a movie, and Daniel refused to sit in the middle of a row. He wanted the end seat, he shrieked, he *needed* the end seat. He took hold of the armrests and tried to pull the seat out of the floor. A hundred blue-lit faces, parents and children, watching us instead of the screen. Carrie moved ten feet away and pretended to belong to another family. And Sam just walked out to the car and left me there. He sat in the driver's seat until we came out. A year later, we were through.

I slept with several men during our marriage, and I know Sam was unfaithful at least once—a woman's gold bracelet left on my bedside table, never claimed. I met mine at the gym, at my various office jobs, in the stands at Carrie's soccer games. Sometimes I felt somebody wanting me, and it woke some ravenous part of my heart that would not sleep until satisfied. I wonder if this is how it felt for my mother at her most divine—how many of her clients she ravished on the rumpled sofa in her office while I was outside going through their cars. Sam knew how my enthusiasms could play out in this arena, and it was never the poison it can be for other couples. He only pretended it was, toward the end, to justify his cowardice. Something to say in a language the divorce lawyer could understand.

I STAND AS close as I can to the wall that is gone and look out at the Atlantic. The tide is going out. Foolish boys are trying to surf in the twilight. The sky is a velvety bluish gray now, fading to ink, and the lights of the boardwalk look superstitious, candles burning against the dark. The Ferris wheel turns slowly. Time is passing, and Daniel is not found. I strain my eyes to make out a shape that could be the salmon man's boat, which I imagine as a small green rowboat, but all I get is a headache and a sense of the wide night flowing together with the dark of my mind.

6

. . . . .

Iᴛ's ᴛʜᴇ ꜰᴏᴜʀᴛʜ of July and I am sprawled in Jake's father's Sunfish, six of us weighing the little boat danger-
ously low in the water. We watch the fireworks, lying in a
human basket weave, our heads on one another's stomachs,
passing a joint. Pink rain, silver flowers exploding. I tip my
head back over the side of the boat to watch our wake: moving lines swimming in and out of contact, drawing moon-
hued diamonds and chevrons on the black water. Jake puts
Pam at the tiller and scrambles over us to the bow, where
his own personal fireworks stash is in his backpack. His calf
grazes mine as he passes.

Private fireworks are illegal in New Jersey, so Jake is
drawn to them, as I will come to understand he is drawn to
all forbidden things. The soar, the glittering violence, the
chemical heat. Tonight, Jake is the source not only of the
boat and the after-fireworks fireworks but also the weed.
This is why I have seen him biking so frequently, following his delivery route to drop off dime bags with stoner kids
at the arcade, the park, the public library, and why I have

seen him hanging around smoker's row in the wintertime, the strip of property across a driveway from Burling where all the bad girls smoke between classes, off school grounds.

Pam passes me the joint, and I take a deep pull. Weed, like so many things, is a welcome surprise of the summer, though it is incidental to the higher highs of friendship and of secrecy. But it makes the fireworks explode in a slower way; I can see their insides as they bust apart. For a few hours, it lets me relax into my mind and trust myself, where my mother's doubt has made me edgy.

Kandy's head is on my stomach. She watches Jake recede and then turns her head up to mine and blows out a mouthful of air. We regard each other across the minor obstructions of my breasts. "Jesus Christ," says Kandy. "His *eyes*." It's true, they are fabulously blue. Blue like a gas burner. By some trick angle of moonlight, you can see them from here when he looks back to stern. I imagine him signaling ships to port. Lighthouse man. I consider his worthiness of Kandy: He is a little haggard, a little skinny, but utterly composed, like somebody who has seen another world and walks through this one with pitying understanding.

Kandy closes her eyes and looks tragic. I don't get it—if she wants Jake, he is right there. I am pretty sure this has nothing to do with the tiger of love or the flea of sex. I have always pictured crushes, instead, as fat, undetected woodland ticks, buried under girls' ponytails, sucking away their strength and resolve.

"Just go fucking do it," I tell her. I have learned where to place my curse words for best effect. "Don't be a pussy."

She makes a face at me but gets up happily and goes after Jake, helps him set up the roman candles and send the first one screeching into the sky. She shifts her weight closer to him, and the boat yaws. My stomach gurgles from the weed and the weight of Kandy's skull and now from the dark biting drink someone has handed me in a plastic cup. I go to Pam and drape myself across her lap. She runs her fingernails across my scalp, and sleep comes at me sideways.

When I wake up, we have tied up to a buoy, and everyone is swimming except Pam and me. "Why are you such party poopers tonight?" Kandy asks, shivering, her chin above the side of the boat.

"Olivia fell asleep, it was too cute," says Pam. I am cared for. Kandy drops and surfaces slick, calling for us to come *on*.

Later, Jake sets off the rest of the fireworks from the boat, and we huddle together, trembling under thin towels, looking up. I think how we must look from space, a tiny bobbing spark at the edge of an interminable darkness.

"WANT TO GO for a walk?" Jake asks me in the marina parking lot as I pull on my jeans over sandy-wet skin. Some kids have split for a diner. Others peel out of the lot in someone's parents' wood-paneled station wagon. I don't want to go home to my mother and her ghosts; I never want to go home anymore.

"Okay," I say. He hands me his hoodie, and I put it on, though I'm not cold.

Pam stands in her open car door. "You coming?"

Jake yells back, "I got her." Pam slides into her seat and watches us recede in the rearview mirror.

I babble as we walk down the beach, like there is something I want to say but it is at the bottom of a box full of trivia. I wonder what I was drinking earlier. I talk about a teacher Jake and I knew from the craft workshop, how he won't let his kids do Halloween, how his boxers always show above his belt: hearts, chili peppers. We keep going past the last pilings of the beaches that are good for swimming, and I take off my Keds to walk on the wet sand, farther from the green glass shards and the sand-submerged diapers and McDonald's cups. We pass the beginning of the boardwalk and all the screaming lights and the people and the powdery mess of funnel cakes dropped on the splintery boards, and then we pass the end of the boardwalk and keep going, past the private beaches, all the way down past the public housing development where Kandy lives, past a city of orange-roofed storage units between which I think I can make out the dark, indefinite shapes of people standing still.

Jake leads me to the skeleton of a house, up at the edge of the sand dunes where the beach becomes the land. Tar paper flutters from naked studs, and tall beach grass grows between moldy fragments of plaster, some faint yellow-diamond wallpaper that might float away on the next high tide. I know without asking that Jake lived here, by the way he navigates between former rooms, creating a hallway where you can no longer discern that a hallway once was. He lights up a cigarette and blows smoke at the ocean, watching me angle and squint at the house, wishing for my camera. We stand where the kitchen must have been, and mud squelches between our toes.

"Come on." He leads me to the back of the house. A staircase spirals up into the darkness, missing five steps out of twelve. I climb up after him, wincing at the creaks of the old, dried, and salted wood of the second floor. The room we enter is more of a room than anything on the ground floor, with two intact green-papered walls and a rusted metal bed frame still supporting a salt-stained, waterlogged mattress.

"This is my bedroom," he tells me as we settle cross-legged on the floor, face-to-face.

"*Was.*" I have it from Kandy that Jake lives in an upscale housing development a mile inland.

"Yeah. I don't like the shit I sleep in now. It's, like, Barbie's Dreamhouse or something."

"When did you live here?"

"We left when I was twelve."

"Why?"

"Beach erosion." The sound of moving water fills the house, and I feel more aware of it, more tuned in, than I have ever felt. This is how the ocean must sound to vacationing midwesterners: rare, enormous, extravagant. Jake flicks ash, and we watch it die in the wet sand. "I mean, look how high the tide comes now. My parents don't even miss it. They think wall-to-wall and fake plants is nicer."

"Why are you telling me this?" I ask.

"I don't know." He grins at me, and I relax. This is a

conversation in which we don't have to know why we say things. I can do that.

"You know what?" he says, and I don't answer, but I know. I think I know. Something is happening. Jake is looking at me. His hair is dark, and the salt smell of the house makes me thirsty. He tips forward onto his knees, one hand on either side of me, and he kisses me.

"You're something else," he says in an anachronistic James Dean way that, in this moment, *kills* me. Kandy doesn't even cross my mind; I am an inexperienced friend. What I am thinking is this: Here is a boy who wants me. Here is a chance to cross a threshold. And I can feel it, I can feel the pull, his body's heat, an interior quiver. My mother buzzes like an insect in my ear: *He won't be worth it. They're never worth it.*

I get up and move to the sodden mattress. I plant my hands behind me and lean back a little. It seems perfect, all the elements of cosmic alignment—there is a bed, the sound of the ocean, and this boy with the beautiful hands, with the lighthouse eyes, wants *me*. Jake comes over and kisses me on his old bed, longer and deeper. We roll locked together, and I can feel a heartbeat between us. His lips are soft, and he tastes as I imagine fireworks taste: cinnamon and metal. I reach to undo his jeans but get only the top button undone, unfamiliar with the mechanics of the button fly, before he pushes my hands away.

"What are you doing?" he asks, muffled, a heat on my neck.

I thought boys wanted to all the time. "You don't want to?"

"I mean, not unless you really want to." He picks up his hoodie from where I've tossed it on the floor, and drapes it over my shoulders. We are quiet for a moment. I hide my embarrassment. I'm not concerned about my failed attempt (the flea, not the tiger), but I don't want Jake to think I'm strange for trying. I'm sure he doesn't know that I'm a virgin, that I was kissed for the first time only weeks ago—it wouldn't seem likely for this wild, fearless duplicate self I have constructed.

We sit at the edge of the room, dangling our legs over the beach grass, talking, for a long time. We talk about our friends and about the tourists and the stars, about our town and what lies beyond it. Each time I think the house will fall down in a gust of wind, it does not. When we finally climb down, hoarse and thirsty, the tide is up to our ankles in the kitchen. I feel like I am already asleep as we walk the long walk back to the marina. He drives me home and drops me off a ways up the road, because I tell him that my mother is strict.

"How strict?" he asks.

"Strict," I say, and he holds my hand for a moment before I get out. That sober handholding in the dewy scrub, the rattle of the highway through the trees, the thin gray light—this is the most real part of the night. He is serious about this, about me. I don't know what to do with it.

All the lights are off in my house. I climb in through my

window and lie in my bed, rolling the whole night around in my dry mouth. Morning comes blue through the slats of my blinds. I wonder if my mother looked in on me during the night. I am a new girl, and she is going to have to see that sooner or later.

JULY WEARS ON, salty and gradual, like an oven on preheat. My two lives diverge, the old one a straight line: mother, nursery, camera, home. The new one a plunging diagonal: nights in the suite, climbing out my bedroom window, the sweet ache of tequila shots. Loitering, messing with tourists, playing kickball, the sweaty heat of boys' hands on my shoulders, helping me up. And my sisters haunting both, anxious as a headache, strong-limbed teenagers fighting in the sand, bawling infants in my mother's empty arms.

By now I have begun to rearrange the nursery. As I clean, I turn things, reorient them, replace them with very similar things to see if my mother will notice. Sometimes I come back to find that the tissue box I have turned forty-five degrees has turned itself back so that its lines parallel the table on which it stands, but every now and then a change of mine becomes permanent: fake tulips in a mason jar by the window become fake roses, the blankets in the crib shift from the east to the west end, so that my sisters sleep now with their heads to the ocean and the rest of America below the soles of their feet. I dust less carefully, and sometimes my mother fails to notice small triangles of dust and sand in the corners of the room, where I have not bothered to do two sweeps of the vacuum cleaner, but have rammed it with careless geometry against the meetings of the walls.

THE BOYFRIENDS ARE most active in summer. They take my mother dancing, they bring us buckets of fried chicken, they feel generous, they help with the electric bill. The door to my mother's bedroom is often closed, and I blast Joy Division on my boom box so I don't have to hear what goes on. My mother makes tortilla soup for Terry and me, and after we eat, I watch Terry dry the dishes, his ponytail moving softly on his meaty back, and pretend for a moment that he is my father. He would try to take me camping, I can see it. He would snore and overcook the fish.

"How are the girls doing?" asks Terry carefully, glancing sidelong at my mother.

"They're okay," she says, stacking blue bowls in the cabinet. "Olivia has been going to a photography camp." This is the story I've spun to account for my days with Kandy's crowd. I'm taking enough photos to make it plausible.

"And," Terry pushes, "how are the little ones?"

My mother studies him and then looks down, shy and smiley like a little girl. "Can't you feel them? They're so happy you're here." She squeezes Terry's hand. "They're so happy."

MY MOTHER'S CLIENTS crowd the house. Footsteps overhead, creaking doors, nervous small talk audible through the basement ceiling: *I heard there will be rain next week, the drive was longer than I thought, do you have a restroom?* The divine-energies chart shows a line steadily rising, which is, as always, both good and bad. We could certainly use the money; we've canceled cable and the newspaper, and I want my MTV.

I am showing Pam my darkroom. When I first told her that I'm into photography, she said that photography is not an art because "there are insufficient fumes." She paints with oils because, she says, acrylic is for pussies. Your art should literally kill you, she says. So now I lead her to my jars of developer and fixative to show her the depth of her error. She sniffs at them, wrinkles her nose, and concedes my status as a fume-plagued artist. She says, hushed and reverent, that Rembrandt died of fumes.

"Who?" I ask. She goes slack-jawed and digs in her backpack for a big square book: paintings of the Dutch masters. She actually has it with her. She watches me like she's worried it might make my head explode, the beauty of it. I spend a long time on my stumpy Salvation Army sofa—the legs sawed off so I could fit it down the basement stairs—examining the girl with a pearl earring, and when I look up, Pam has spread a number of my prints across my door-desk and is moving them around, making piles.

Among the photos she is looking at, the ones she has not piled up and pushed aside, are the photos of my sisters on the beach. I drag over a wooden stool to sit opposite her and look at the upside-down photos.

"Who are these girls?" she asks me. "Why did you take so many of them?"

"You don't know them?"

"No. Why, should I?" She looks more closely. I taste blood and try to stop chewing the inside of my cheek. It is terrible to see my sisters exposed like this, but it is also a relief, like I have been alone in a room for months, and now Pam has opened the door and walked inside.

She picks up the one where Courtney is airborne, curled in a downward-facing C shape, and Laura is kneeling, reaching out, about to be collected into Courtney's fall. "These are really good."

Pam trips over to the sofa and collapses, produces a dime bag of weed, dangles it out in front of her enticingly.

"So you've never seen those girls?" I dare to ask.

She shakes her head distractedly, feels her pockets. "Shit," she says. "I forgot my lighter." I want the fact that Pam doesn't recognize my sisters to mean something, but I'm not sure it does. My new friends have failed to notice plenty of living girls. Me, for instance, until quite recently.

I run upstairs to get some matches, and my mother is in the kitchen running a glass of ice water, which means she has an overheated client. Possibly she has told someone very ill that he will soon embark on a great journey. I open the fridge and rummage, since I can't go for the matches until she leaves the room.

She starts to go but then turns back. She has been careful of me for a few days, and I'm not sure why. I am a fragile piece of china.

"I want you to know it's all right with me." She gestures at the basement stairs with the water glass, the ice cubes clinking. "You two."

"Hmm?"

"Whatever you feel is okay with me."

"What do you mean?"

"Just that I support you. I like Pam."

I cough and bend over, watching the swirling kaleidoscope of floaters inside my eyelids. I don't want her to see me laugh. I cannot resist saying, "Such clairvoyance," as I close myself back into the basement stairway without any matches.

"Pam," I say, exploding with mirth as I barrel down the stairs. "From now on we're lesbian lovers, okay?"

She looks at me flatly, and I blanch. "Or not. My mom just thinks we are."

"Okay."

"We have her blessing," I say, dissolving again into giggles. Pam stands up and approaches me dramatically, dragging her steps, crossing one foot in front of the other, and inclining her head in an attitude of mock seduction. Then she stops a foot in front of me, lengthens her pale neck, puckers her lips, and closes her eyes. I laugh. She opens her eyes and says, the corners of her mouth twitching playfully, "Fucking chicken," so I take the step in boldly and I kiss her. Our teeth bang together because we are laughing. Very close up, I can see the tiny soft hairs on her jawbone, swirling and snaking up to meet the dark of her hair. The vague craters on the hollows of her cheeks are like topographical maps.

For the next few weeks, whenever Pam drops me off at my house, we kiss on the lips, my mother watching through the living room blinds. I bite my lip to keep from laughing;

one time I bite *her* lip. Pam tells me I have to open my mouth more or it won't look real. "Come on," she says, "fake better." I find this game hilarious, and it won't occur to me for years that Pam doesn't.

When I go into the house, my mother pretends that she was at the kitchen table, paging through L.L. Bean the whole time, but she looks at me with a wild relief, and later she will bring me a mug full of ice cream or a cinnamon bun she has made from scratch and chat forcibly, as if to prove that we are okay, that everything is going just as it should.

MID-JULY I DROP by the grocery store to get some cash. I chain up my bike and wait for the slow automatic door to allow me inside. Through the glass panes to my right, I see my mother in the hallway by the employee break room and the basement stairs, talking to a tall woman with wavy chestnut hair. My mother is gesturing with both hands. The woman reaches out and touches her shoulder. I pause to watch, and the automatic doors close, forgetful of me. The woman's face is handsome but drawn, the skin around her eyes pink and papery. Her loveliness—her straight nose and her dark, bright eyes—seems worried away, like that of an aged ballerina. She is speaking urgently to my mother.

I wave my arms, and when the doors slide open, I walk through the front of the store to join them, past the four cashier stations, down the produce aisle, and back by the approach side of the checkout lines. When I turn the corner to the hallway where I saw them standing, they are gone. I see my mother where I just was, at the front, manning the third register. She is halfway through checking out a customer; how can that be?

"Olivia!" She scans cans of chickpeas in her lazy way, and the customer, a drab khaki man, stares at the hypnotic movements of her hands. "It's so nice when you come see me." This is her public voice, too bright.

"Who were you just talking to?"

"Hm?"

"That woman back there." I point to the break room, but she doesn't look.

"Sweetie, I haven't had a break today."

"But you were just standing over there."

She hands the khaki man his receipt, and he trundles off. She frowns at me. Her arm snakes out to wrench my head in for a diagnostic forehead kiss. "Do you think you had another experience?"

I know what she means by *experience*. Neither is the subtlety of *do you think you had* instead of *did you have* lost on me. I saw the chestnut-haired woman with the precision of reality, but then, that is how my mother describes her vision of the twins, and that is how I have seen them, too.

"Nope," I say, loudly enough to turn a few heads. I stare over my mother's shoulder into the store, where women are mothering the produce. They run their fingers over the eggplants, checking for soft spots. They heft cantaloupes and heads of lettuce in their arms. They hold apples up to the light to inspect them for bruising.

My mother hands me a twenty from her back pocket, and I stuff it in my front one. Even this basic transaction galls me. She knows when I need some cash, and she knows how much. And she is telling me that things I see are not there. It makes the whole grocery store tremble like a sheet of water. I don't want to think about it.

"You know, you were right before, about my sisters," I say, a creeping malice in my heart. "I was *mistaken*."

"Yes," she says quietly.

"I'm not like you. I don't see shit that's not there." If she can hear the talk underneath my talk right now, then she knows the depth of my contrariness, for my interior voice is compelled to speak for my sisters even as I slight them: Don't listen to me! I see you, I know you!

My mother is rearranging a small display box of plastic penguin key chains, making them all face her instead of the customer. "Good."

"Good," I say, but it feels like she has won, so I add, "I'm not a fucking psycho." Everyone in the store looks up.

My mother smacks the moving belt with her palm, and it comes alive, cycling slowly and inexorably toward the end of the checkout counter. Her eyes narrow, her jaw clenches, she sucks herself in and becomes somehow taller. I am struck motionless with a familiar little-girl terror. Having drawn herself up in such a fearsome way, my mother says only, "You are skating on thin ice," which seems folksy and weak and insufficient to describe the peril I feel in my gut.

Following this feeble pronouncement, her mind closes on me with the slow absoluteness of those automatic doors, and I cease to exist. I punch the slanted shelf of grapefruit on my way out, and my fist is sticky with exploded pink fruit guts. A woman with a shopping basket stares at the mangled grapefruit and then at me. I get on my bike and pump the pedals until I am flying past lines of parked cars toward the ocean, away from my mother, and back out into my glittering, unsupervised life.

THE NEXT DAY around the same time, as if to prove themselves to me, my sisters reappear. I brake hard on the pebbly sidewalk. I was headed home for dinner, but my appetite whooshes out of me as soon as I see them. They are in a group of kids I don't know, waiting for the third hole at Peter Pan Mini-Golf. Peter Pan is a few blocks off the boardwalk, a shoddy, bad-dream Neverland. You putt through Tinker Bell's miniature house and past Tiger Lily's forest, where crumbling, wild-eyed plaster Indians lie on their elbows in the grass and shoot retractable arrows onto the green, and finally through the crocodile's great jaws, which open and close on the hand of a giant Captain Hook, his eyes widening over and over in surprise. The course is surrounded by a high chain-link fence, and within that, a wooden split-rail fence, a vestige from a more honest time. My sisters are sitting on the wooden fence, leaning back against the chain link, waiting for their turn to putt past the Indians. They are ten feet away from me, if that. I can see the diamond rumpling of their shirt backs through the chain link, the pink elastic around Courtney's ponytail, the silver hoops in Laura's ears, oval sweat stains beneath her arms. Ghosts don't sweat. Do they?

I feel emboldened by the past month; I am no longer the

timid girl on the beach. As I move toward them, I feel almost angry: Stop terrorizing me. Be or don't be. Get off the fence. I let my bike clatter to the sidewalk. There is a little incline from the sidewalk up to the base of the fence, and I take it in a leap. One of their companions, a too-tan blonde, barks a warning "Hey!" that causes my sisters to twist around in their perches and then leap down. I am danger rolling in.

"You're Laura and Courtney, right?" I ask. It's the wrong question, but it's what comes out.

A boy asks them, "You know this girl?" and though they shake their heads, they look at each other, and a message passes between them.

"Where do you live?" I ask. A serial killer's question. "I mean, where do you come from?"

"Fuck off," the boy tells me, and puts his arm around Courtney. She shivers him off, and she and Laura walk briskly away from me toward the interior of the park. Their putters lean up against the fence. Their hair swings. Their friends shift on the fence and glare at me. My sisters disappear behind the crocodile, where the park office is. The boy who spoke ambles over to leer through the chain link. His nostrils are wide and round, and his lip is hairless. He says, "Weird girl, I'm coming over the fence for you." He mimes it, tensing his muscles as if to jump. "I'm coming. You better run. I'm coming." It is beneath me to respond. I can hear him gloating as I collect my bike.

I wait for my sisters outside the gate, but they don't emerge, and soon I see the manager's big bald head bobbing toward me behind the rigging of the pirate ship. He doesn't have to tell me to scram; by the time he gets to the gate, I'm gone. My sisters don't want to talk to me. They disdain me. Maybe they are nothing more than normal city girls on vacation, like the girls who sometimes crash our parties, drink all the beer, and stand in a knot in the corner, laughing. Maybe their familiarity is only in my head, a healthy thing that everyone experiences, like déjà vu. Maybe the best, most sane thing I can do is to forget all about them.

I SIT IN the kitchen with my summer geometry catch-up worksheets, and my mother sits knitting me a cardigan, blue and brown. Blanche lies panting at her feet. I stare at a diagram of an isosceles triangle, and I think of how new everything is, how changed, how many-angled. But here I sit, reeking of kisses and the respect of my peers, grown five foot five, and still, the house is quiet and changeless. My mother hums over the crackle of the radio-broadcast news, and a pot of water for pasta boils over behind her, spitting and seething. If this were a photograph, I could cut myself out and replace myself with five-year-old Olivia, ten-year-old Olivia, any Olivia. I could paste in a picture of Laura, a picture of Courtney, and there would be my mother, knitting blue and brown stripes, ignoring the boiling water. It is difficult to bear.

UNTIL THIS SUMMER, I have submitted to nonsensical obligations, as children must. I have cleaned empty cribs in the same spirit in which I have slapped the roof of the car at yellow traffic lights and worn nylon stockings: just following instructions. And in this spirit, I have submitted for as long as I can remember to church. James picks me up every Sunday in his algae-green Lincoln Town Car and drives me two towns over to St. Michael's Presbyterian, where I absorb very little theology, preferring to make up my own stories to explain the configurations of stained-glass saints on the great, glowing windows. The minister speaks with a cotton-mouthed rasp, and the other kids in the congregation all know one another from years of Sunday school.

Around the age of ten, I realized that church was something from which most attending kids' mothers were not excused, and I started throwing weekly fits. "Mo-om," I whined. "How come I have to go if you don't go?"

My mother enjoyed this weekly chance to show me the breadth and depth of her sacrifice. I could say it along with her: "I didn't move all the way out to Ocean Vista to raise a godless daughter. God doesn't want me in that church, but He sure as hell wants you."

When I was very young, I thought that meant she was going to hell instead of heaven. I had a nightmare in which I searched for her through a town built of brimstone, full of snakes and ladies in red bikinis. I woke up crying and asked my mother if she was really going to hell. She sat on the edge of my bed and told me how it was possible to cast aside all your sins on your deathbed and go right up to heaven. She tapped my chin three times, our special kiss, and said she had a trick up her sleeve. I asked why I couldn't do that, too, why I didn't have a trick. "You could, but it's better not to have to. Sin hurts," said my mother. I asked if it hurt like a bee sting. She said, "More."

Today, James pulls up and I am hopelessly hungover. My mother is cutting coupons in the kitchen while she waits for a client. I can hear the zing of her scissors. I assume she has intuited my delinquency these last few weeks, but I am puzzled by her strategic pause. When will she pounce? At fifteen, I don't consider the possibility that my mother has other things on her mind than me.

"Hey, kiddo," says James as I sink into the passenger seat. He squints at my outfit: ripped white jeans and one of Pam's screen-printed T-shirts, a giant ant drinking a Coke. Not church attire.

"Here's the deal," I say once we're on the road, coasting inland. "I'm not doing church anymore. Maybe you'd like to go with your real family?"

He shakes his head. "Jewish. Busy."

"Whatever. Drop me at the boardwalk?"

He gives me a long look as he makes his inevitable decision. Shrugs. As we U-turn, he asks me, "You been sleeping?"

"Yup." I have been, though passing out more frequently than drifting off. It seems like an odd question until I recall that hot anxious sleepless time at the beginning of the summer. Amazing to think that it was only six weeks ago; my whole life has started up since then.

"Your mom been sleeping?"

"God, what is it with you and sleep? What's your damage?"

He chuckles and repeats my new phrase, "What's your damage," in his soft, nasal voice, and it is so dorky that it makes me smile.

I shout out the window, "Sleep when you're dead!" and we ride along in companionable silence.

We pull up to the curb by the big pedestrian boardwalk ramp, where Stan the Deserter and a few other crazies are pestering a busload of summer-camp kids in matching purple T-shirts. Kandy is walking up the ramp toward our usual arcade hangout spot and doubles back when she sees me getting out of the car.

"Hey, sugar tits," she yells. "This your dad?"

James rests his arm in the car window and smiles broadly, which makes him look different—less slumpy-sad—than usual. "Just a friend," he says.

Kandy struts over to lean against the car. She is wearing, of all things, a denim one-piece jumpsuit with a halter neckline. She sees me looking at it and says, "It's vintage."

"I remember that look," says James before I can think of something snarky to say. "That was very hip. It suits you." He turns off the engine.

Kandy's lip curls with pleasure. "Thanks, old man. You coming up?"

I am horrified. James? Coming up where? The arcade? The boardwalk? What is she talking about? I slam the passenger-side door and pound twice on the car. "Oh, no, he has knee replacement surgery this afternoon, he can't come." They both stare at me, failing to pick up on my fine humor. "He has to have his dentures filed down. After his coffin fitting."

James laughs, tucking his chin down turtlishly, back to the James I know. I look between them, waiting for Kandy to start walking or James to turn the car back on. Nothing happens, so I head up to the boardwalk alone, and when Kandy comes up twenty minutes later with a soda I bet she didn't buy, I ask, "What the fuck was that?"

"He's nice."

"He's, like, fifty."

"*Ew.* I just said he's nice. What are you, ageist?"

I shudder. I guess I am ageist.

Kandy leans against the boardwalk fence and throws her head back, takes a drag of her cigarette. "Jim thinks I could model," she says.

"James."

"Whatever."

THIS IS WHAT we do at Emerald parties: We drink, we talk about ourselves, we make jokes, we catch each other's eye and think, *What if?* We do a power hour—a shot of beer every minute, the minutes marked by song changes, a boy wearing eyeliner and army boots manning the boom box. Kandy invites new boys, always: shy JV athletes, stoners, philosophizing honors boys with facial moles and legs hairless as girls', and they flutter around her while she postures for Jake. Inevitably, one of these boys passes out, and we put makeup and a bra on him, and I take pictures.

Tonight somebody brought an old childhood copy of Magic Telephone, a game where you figure out, from clues spoken by a giant pink plastic telephone, which one of twenty-five fictional boys has a crush on you. On laminated cards, they clutch surfboards and electric guitars; their skin gleams acne-free. We are playing *ironically*. We take shots of Jägermeister whenever we guess wrong. I am pulling for Will, the hot poet-athlete, because the other girls seem to like him most. I haven't seen my sisters since the Peter Pan encounter, and I am feeling successfully normal.

"Look at that," says Pam, and points through the doorway to the bedroom, where Kandy and Jake are slow-dancing, Kandy with her head on Jake's shoulder and her eyes closed, looking like a doll; Jake smoking a cigarette. I snap a photo. Jake notices the flash and waves his pinkie at us. He makes a drinking sign with his cigarette hand, rolls his eyes, and points at Kandy's head. I laugh. Pam stares at me and gets up.

The music is good, and the air is salty and cool, and everywhere people are laughing; it is one of the good nights. After our game has broken up, Jake comes over to where I'm dancing with a knot of kids. He lifts my hand, spreads it open, and drops a round pink pill into my palm. His eyes so blue they seem clear to me, like lenses through which I am seeing an interior sky. "But Doctor," I ask, "what will it do?"

"It will give you joy," he tells me, and that is good enough.

WE DON'T HEAR them come in. All of a sudden there are
five giant cops flanking the door to the suite, yelling that we
kids are in big trouble and this building is condemned and
did we do this to the walls? I see it happen in slow motion,
these men bellowing, pointing, striding into the heart of my
new world, fluttering their fingers over the butts of black
guns tucked into belt holsters. One of them pries a Barbie
doll out of the gunked paint on the wall and shows it to another one. My eyes focus on a pink color behind the cops,
such a familiar pink, moving, following them into the suite:
That's a dress my mother has. No.

That's my mother.

There she stands, trembling, glassy-eyed. She followed
me. It is one of the good nights, maybe the *best* night, and
she is out to ruin everything. Her cheeks are flushed, and
as she sees me take her in, her right hand rises to her hip
and her jaw sets square. Rage blooms on her high cheekbones. Pam is suddenly beside me, her shoulder pressed to
mine. Ready to defend. Everywhere, confusion. Some kids,
too wasted to notice, keep on dancing, and some kids, too
wasted to think straight, cry. The ratty boys make for the
door, but a cop blocks them. They jostle my mother, who
doesn't seem to notice, her eyes locked on me.

The cops are yelling something, but it is hard to pay attention. I feel aware of the patterns of blood moving inside
all of our bodies: Möbius ribbons of fluid rush. This is how
I realize the drug is working. The room seems larger and
everything more committed to itself: blue more surely blue,
red more surely red, sofas as sofa as they can be. And my

mother, more herself than I can stand, more tender and embarrassing and terrible, storms raining hail from her look, rearing up to smash me down, scrape me up from the floor, and pack me into a box to keep on her windowsill. A witch.

She comes toward me, talking fast. One of the cops says something to her. She throws him a gorgeous lit-up smile and says something, and he nods and turns back.

"Don't you think I know what you've been up to?" she asks. "On this mission, do you think I am unguided? Do you think you are so smart?"

"Stop," I hiss.

She pushes on without pause, into a dense field of anger. "These kids are trash, these kids will ruin you, you have to come home now, I can keep you safe but they cannot keep you safe, and if you don't come home, how can I keep you safe?"

The music dies; one of the cops has found the boom box. My mother's voice is everywhere, and everyone is watching us and realizing who she is and who I am and what it means.

"Is this her?" a cop says to my mother, and my mother says yes it is. "Go on." The cop points me toward my mother.

The faces all around me sour. I will be the one who ruined the summer, the one who infiltrated the club just to narc on everyone. I will be alone again.

I feel an impulse to go with my mother, just to get it over with. I am unmasked. There is that eking feeling of burning eye socket and toddler contrition, that instant shame response that makes me want to lie facedown in bed and cry until she comes in to rub my back and tell me that it's okay after all.

But then my mother claps a hand on my shoulder, puts her flushed face up to mine, and yells, "You have no idea what you're getting into, you think you know but you're a child, what makes you think you can sleep with dogs and not get fleas?"

Dogs. Pam has moved back slightly. The look of doubt on her face breaks my heart. Is that the drug or just my head, everything feeling so powerful? My mother's hand on my shoulder is like doom; I can feel her nails pressing crescent cuts into my skin through my T-shirt. I have a thought, and I do it without thinking.

"Who are you?" I ask my mother. She gapes at me like a drowning fish. I turn to the cop. "I don't know this lady."

The cop groans. "Okay, kid." He puts his hand behind my shoulder as if he is going to push me closer to my mother. He doesn't, though; I guess cops aren't supposed to push. His hand just floats there, and I look him in the eye and try to look confused, which is not hard because the drug makes his face seem more like his face, which is sagged and bristled like an old cartoon hound dog's. *Sleep with dogs,* she said.

"I really don't know her," I say, and there is some credibility to the rise in my voice. He stands back and looks at my mother, who is stamping with frustration.

She yells, "I can't believe this bullshit! You're all bull-shit!"

The officer cocks his cartoon head and says, "What?" just under the volume of my mother's continued indignation.

"She absolutely is my daughter, Olivia Reed, born November second, 1972. She is in danger, these kids are in danger, and why am I the only one who wants to stop this danger?" She bites her lip. The cop eyes her, considering. I can see the kind of rage she has cooking, a beloved-of-God, towering rage.

The cop can see it, too. "Okay, then, what's your name?"

I give the name Desiree Kandinsky and a fake address, and he writes it down. He turns to Pam. "Name?"

My mother surges forward. "She's lying! Can't you see she's lying?" She is crying in frustration, and she lets her fist come down on the officer's chest. Pounding on the chest of a police officer in grief is something I have seen women do in movies, but real police officers don't like it. He takes on a deeper voice to say, "Ma'am, I need you to step back." Everyone stares at my mother to see what she'll do, or that's how it seems, though I know there are other cops taking down other kids' names, making kids sit in different chairs, calling their parents.

"I'll complain," my mother starts, and I take the opportunity to retreat toward the next room in the suite, where the tall windows look out over the ocean-facing side of the Emerald. "You fucking pigs, I'll complain. How can you trust a liar and a child, I will give you her birth certificate, she is absolutely mine." Then she dashes forward, toward me, and the cops move to block her, and that is the last thing I see: her hair snaking out as she whips her head around, trying to wriggle past the giant cartoon police dogs, her eyes huge with horror as I disappear around the corner.

Somewhere, I can hear somebody puking. I grab Pam's hand and pull her over to the window. We peer out. There is a drop to the slanting roof and dormer windows jutting from each of the floors below us. I can do it. "Kandy?"

Pam gestures toward the other room. Kandy is passed out on the bed, her golden hair spread out like a sun. Behind her, all of our small paint selves stand watch. "Don't worry, she gets arrested all the time." Pam looks at me, flushed, one eyelid twitching. "Don't drop me."

I swing down to the roof and slide the few feet to the top of the highest dormer window. From there, I talk Pam down to me: *Hang, straighten your body out long, now drop, get low, take my hand.* We do it four times, down to the ground, Pam shaking all over. When her feet hit the ground, she crumples like a dropped cloth and sits like that with her hands fisted. I feel elation when I hit the ground after a climb; she feels only a release from fear. I hold her head to my chest and tell her she is all right, and she seems so very slender and fragile, like a wounded bird, and I can feel her trust and her love all through my body, and I think *this* is the thing. We turn to go.

Someone calls, "Wait!" from the window, and Jake swings out, graceful tonight, his long body compressing and releasing like a spring. Behind him, kids spill out one after another after another, some of them very close to falling. I move beneath them instinctively, my arms held out to catch. When the last one grounds, I hug him out of relief. The moon is gibbous and grave, and we can hear the boardwalk even from here, the distant lights garish: some other careless world.

"Let's go," I say, and we run like hell until we are behind the dark pilings on the beach.

"Did they follow us?" somebody whispers.

"No, they don't care," says Jake. He throws out his elbows to crack his back. "They don't care where we go."

So we go swimming.

We leave our clothes wedged between sandy boulders and swim in our underwear. I am wearing a white cotton bra, no underwire, the only kind I own. The water feels like cold silk to my switched-on brain, as if I am rolling tangled in the long silk skirts of a crowd of giantesses. I try to convey this to Pam, and she asks Jake what he gave me. They murmur low and watch me swim. I am so angry with my mother that it feels like part of me rather than an emotion that might come and go. I thrash and dive. The salt water in my mouth is like food.

"Don't swallow." Jake holds me by my shoulders, and his hands on my bare skin feel incredible. "Olivia. Don't swallow so much, okay?" I spit out the water in my mouth and let Jake carry me like a weightless baby through the waves. Someone yells, "Marco!" and the echo, "Polo," rings back multiply.

I look up at Jake's face against the star-exploded sky. "You picked me," I say. "Why me?"

He is more Jake than usual tonight. His skin is white and his mouth is dark and the water is the color of the sky. "I just like you," he says. He is larger and larger, and then I realize larger is only nearer, and he is kissing me. The breeze is prickly cool and the heat of his lips so ecstatic I wish I could crawl inside of it. *Oh*, I think. *Oh.*

I dive away, and when I come up, Pam looms over me darkly. "Do you realize what you're doing?" she whispers, pulling me back toward shallow water. Her face is very close, gleaming wet and desperate. "This is Jake. This is not just anyone."

I giggle and dive, resurface. "How long has it been going on?" she asks, so I dive again. This time she grabs me under the armpits and hoists me back up.

"Fuck you," I say—in a friendly way, like "thank you," like we say it all the time—and she drops me and walks back to the shore, rising streaming from the waves. Her back is narrow and pale as the moon, and her underwear clings invisible. She is a goddess, I think. She is a Vermeer girl. She is a mermaid's first time on land. I turn around and swim to Jake, but by the time I reach him, we are all getting out, and when I call for Pam, she isn't there anymore.

7

. . . . .

WHEN I EMERGE from the Emerald, Carrie has already called the police. She is sitting on the steps, hugging the beach bag to her chest. "Are you mad?" she asks.

"No, you're right, it's the next thing to do." We are both thinking, I suspect, that it was the first thing to do and that I am doing badly at this. I feel guilty as we drive to the station house. One count of aggravated carelessness. One count of poor mothering.

The station house is just as I remember it, a squat brick building full of blond benches and fluorescent lighting. Distance from the beach sharpens my panic, my sense of the real, and Carrie seems satisfied to see me properly fretful, drumming my fingers on the front desk. A policeman shows us to a small office, where we sit on black plastic chairs as I fill out the missing persons report. Height: four-three. Eyes: brown. I rest my head on my hand. Carrie is texting, and I don't say a word.

A man with a gelled wave of brown hair enters and

introduces himself as Detective something. Something Polish. I am not really listening. I am seized by imagery: Daniel cowering in a peeling green rowboat, the salmon man reaching for him. Daniel clinging koala-like to a piling as the water rises around him. Daniel in a basement, in a dog crate, rocking back and forth to clank the metal on the ground. Terrible, unstoppable, these thoughts. I am suddenly afraid I will cry.

The detective puts down the missing persons sheet and leans across his desk, crinkling his eyes in a practiced show of sympathy. "I have no doubt that we'll find him. It's only been an hour. First thing I'm going to do is alert my guys." He pulls a radio from his belt and gives a short description of Daniel: nine-year-old white male, lime-green swim trunks. Officers respond in crackly code. The only thing I catch is 10-4.

"What about the father?" the detective asks me.

"What do you mean?"

"Would your son's father have any reason to come looking for him?"

"Oh. No."

"I understand it's uncomfortable to consider, ma'am, but it happens."

"No," I say again. "His father didn't come for him. That's one thing I'm sure of." Carrie gives me a spiteful look.

"Any other family members you think might want to . . ." He draws circles in the air with his hand. Dot dot dot. "Grandparents, maybe? Aunts, uncles?"

"No." I feel like he's fishing for something, like maybe he

thinks I have kidnapped my children and there are sane, responsible people out there tracking us down. I have broken out of the asylum, stolen street clothes from a clothesline, something like that. I'm getting carried away. Why would he think that? I let an hour go by without calling the police, is that so unusual? I thought I could find him myself.

"It's a possibility we have to consider."

"All of his grandparents are dead."

"That rules them out, huh." The detective chuckles and then looks at my face and stops. I have lied a little bit; Sam's mother is alive but poses no such threat, sucking oxygen from a tube in a retirement village in Arizona. It's hardly a village. Whenever we visited, she said they were making her play the tambourine, and couldn't we speak to someone about that? She would weep with frustration. Sam would read his father's letters out to her, old letters she kept in a Velcro giveaway binder from a car dealership, and she would fall asleep and never remember which ones he had read.

In my family, grandparents go faster. My great-grandparents dropped like flies before my mother turned ten, two in a car crash, one of cancer, and one simply vanished, crawled, perhaps, beneath a porch like a cat would, to avoid a fuss. I never met my grandparents. My mother told me how they died, he of adrenal failure, and she of love, ten days later. My mother only ever showed me two pictures of them. She was in one of them, a chubby kid in a white dress with a frilly smock, blowing out birthday candles. My grandmother, her dark hair bobbed and waved, leaned over the cake, too, with a close-lipped smile, ready to blow out the last candles if her daughter didn't have enough breath. My grandfather stood behind them in suspenders, with a dark beard, his expression unreadable due to photo glare on his glasses, like crazy neon bug eyes. The other picture was black and white, and in it my grandparents were younger. They were skating on a frozen lake. He was behind her, holding her around the waist, and she was clutching his arms for balance. They both wore earmuffs. Other people were skating behind them, a blur of motion against which my grandparents looked frozen.

I DON'T HAVE a single picture of my mother as I remember her. I never took one. The only pictures I have are the ones in my head. She didn't have a camera, herself, so neither are there pictures of me as a baby. It pains me now that, while I snapped away at everything else in Ocean Vista, I didn't take a picture of her lounging on the sofa in a square of light or kneeling to garden, kerchief-headed, a drop of sweat eking along her jawline. She was always with me. I didn't think I needed any proof of her.

Later, I came into a stack of photos from her childhood, and these are what I've shown my kids. How strange for them to see a grandmother their own age, grinning tooth-less from the back of a horse. I told them that she died before they were born, and this satisfied them. She is gone and will not impose wet geriatric kisses or send preppy Christmas sweaters like Sam's mother used to. They know that she is the source of my moods and of Carrie's red hair, and that she and I fought, and that I left home young. Though I have been very clear that they may ask me anything about our family or about my past—that I had a withholding mother and they do not—they have asked me little. When a teacher directed Daniel to draw a family tree, in the branch that sprouted the Mom twig, he wrote: *Grandmother. Red hair. Missing tooth. Rode horses. Mean.*

I am sorry that he will never know her as she really was: a burning star, a tigress, a prophet. The heartbeat that fills the house.

THE DETECTIVE DRIVES us to the boardwalk in his squad car. We sit in the back, and I'm embarrassed. Carrie is enjoying it. She crosses her arms and sets her jaw, and I can tell she's playing out some bad-girl daydream in her head.

We stand on the boards amid the happy throng and show the detective just where we lost Daniel, beside the snack stand. "I thought he was watching the grill cook," I tell him. "I thought he was right there." I think I see his green trunks through the crowd, but it's a girl in a green sundress. Two cops mount the turnstile and turn onto the boards. On the street behind us, I see a cruiser stopped at a red light. I feel hunted, even though I know they are supposed to be helping me.

"Ms. Reed?" the detective is saying.

Carrie is glaring at me. "Mom!"

"I'm sorry."

"That's okay. Where were you folks headed tonight?"

"That's our business." There is something droopy about

his face, some irritating sitcom goodwill that can't be for real. I picture him with a three-day beard, and there he is, the cartoony hound dog, holding my mother back as she whips her hair from side to side and shrieks, reaching for me, as I back toward the great window of the honeymoon suite, toward the night sky and the promise of freedom. But of course he can't be the same cop. I stumble backward a few steps, and my calf hits the seat of a bench. As I fall, I try to make it look like I am purposefully sitting down, but I can see in Carrie's expression that I am acting weird. She crosses her arms over her chest and looks away. She hates me. She is wishing for her father.

The detective sits down beside me and engineers a moment of respectful silence. I could strangle him. "Do you need a hotel for the night?" he asks. "We need to know where you're going to be in case we can't get you on the phone."

"We'll be with you until you find him. Since you're so confident."

He sighs. "Ma'am, did your son know where you were headed?"

You can almost see the lightbulb blink on above Carrie's head. "He could have read Kandy's address off the GPS!"

The detective nods gratefully. "Then that's where I need you to be, in case he's on his way there. All right? You ladies had some dinner?"

Carrie shakes her head. The detective stands and holds out a hand to help me up. "I'll escort you on over there. We'll find your son."

I stand up without taking his hand. As we walk to the squad car, I reach for Carrie, and she skitters away from me. We duck into the backseat and roll quietly through Ocean Vista. We are going to the station house for the car, but it feels for all the world like I am being driven home, contrite, to be escorted along the crooked flagstone path to my mother's door, where I will hang my head and say, *I'm so sorry I lost Daniel, I don't know how it happened*, and she will walk back into the house and never speak a word.

8

.　.　.　.　.

FOR THREE DAYS after the Emerald bust, I don't go home. We can't go back to the Emerald, at least not so soon, and our world is splintered, centerless. Certain kids look at me with dislike. Pam watches me closely when Jake is around, but she hasn't breathed a word to Kandy. I spend nights writhing sleepless on Kandy's sandy sofa and days hanging out on the beach. I hear nothing from my mother. Every moment, I expect her to come barging into the arcade or into Kandy's living room, pushing aside all the lazy, smelly brothers to get to me. Her failure to do so wears me down, and soon I am yearning for my sun-and-moon bedsheets, a plate of good food. A fresh strawberry. Sleep.

I leave Kandy's sofa in the early morning and bike to my house, half-pretending that I'm sneaking in after an Emerald party and nothing has changed. There is a hose tap under my bedroom window that I use as a toehold so I don't make telling footprints in the garden soil. I pop the screen inward and swing myself up with unusual gusto to get out of the lukewarm prickling rain that has begun to fall. I am halfway through and wriggling my hips over the ledge before I see my mother. She is lying on my bed, wrapped in her pink silk bathrobe, sad-eyed, cheek to my greasy pillow. An empty wineglass on my bedside table and a thumbed copy of *Great Expectations* speak to her vigil. I tumble in and replace the screen behind me.

She looks at me, but I don't seem to register. I wait. Maybe she wants me to speak first. After a few minutes of standoff, she says with a chilling lack of affect, "I know you're not stupid, so I assume that you are *choosing* to throw your life away." She swings herself to a seated position and finds her slippers with her feet. "Everything I've ever done is for you. My whole life."

She stalks out of my bedroom and slams the door behind her. It makes a huge wooden *crack,* and then there is the turn of a key I didn't know existed in the antique iron lock below the doorknob.

This is not the first time she's caught me sneaking out at night; last year there was a fashion among the youth of Ocean Vista to visit the bakery at four in the morning, when the baker would sell hot pastries for a quarter—the broken ones, the ones with burned edges. I heard about it at school and decided to go myself, not in a giggling group, like other kids, but alone. I loved it: the otherworldly feel of the night bakery—the yellow light and the smell of bread, so rich you forgot there had ever been another smell. The baker told me knock-knock jokes and let me sit on the floured counter. He knew my mother but wouldn't say how.

When she caught me slipping through the screen door

late one night and learned my destination, her eyes went soft, and she cried into her hands on the living room sofa. "Has he ever tried to touch you?" she asked me. Her tears left dull pink tracks from her eyes to the corners of her mouth.

"No! God, Mom, *no*." This was a painfully embarrassing question. "Gross. He's, like, *sixty*. He's my friend."

"You can't be friends with men." She said this softly, as if she knew it would have no impact—that I was already too far gone. She took my hand and traced my lifeline with her finger. "Your life is long, Olivia. Don't walk by the highway at night. Promise me that you will never, ever do anything so stupid again." My mother clasped her hands around the back of my neck and leaned her forehead against mine, our same-green eyes very close.

"I promise," I said. Then, half an hour after she clicked off her reading light, I tiptoed out of the house and sprinted along the parkway, cutting into the wind so fast I couldn't smell the salt. My rebellion had started so quietly that it surprised me, at moments like this, to find myself sprinting in the dark away from a warm house.

I DREAM WILDLY: I am on a bus sliding backward down hills, I am in a dark house with a door that bangs open and shut in a high wind, I am setting off a long line of Roman candles with Jake, one after the next after the next in an interminable row stretching to the horizon. They make a rhythmic firing sound: thunk-thunk-thunk-thunk . . .

An X shadows the midmorning sun patch on the floor of

my bedroom, and I rise to see two plywood bars across the outside of the window frame. My mother is outside, pounding nails into the clapboard, sweaty in the old Yankees jersey she saves for dirty jobs.

"Are you kidding me?" I shout at her, and she clenches her jaw victoriously. I try my bedroom door and find it unlocked, and a hot plate of eggs and bacon waiting on the kitchen table. The front and back doors are locked from the outside. The windows will not budge. She has unplugged and hidden the telephone. I sit and eat furiously, too much, until I feel ill. With the windows closed, it is hot and stale, and the smell of the nursery pervades the house: close, faintly antiseptic, a kind of sweet that is neither flowers nor food.

I am spitting mad at my mother. I am sorry I came back. I will not be contained, I will not be included. I do not belong to her. A picture develops in my mind of a future Olivia holding out a match in the middle of the nursery, lighting the spirit world on fire, burning away all the babies and the just-dead fathers, the cards and the runes and the old photographs, while the real and certain furniture of the world remains—clean, inviolate.

I AM LOCKED in for thirty-six hours. If I were still the obedient daughter of yesteryear, I might have been locked in forever. I spend the first morning ignoring my mother, who is, judging by the sustained banging of pans and hissing of burners, cooking a banquet for thirty. I watch the daytime talk shows (topics: "Runaway Homecomings," "He

Cheated with My Sister," "Exes with AIDS") until she comes to me, as I knew she would.

"Okay," she says, settling beside me on the sofa. "Tell me all about it."

"It?"

"What you've been up to." She blinks too quickly. I don't believe her when she says she isn't angry, only *concerned.* "This boy."

So she has figured me out. There is nothing to say. In my mother's mind, the danger that Jake poses would far exceed the more legitimate dangers of a sudden adolescence: the alcohol, the group mind, the availability of mysterious pills. Worse, she would understand the pang I feel when I smell Jake's dark boy-smell as he leans in to kiss me, and this new desire to feel his particular hands on the curves of my neck and the pooling places behind my collarbones. She would know just what I mean when I say that this feeling struck me fast and hard, the stroke of a hammer on a nail. She would understand me perfectly and tell me I am making a mistake. I imagine my sisters sitting opposite us in the brown corduroy armchairs, shaking their heads in solidarity with me. *Don't tell her anything*, they say. *She won't understand.*

My mother lets go a train-whistle sigh and pads over to the dining room hutch to fetch a tarot deck. She lays out my signifier, the Page of Wands, and hands me the cards. We take our places on the carpet. Imaginary Courtney crosses her arms over her chest and raises her eyebrows at me to say, *Really?*

"I want the queen." I hand the cards back.

My mother shuffles through the deck, switches out the Page for the Queen of Wands. I can tell she doesn't like this by the soundless tightening of her throat. I will be her Page of Wands forever. "Fine. Shuffle it in," she says, meaning that I should shuffle in my question. I shuffle automatically, trying to think of nothing at all, to keep her out of my head. She lays out the spread.

Most of her reading is predictable (I am lost and confused, I should turn to my loved ones for guidance), but I zero in on the Knight of Swords, the charismatic lover, in the position that indicates the uncertain future. Reversed, the Knight of Swords brings instability, heartbreak. My mother and I sit across from each other over the cards so that what she sees straight on is reversed for me and vice versa. I am convinced that I am in the best position to see the truth of my future.

"Can I go now?" I ask when she is finished.

"You lied to me. You might never leave the house again." I have no way of knowing how serious she is, but she has done a remarkably good job of escape-proofing the house, and I am truly locked in. Tonight everyone is going up to Asbury Park to see a punk show. I'm supposed to ride with Pam. Jake knows the bassist from the opening band, and he's promised to get us backstage.

At three my mother has a shift at the store, and she leaves me locked in with Blanche. I go from room to room, doing damage. The kitchen surfaces are covered with her morning's work: quiches, coq au vin. Cake. I put it all on the floor for Blanche, who goes into a feeding frenzy, but then, when she whines and paws my knee, I realize I can't let her out. She dances at my feet. Her whining escalates to a howl. I put newspaper on the bathroom floor, but she doesn't understand. She is in pain.

This is worse than anything that has happened. I lie face-down on my bed and shout into my pillow. Blanche cries and cries. Eventually, the house smells like shit. Blanche jumps up on my bed and curls up against the back of my knees, and I rub her silky ears. She doesn't even know she should be mad at me.

None of my friends come by to break me out. They don't know I need breaking out. So eight o'clock rolls by, then nine and ten. My mother comes home, and I hear her stop short in the kitchen, taking it in. I fall back asleep. I must have tapped in to some emergency hibernation instinct, for I don't wake up until the next afternoon, when I can hear my mother explaining the boarded-up windows to a client as she walks him into her study. "It's a vermin problem," she says. "Possums." I am possums!

When I do emerge from my room to scavenge for food, in the middle of the night, the nursery door is closed and framed all around with light. The kitchen mess is untouched, chicken bones and frosting all over the floor. I pick my way through and put my eye to the keyhole. My mother is kneeling, and I can see only the back half of her: a cotton peasant skirt draping over her calves, her feet protruding behind her, dirty and bare like my own. She is lit by a warm, flickering light. For a moment I think she has beaten me to it and set the nursery on fire. I open the door.

What at first glance appears to be a heap of random objects in front of my mother has been, I see, arranged carefully. Candles stand on makeshift pedestals: stacks of books, Kleenex boxes set on end. Certain objects I recognize from elsewhere in the house: the three ballet-slipper ornaments, the dried baby's breath flowers from the living room side table. But there is more. A red plastic steering wheel, a crocheted blanket, tiny dolls made of thread and cigarettes. There is a plain wooden cross in the center, wrapped in Christmas-tree lights.

My mother is moving her lips in quick silent speech. She has lipstick and mascara on. She doesn't respond to my presence at all. I stand there until I feel stupid, and then I ask her what she's doing.

She holds up a hand to shush me, cocks her head sideways, and squints, her forehead trembling with strain. "I can't hear him when you talk," she says without looking at me.

"Hear who?" I ask, though I already know. I want to hear her say the things that damn her most.

"God."

I leave her to it.

I wonder now what God said to my mother at these times. It was easy then, and it is easy in memory, to dismiss her religious fervors, bound up as they were in her dramas of mood. But she said that God spoke to her, and so it must have seemed. And so it was, for what else do we have but the seeming world?

BY THE SECOND evening, Imaginary Laura and Imaginary Courtney are seething. *What a fucking bitch!* they say. *I can't believe she would do this to you. Maybe she did this to us, too, maybe she smothered us to death.* They laugh and give each other a high five. The house still smells awful, though my mother has shoveled the worst of the mess into the kitchen and is going about business as usual, showing clients in and out.

My claustrophobia peaks. I kick a hole through the drywall of my room. I have begun to hate the house, its very walls, and it feels good, the white dust clouding and settling on the hairs on my arms like a fine snow. Your walls cannot hold me! I think, and bare my biceps in the mirror. It is a lucky kick: right between two wall studs. I snip the chicken-wire drywall backing, kick through the clapboard, duck under a snaking bundle of wires, and I am through. Mice will nest in the walls now, but I don't care. Let them have a warm, dry place. Let them invade.

I CONTINUE SLEEPING at home to prove that my mother can't stop me from coming and going as I like. I tack a dry cleaner's plastic garment bag over the hole to keep the rain out, and my mother, defeated, lets it be. Jake comes by to pick me up or drop me off, and my mother stands in the doorway as I jump into the passenger seat or as Jake gets out of the car to open the trunk so I can grab my backpack. They stare at each other, Jake with a daring curiosity and my mother with a lively hate, her eyes bright and her hands planted on her hips, the only motion in the waves of her hair rising and falling on the breeze.

Jake is aware of Kandy's affection and of what would happen if she felt herself betrayed, so our connection grows in secret, in glances and trysts. We go to the beach or drive on the lonely back roads, going nowhere, making plans. When we leave this town, we say, we'll go to Brazil and win a samba competition, get filthy rich, and buy a bungalow dripping with trumpet-blossom flowers. Or we'll hijack an airplane and land it in Las Vegas, where we will become notorious casino robbers, making our escapes by air. But, I stipulate practically, why not just kidnap a pilot? Why take the hostages at all? Jake says it would be easier to hijack a passenger plane on the way to Vegas, security-wise. He smiles and plants his fingers in my hair at the nape of my neck, drawing me toward him. "Don't worry, baby," he says, "we'll give the passengers parachutes and let them jump into the Grand Canyon, and they will see such beauty on their way down that their lives will change, and they will thank us." This is how Jake thinks. I can get lost in it.

Sometimes I risk discovery by an Emerald spy to steer Jake to the bike rack in front of the grocery store, where I know my mother can see me through the glass windows from her checkout counter, and I hook my thumbs through his belt loops and kiss him hard. There it is, love, that tightening stomach feeling. Maybe only one person can love me at a time, I consider, and my mother has had the job too long. Jake must feel it, too, for he locks his arms around my waist and holds me tighter. How perfectly sinful all of this must look to my furious jailer mother as she scans cans of soup and hurls them clinking into a pile at the end of the moving belt.

FOR A FEW days after I broke through the wall, my mother ceased to see me. I turned ghost. We spoke sometimes like strangers, asking each other the time or where something lost might be. Now she has begun to acknowledge me again with her body and her face. When she thinks I am distracted, she watches me closely, a scientist tending a failed experiment. When she puts her hand on her hip, waiting for my answer to a question she has asked, she looks like such a normal American mom, in socks that come from the Hanes catalog. It makes me furious, how she can look so normal.

We drop the formalities and traditions, each, perhaps, afraid that to make Sunday-morning pancakes or to tend together to the roof garden might ruin these things forever, might ruin even the memories of them. We shed the layers of our family life, and as we approach August, there seems to be very little between us but this new animosity, this inarticulate anger that has become our food, that powers our appliances, that keeps us strong and separate.

Small tortures: I will not take her messages. I give her messages that do not exist, like, *Danielle from the pharmacy said you dropped some cash when you bought that Tylenol— she has it at the register.* Sometimes I throw in a real one to keep her guessing. She does not invite the boyfriends over to witness my betrayal. She goes out. She leaves my meals on the table at six o'clock sharp even when I am not there, instead of refrigerating them, a punishment for poor attendance. Once I eat a fly with my mashed potatoes. I leave the toilet seat up. I think this will bother her somehow, the illogic of it.

My mother is spending more time in the nursery. I thought at first that she was back to cleaning; I have stopped entirely. Tumbleweeds of dust and dog hair float across my bare toes, and in the kitchen, cockroaches die happy deaths, mired in ketchup on old plates. One night she doesn't come home after her shift, and as a joke, I make a stir-fry and leave a bowl of it on the table in her place. When I come in at two A.M., I find her eating it stone cold.

IT IS A sweltering afternoon, and my friends and I are moving in a pack. We have heard that some city kids ganged up on one of the ratty boys' little brothers and broke his nose last night, and we are ready for a fight. Jake is into it, calling us the Townie Army, and I am amped up on the drama. Pam has made me promise that I will find a way to let Kandy down about Jake this week, but I have no idea how to do it, and I don't see myself trying to figure it out. Jake and I communicate by glance and by an energy that seems tangible to me: gossamer threads growing between us, connecting us. Even with my back turned, I can tell where he is. Kandy walks beside me in lace gloves, with war paint on her tan cheeks, enjoying the hunt. Oblivious.

As our war party rages down Second Street, making mothers hurry their children into stores, eliciting clucks of displeasure from old ladies at the bus stop, I see my mother. She is on her hands and knees, reaching behind a pile of garbage bags and broken-down boxes in the mouth of a long alley that winds behind a row of restaurants, nail salons, and real estate offices. The alley is sheltered by these buildings' wide eaves, and at night it is the best place to sleep if you have to sleep outside. All summer it is a dormitory for runaways and bums, raided occasionally and halfheartedly by the cops. Beside my mother is a bulging canvas beach bag.

I fall back, hoping that nobody will notice, and duck into the alley. My mother is dressed beautifully in crisp black pants and a fuchsia blouse with a tie neck—expensive old clothes from her New York life. Long dark ovals of sweat stretch beneath her armpits. Her hair is ribboned neatly back, as she wears it for holidays. Her elbows move as if she is doing some work with her hands, obscured by the trash pile.

"What are you doing?" I ask over her shoulder, and she jumps.

"Jesus Christ!"

"Nope, just me."

"Help me with this. I can't reach the thing." I peer behind the trash bags, and it still doesn't make sense. She is positioning a gift box in the open mouth of a drainpipe. The box is wrapped in shiny red paper and tied with curled white ribbons. This has always been her gift-wrapping style; she taught me how to rough the scissor blade across the ridged ribbon and watch it curl.

"What are you doing?" I ask again, loudly. I move to the other side of the trash pile, by the building, and grab the box. "What is this?" A glimpse of red catches my eye, and I focus on her canvas bag, full of these boxes.

She stands up, wincing as her knees crackle. "Olivia Reed, put that back."

Kandy's voice, behind me: "Hey, what's she doing?"

"Charity," says my mother, and smiles broadly. She hasn't smiled like that all week; she is on to something bigger than our feud, and that is bad.

I rip the red paper off the box as my mother advances on me, incanting, "Don't you dare don't you dare don't you dare *Olivia!*"

Inside the box is a tiny purple flower in a moist peat pot, a Russell Stover chocolate assortment, and a small sealed envelope on which my mother has written in her elegant looping script, *To give you joy.* It's almost exactly what Jake said to me when he gave me the pink pill on our last night at the Emerald; did she find that phrase in my mind? I rip open the envelope as my mother snatches the box back, and I pull out a hundred-dollar bill. I picture, fleetingly, my mother robbing the grocery store in a stocking cap, with a fake gun (the kind with the flag that says BANG!) But then I understand. Our savings. She is giving away our savings.

This is not the first time my mother has felt generous. It's the reason she keeps our balance low and the bulk of our savings tied up in two-year CDs, so it won't be too hard to spring back from a generous mood. I count back, and a dead feeling blossoms in the pit of my stomach—the anticipation of hunger. Her last investment must have matured. The timing is just that wrong.

Kandy edges forward, curious, and I realize that Pam is here, too, and the public school girl. A few bums sit on milk crates, talking, a ways down the alley. At their feet are shreds of red wrapping paper.

"What's that?" Kandy asks harmlessly.

My mother's eyes travel back and forth as if she is reading a print version of Kandy's motives scrolling across her face. She drops the ripped box into Kandy's hands. "It's a joy box. A person who finds one will have the best day of his or her life." *His or her.* How she wrestles with language in a mood like this one.

"Mom? How many people are going to have the best day of their lives today?"

She bares her teeth at me. It's almost a smile, but it's not. "Full of deceit," she says. "You are full of snakes today."

"A hundred dollars!" I yell. "What if the garbageman took it?"

"Then bully for him, that's the whole idea!"

"I mean, with the trash? And it got compacted?"

"God will guide it to its right person, and maybe it's the garbageman."

Pam, Kandy, and the public school girl have moved to stand behind me, whether consciously or by instinct. I appeal hopefully to the logic buried somewhere deep within my mother; I rattle off a list of things for which we need money: food, clothing, bills, the final two years of mortgage on our house. My school tuition. When I mention tuition, her forehead furrows.

"Maybe I should go to public school," I say. "With boys."

"Slut," my mother hisses. The one word. The pure meanness of it. I have been her sweet pea, her puppy-face, her daughterling, her tiny bunny rabbit. I can feel the part in my hair growing pink and tender. I don't realize how upset I'm getting until I'm almost overcome.

I thrust the bill I'm holding into my pocket. I dash down the alley and grab the little envelope out of an old man's hands, hands that cannot hold on. One of the other bums tries to swipe at me. I skin a knee on the asphalt getting away, but then I am up. I hold the envelope up to the light and see the dark bill inside. Two retrieved. The bums call after me, "You bitch, you thief. You mean, mean little girl."

My mother grabs me by the back of my T-shirt and spins me around. Her hand flies up and she slaps my face: a hot rush, a bee sting. Then she weeps there in the open, my friends looking on, and I feel tears coming, too, only I won't share this with her, not even this. I could kill her. I imagine it. With my hands.

I turn and walk away as fast as I can until I am around a corner, and then I run. In my head, my sisters whisper: *Get away, get away, get away.* I forget where I am going and sit down on the sidewalk and close my eyes, and I don't open them until Pam is beside me, rubbing her hand in circles on my back.

"Sweetheart," she says, "you're panicking. It's okay."

She sits beside me and says that over and over, "It's okay, it's okay, it's okay," until there is nothing but her and the sidewalk and a tuft of grass, and an ant making a long trek toward that tuft of grass, and the coolness of the places my shadow touches on the concrete, and the burn of the places in the sun.

WHEN I RETURN to myself, I am parched and it's six o'clock, the shadows lengthening. Pam buys me a Coke slushie, and it is the nectar of the gods. Kandy had the presence of mind to grab the canvas bag, which I dump to find three wrapped boxes amid the detritus of the project: the ends of ribbon, the extra peat pots.

I go to the pay phone behind West Coast Video and call James. He says to stay by the phone, and I do, though I can hardly sit still, while Kandy rallies the Townie Army to our greater cause. They have found their quarry anyway, and are satisfied. James calls back to say my mother isn't at the house, and then he shows up in the West Coast Video parking lot, hands in his pockets. We split up and fan out, hunting for red boxes. I know a few of these kids will pocket the cash, but what can I do?

Jake comes with me as I hunt breathlessly, following my mother's logic. She wants to give joy to sad people—where do sad people go? I check dumpsters and alleys, I head south toward the crack houses and littered lots of the poorest part of town. It is a terrible Easter-egg hunt. I spot something red wedged in the mouth of a storm drain. When I get close enough, I see that it is just the wrapping paper and the box, ripped apart. The money is long gone. The plant, too, which softens me momentarily.

Jake points out a joy box on a windowsill across the street. We sprint. The window is open, and as we swipe the box, we see a fat woman sleeping on a low couch, an oxygen tank, tubes, an IV drip. We continue to hunt, fruitlessly, for I don't know how long until Jake says he is going to get us some pizza and meet me at the boardwalk ramp in twenty. It is twilight, and the boardwalk crowd is changing: couples and prowling sunburned men and fearful little gangs of women in short denim skirts. I go to the ramp and hunt as I wait, peering in trash cans and kneeling to see between the boards and scan the undersides of benches, when the night veers off in another direction altogether.

My sisters emerge from a turnstile and turn onto the boardwalk, talking, holding beach bags. This time they don't see me. They won't know to run.

I will learn where they go. Jake will wonder where I've gone, but I don't care. There isn't time to wait for him.

I continue as before, only the hunt has changed character. My sisters stroll down the boardwalk, stopping once for Courtney to buy a box of saltwater taffy. I idle on a bench twenty feet away. Kids from Ocean Vista don't eat taffy. Sometimes we spit gum into the giant taffy vats in the novelty stores, where mechanical paddles move in figure eights, twisting the candy, keeping it supple and warm.

My sisters walk a block west, then north on Allison Street. The streets in this section of town are alphabetical and female: Allison, Bettina, Catherine, Delia. Allison is a dusty little street where families from Pennsylvania and Connecticut rent tiny clapboard beach homes with outdoor showers. My sisters kick their way through the dust in flip-flops and I amble behind them, keeping my head down. I keep my head down for a moment too long; I lose them and worry—will they be standing around a corner with a base-ball bat, waiting to confront me? No, there. A flash of red through a prickly hedge, and then, rising step by step above the hedge, those two auburn heads. I take in the house: a pink-trimmed white beach house with a small screened-in porch containing a clutter of chairs and tables, beach towels laid out to dry, packs of cards, left-out glasses. Old lemon slices in the glasses, sweating sticky juice, bees that have found passage through the screen.

As Laura and Courtney rise to the level of the porch door, I realize I am standing in plain sight. I dive behind a parked car and try not to breathe. My feet must be visible under the car, I think, and then stop myself. This is not an episode of *MacGyver*. Nobody is looking for me. My sisters move across the porch, and Laura knocks on the front door. Through the screen, they look as ghosts should look: filmy, remote. Sepia-toned. Laura yells, "Mo-oooom."

The door swings inward, revealing the soft dark of an unlit daytime house, and a woman appears. My sisters move toward the woman with clear familiarity. They move as if they love her. This woman: the pale, tall woman with the chestnut hair. The grocery-store woman. "Did you lose your key?" she asks them.

Laura and Courtney step out of their flip-flops and

smack them against the porch screen, showering sand. "No pockets," says Courtney. "We rented a movie." And then the house swallows my sisters, these sisters who are not my sisters, and I am an only child once more. The door shuts with the groan of heat-swollen wood, and I stand up in the street.

My sisters have a mother who is not my mother. The faith that I have held, the hope, magical or insane, that the tall tales of my childhood are true, vanishes through the closing door of a rented beach house. As I stand staring at the house in the failing afternoon, I clasp my hands together and squeeze because I have never felt so disconnected from people. There are no ghosts, there are no guardians, there is no God, no father, no whispers from a general consciousness. There is only this newly severed mind of mine, shivering with logic and with loneliness.

ALTOGETHER, WE RECOVER only nine of the joy boxes. When the utilities start shutting off, I dig through the piles of junk mail and bills on the coffee table and learn that what we have would only begin to cover what we owe. It takes all my willpower to speak to my mother, but I make myself ask the necessary questions: "Is there any other account? Is this all we have?"

She pauses for a long time, holding her scissors aloft above the coupon page of the Pennysaver, and then says yes, it is. The electricity goes first, and then the gas. She digs a fire pit in the backyard like a Boy Scout. She rings it with stones and fills it with sand. She cooks a risotto this way and sets the table with our holiday silverware just to show me that she will not be beaten by gas or light. Her strength, she says, comes from the earth itself, from the mercy and the will of God.

9

. . . . .

KANDY'S DAUGHTER, MELANIE, climbs onto her lap where we sit in the screened-in sunroom, braces her small bare feet against the wicker sofa, and nestles. Kandy nudges the plate of chips and salsa closer to me on the table. "You should eat something," she says. All the unbroken chips are gone; we have delayed dinner for hours. I stuff my mouth obediently. Carrie takes a single chip and holds it in her hands. The cordless phone sits on the table, poised to ring. I feel irrelevant now that Kandy is here to take police phone calls, to make up our beds, to feed my daughter.

Every time I see Kandy, I have to relearn her: no longer the bleached-blond sexpot of my adolescence but this softened, effective brunette person. After she ran out of new drugs to try, after her father died, after she watched her disciples from our old Emerald crew burn out one by one and turn into parking-lot loiterers, assembly-liners, data-entry clerks nursing terrorist fantasies, she surprised everyone by applying to college at twenty-two. By her senior year, she was utterly changed. She went on to earn a master's in social work, and now she is a grief counselor. Her mother still lives in Ocean Vista, which is why she came back to settle here after all her brothers fled. She married a gentle electrician ten years her senior, and she seems wholly satisfied with her life. It boggles my little mind.

When we got Daniel's diagnosis, Kandy was the only person I told outside the family. It wasn't that other people didn't sympathize, but there was always that note of condescension in their "oh nos" and their "mm-hmms" when I told them that Daniel had bitten me or thrown a fit on the school bus. That twinge of not-my-problem. Kandy just listened. It's possible that I was better able to talk to her because she'd known me when I was wild myself, and I'd known her when she was wilder still. For sixteen years we have talked on the phone most Sunday nights.

I make female friends rarely, but when I do, I find myself acting slightly different: bubblier or quieter or more intellectual, or less. These small calibrations wear me out; I am exhausted after spending time with women. With Kandy, I don't have to recalibrate, and I feel the danger of that authenticity now. I am untethered.

In the backyard, among the artificial boulders and potted shrubs, Kandy's son, Ricky, is tending an enormous propane grill. He's a good-looking kid, quiet and quick with strength. A baseball kid, not a football kid, and just the right number of years older than Carrie to make her visibly nervous. She texts fiercely to prove she's not looking at him.

Kandy gets up to check on something in the kitchen, and little Melanie stares at us baldly. "Maybe somebody kidnapped Daniel," she says, and waits for the explosion of this idea into our unprepared minds. "At school we had an assembly about how sometimes there are kidnappers and they give you something, like candy or something, and they tell you they'll give you a ride home."

"And then what happens?" I ask. Carrie gives me a disgusted look.

"Then they take you away."

"Where do they take you?"

"Their house."

"What do you do there?"

Melanie watches herself point and flex her feet on the Hawaiian-floral sofa cushions until she thinks of an answer. "Watch TV."

I laugh. Carrie gets up abruptly and storms through the screen door into the backyard. The patio is lit by a row of floodlights. I watch her wander along the dark perimeter, kicking small stones. The evening has turned chill, and she has put on a black hoodie with a glittering skull and crossbones on the back. Ricky turns and says something to her, and she ambles over, letting her hair fall in her face, gesturing dismissively toward the house. She hooks her fingers in her belt loops and hunches, trying to be shorter than he is. I want to call her back inside, but I can't think of a pretense.

I DON'T KNOW when Carrie became this new person, and that is exactly what implicates me. Where was I? What was I doing? Slipping off in secret, driving from office to gym to store, over-occupied by the small things, worrying about

Daniel, dealing with Daniel, placating Daniel? In what sand did I bury my head so deeply that I missed it? I imagine her writhing on her bed, shedding her skin, moving from a larval to a pupal state, Sam sitting at her bedside and me off somewhere, oblivious, fucking the bike-store guy.

I remember Carrie's face as she got off the bus after her first day of sixth grade, gravely concerned. There was some kind of virus going around. It was a virus only girls could catch. It made the rims of their eyes all black. After I recovered from a long teary-eyed laugh in the backyard with Sam, I showed her a stick of eyeliner, how to put it on, what it looks like when you put on too much. We made ourselves into ghouls in the bathroom mirror. She wasn't so tall then; the top of her head fit under my chin. We pretended to be a totem pole.

Now she highlights the tear duct; she knows how to blend and foil. She uses the cosmetics companies' color language: aubergine, slate, champagne. I am not the kind of mom to forbid a little pigment, but the aggregation of this and other small changes has made Carrie difficult to recognize. She is embarrassed to use Kleenex in public and so just sniffles. The corners of her mouth turn down when she is aware of herself; she hides her face behind hair that she allows to tangle and muss. She wears legging jeans and belted tunics, and I have no idea where she gets them. I could never read her thoughts, or anyone's, but I used to be able to read her face. In my mind, her true thoughts pour into her phone through her quick-tapping fingers, and every word she says to me is false.

What will I do the next time I eat Froot Loops and Sam is not there? Who will steer the ship? I had hoped it would be Carrie, but now I see that I can't impose that on her, too. When there were four of us, she leaned heavily on Sam. Someone to share a grimace with when Daniel or I went snappish, someone to remind us all of rules and regulations. If she knew that I had been unfaithful to Sam, it would push her over the edge. She'd be his entirely, and lost to me.

Even before Daniel's diagnosis, there was a sense that he and I were of a kind, and Sam and Carrie were something else. Daniel stepped on a bee when he was three just to see what it would feel like. Carrie was afraid of everything. She wouldn't get on half the playground equipment. When I call Daniel into the kitchen for pill time, Carrie buries her face in a magazine. At first I thought she was ashamed of us. But I don't think that's it. Daniel and I get to blame our bad days on chemicals in the brain. There are pills for what ails us. But for Carrie there is nothing. She must soldier on through life, alone and normal.

WE EAT AROUND Kandy's oval dining room table. Her husband, the electrician, plunges a fork into his chili with enviable resolve. Carrie is moving salad around on her plate and communicating nonverbally with Ricky. They are having a whole conversation of eyebrow twitches and mouth shapes. Carrie: incredulous grimace. Ricky: comforting shrug. Carrie, with her eyes: *Did you see that stupid thing my mom just did?* (What? What did I do?) Ricky, with a slight clench of jaw: acknowledges humor. Carrie manifests attractive sadness. I can see them drawn together by circumstance. He will comfort her, she will pretend to need comforting. Later she will slip out some agreed-upon side door to rendezvous with him and roar off in someone's parents' station wagon for a night of empty and premature firsts.

Kandy is talking about Melanie's recent school play, in which she played both Maria von Trapp and a piglet somehow. I missed the beginning. Kandy is trying to keep it light. The chili is mostly beans and makes me miss Texas-style. I keep spooning through, hoping for meat. It's not working like food is supposed to work; each bite makes me hungrier. I push back my chair, and Kandy stops talking midsentence.

"I can't stay in here when he's still out there," I say. The electrician is the only one who nods understandingly. "Come on, Carrie."

"Mo-om!"

"What?" I feel sweaty and contradictory. It's getting Carrie out of the house that I'm interested in, as much as looking for Daniel and getting away from this pleasant, claustrophobic home. My sisters glimmer at the corners of my mind, their hair under the street lamps, their forms receding into shadow.

"I'm staying here," says Carrie in a sharp sliver of a voice. "That's what the policeman said to do."

"I need you to come with me," I say. Ricky and Melanie watch our volley, fascinated. Disobedience is unfamiliar to them. How has Kandy pulled that off?

"Why should I?"

"I'm not asking."

"Fuck you!" Carrie yells, and runs from the room, accidentally snagging the tablecloth so that her fork clatters to the floor and flecks the baseboard with chili.

Kandy sets her napkin on the table, though she has barely had a chance to taste the food she cooked. "Why don't *I* come with you?" she suggests, and I know it is the kind of suggestion that nurses make on closed wards: Why don't you take this pill? Though of course she is trying to help. Everyone is trying to help.

When we get out to the car, Carrie is sitting on the hood with her head in her hands. She jumps down and bugs her eyes out at me. "I don't have the thingy." She mimes the clicker with her hand. I fish it out of my purse and unlock the car, and as I walk around to the driver's side, I hear my daughter tell Kandy she can have the front seat. On the way into town, the stoplights are all green.

. . . . .

10

T HE OFFICIAL POLICE reports will say that the fire at
the Emerald started around ten P.M., that the probable
cause was bad wiring, and that it was purely accidental. If
you ask any cop in Ocean Vista, though, he'll say that the
actual cause was my mother, who showed up grease-stained
and filthy at the fire department, rang the bell for service,
and rode in the fire truck back to the blaze. "I was cleaning,"
she said. "Is cleaning a crime?"

I am at Pam's when it happens. Kandy has begged off due
to some family obligation, and Pam and I are lying on her
bed on our elbows, talking over reruns of *I Love Lucy* on her
little rabbit-ears TV. There is a knock on Pam's window,
and she tumbles over to open it, revealing that public school
girl with all the piercings. Does she often come by?

"Hey." The girl's face is sweaty. "Hey. The Emerald's
fucking burning down. Right fucking now. Come on."

We fly out the back door, Pam's mother calling after us,
"Girls? Girls?," and we don't stop—Pam knows where to
cut through backyards to get there the fastest. Her house is

much closer to the water than mine is, so we just run for it, almost as if the Emerald is a friend in peril whom we must save. We stop to pick up the public school girl when she trips over uneven sidewalk, and we laugh, punchy with excitement.

We approach the Emerald from the rear, and there is already a crowd gathered to watch in that scrubby field. The fire truck is parked up close, firemen yelling to one another and reeling out a yellow hose flat as Scotch tape. The windows on the sixth floor glow, and there is a crackling, rumbling sound that we might attribute to a heavy vehicle on gravel far away if we couldn't see that the loudest noises correspond to bursts of flame through the windows of the honeymoon suite. The fire lights the field to an uncanny gold, and outside its reach, the darkness deepens. Pam and I stand close together and watch, exclaiming sometimes over debris falling from the high windows, or the incredible power of the stream of water that the firemen send through the window of the honeymoon suite, that same window we swung out of only weeks ago.

It takes the firemen half an hour to tame the fire. It is more contained than it first appeared. From our vantage point on the ground, the fifth floor seems to be charred, but the fourth looks all right, and the building stands. What a miracle, people whisper in the field, that this never happened with all those teenagers inside. Later, after they investigate, they will tell us that the Emerald is full of death-trap wiring: old ungrounded power outlets and dangling ends of copper wire. It could have burst into flame at any moment, unaided.

The toys have all melted out of the paint and the paint escaped skyward in toxic fumes. The sofas are skeletal. The mural is gone. That whole wall is gone. They will find buckets melted fast to the exposed floor struts, and traces of various household solvents, as well as a nylon-bristle scrub brush charred bald.

When I go home, exhausted and a little somber, I find cops waiting outside my house. "Are you Olivia Reed?" they ask me. "Your mother's at the station house. We need you to come with us."

OF COURSE IT is not a crime to clean, but it is a crime to trespass, so my mother is charged with a misdemeanor and held all night. I imagine that her misdemeanor is the very same one I wiggled out of by jumping out the window at the Emerald that night; it has been hovering mosquitolike, waiting for a Reed, any Reed, having gotten the taste for us. The police question my mother at length while I sit in the gray-green bucket chairs of the room reserved for the detention of minors. A chubby policewoman babysits me, every now and then offering me a magazine or a stick of gum. I am asked if I would like to be picked up by a responsible third party—a neighbor or a friend—but I say no, there is nobody. I want to see her face, to know for sure.

Here's what I think happened: The mural wouldn't come off the wall with Brillo pads and turpentine or Drano or acetone paint thinner, so she tried heat. Just like that. The next logical step. She wanted to erase my new life.

A police officer enters the room. It's the cartoon hound

dog, though he looks more or less human tonight. He sighs, recognizing me, but goes ahead with his question: "Does your mother have any medicines she needs with her?"

I shake my head.

"Any pill bottles in the bathroom, anything like that?"

"I know what medicine is."

He leaves, and I am dozing when the door opens again. James is there in the doorway, looking mussed and woebegone. The policewoman hands him a clipboard so he can sign me out like a library book.

"Where is she?" I ask him. "Is she arrested?"

"I don't know. Let's get you home." I am not supposed to see my mother, but I do as we pass the cell block, through a glass pane in a door. She is pacing like a jungle cat behind a black aluminum folding table. I have my answer in the sly squint of her eyes, her dry-gummed grin. I am tired of being this woman's daughter. I look at her and think, *This woman.* "What did you do?" I shout through the glass, and she rushes to the door.

James puts his hands on my shoulders to steer me away, but I am already going as she shouts a string of our old jokes in response, "Olivia bunny rabbit light of my life!" and then, "Be safe, my love! Be safe, be safe, be safe!"

James drops me off at home and doesn't even come in the house. This stings; I was counting on his insistence that I eat and then sleep, his disapproval of the filth in our house, his snore. I wonder what he told the police to be able to sign me out. Alone, I have nobody to push against, and the house feels full of watchful and malevolent ghosts. I whistle for

Blanche, and we run together all the way to Kandy's house, where at least I can watch TV unobserved, and do, until morning, when her brothers descend on the living room and change the channel to wrestling.

MY MOTHER DOESN'T come home. I send Jake into the precinct to ask after her, since my going would risk the disclosure that I am unattended. He comes out, blinking in the sun, to our rendezvous point in the park across the street, and says that she was released with a warning at seven in the morning. Jake cups my jaw with his hand in a gesture that is too full of tenderness for me to bear right now. I spit in the grass. "Fuck her," I say.

Later I search my mother's bedroom and see that her suitcase is gone, and a few clothes. James must have come in the night. I wonder what it would be like if she never came back. I picture our house swallowed by ivy and the tomatoes gone wild. I make pancakes on a griddle over the fire pit and sit alone in the backyard eating them, watching the neighbor boys watch me from their living room window. Their little eyes rise beady above the level of the couch back, wide in horror, I think, at the way I have to live. I raise a pancake to my brow in salute, and they duck out of frame.

THE MORE I know about Jake, the more exotic he seems: a boy born to privilege slumming it with shore scum like me and Kandy, and managing to come off like the worst of us. He played Little League as a kid but quit over an unjust call. He lost his virginity when he was fourteen to his adult cousin's date at a wedding in Colorado. I'm the only one who knows how much better he does in school than the slackers he hangs out with; he makes A's when he doesn't cut.

Ever since the joy boxes, Jake has been buying me things. He makes a killing selling weed. He says he is saving for something big and that he'll know it when he sees it, which sounds to me like a fantastic luxury. Every couple of months, he drives to New York to pick up a package from his dealer, whom he refers to, reverently and frequently, as Max. Usually, a package costs him about two thousand dollars, and he makes four times that from the suckers in our town.

"How much do you have saved?" I ask him.

"Sixteen thousand."

"From *weed?*"

"And work. And bar mitzvah."

Max gets shipments of weed from a grower and distributes them to dealers, some small-time underage kids like Jake, some full-timers. Jake explains how he met Max at a Bad Religion show in Brooklyn last summer, how they hung out socially before Max cut him in, so he'll always get a good rate. *Cut him in.* It sounds to me like a gangster movie, all glitz and plans gone awry, late-night trysts, ducking into trash cans as packs of muscle-bound cops thunder by.

Jake has been to Holland, Japan, Mexico, and Vietnam. On these vacations, he has gone bike trekking and gotten scuba-certified. At a restaurant in Mexico, he danced salsa with dark-haired women who stroked his neck and giggled to each other in Spanish. In Vietnam, his dad dared him to eat a still-beating snake's heart in a shot of snake's blood, and he did it.

Jake takes me to his house. It is like my house only insofar as it has been a closed museum. I am the first girl he has let inside, he tells me. It is like walking into a furniture catalog, everything clean, a generic architecture book square to the corner of the coffee table. I see his bed, I sit on it, I lie on it, we whisper in it. Jake says he can't sleep here—he misses the rusty bed in the dead green room on the beach. It is so private to lie in someone else's bed. I can feel his thoughts rising from the pillow.

He asks me if I like it, his house, and I say sure. How can I find fault with this place? How can it make me anything but jealous? It is a palace with carpets that feel like fur on bare feet and cutting-edge design elements, a chandelier of prisms in the kitchen that cast tiny rainbows across the creamy marble counters. Everything in shades of white. Jake's mother lists these shades for me, leaning against her electric cooktop in a charcoal skirt suit: ecru, eggshell, snow, off-white, pure white, white sand, lily.

Jake holds his hands behind his back and keeps from looking at me while his mother leads me on a brisk tour. "This is the dining room!" she says. "This is the downstairs bath!" I count the rooms: twenty, not including storage closets and the two staircases, one straight, one spiral. "And this," Jake's mother says, holding up her arm like Vanna White to showcase the shelves of canned artichoke hearts and the bulk bags of basmati rice, "is the pantry!"

I ask her why they live in Ocean Vista year-round when

they could afford a suburban plot in Connecticut or a Brooklyn brownstone.

"She doesn't pull any punches," she says to Jake. "I like her, Jacob!" Jake stares at the floor. I have never seen him like this. His mother goes on to say, curling her hair around her pinkie finger, that it's the air. The sea air is good for Jake's father's system. When Jake's mother says "system," he will explain later, she is referring to his father's cancer of the intestine, which requires him to drive to New York City once a week for an afternoon of radiation.

Jake's father works at a flavor factory in the big industrial park a few miles down the parkway, engineering the tastes of everyday food. He sits at the kitchen table with a newspaper unfolded around the mass of his belly, and when Jake introduces me, he offers me a tiny packet of yellow liquid. "You know how they say everything tastes like chicken?" I nod, unsure. "You know, 'Mmm, tastes like chicken'? Taste that. Taste it."

Jake rolls his eyes. I squeeze a drop of the liquid onto the back of my hand and lick it off. Rotisserie chicken.

"Well, there's a reason." Jake's father hooks his thumbs in the belt loops of his khakis and rocks back on his heels, his laughter ricocheting off the white surfaces. Later we make chicken-flavored milkshakes, and when Jake says he can't wait to get out of this shithole, I pretend to commiserate. He has no idea how good he has it.

ONCE AGAIN, I own my mother's house. I come and go as I please, through the front door. I chat with my sisters sometimes. I drink my mother's wine. I raise a glass to the babies, I spill a drop on their pillows not to be withholding. I realize quickly what I have to offer. It was my fault that we lost the Emerald, and now I can prove my loyalty and trust-worthiness to my crowd. I put out the word: We need a new place, I got one, but give me twenty-four hours to clean.

When I say this to Kandy, she laughs, but she hasn't been over in weeks, not since I made the hole in the wall. She almost vomits when she walks in. Dog shit and rotting food, maggoty scraps of chicken skin, moths beating their wings at all the lamps. The water has been turned off, so the toilet won't flush. Pam brings surgical masks and brooms. James comes by to check on me just as we are starting, and when he sees what we're up against, he goes home for his Shop-Vac and a supply of gloves. Nobody seems to blame me for the filth. It seems organic to the house and the situation.

It is hot and vile work, and the single battery-powered oscillating fan cools only one person for one moment before moving on. Pam and I take a break to lie on our backs in the yard and chug soda. Blanche chews on a Nylabone; all her legitimate dog toys are stolen from other dogs' yards. Pam grabs the Nylabone and waves it around in a way that frustrates Blanche, who wants to chew, not play. Pam gives up and props herself on her elbow beside me. She puts her hand behind my neck and pulls my head toward hers. I resist. Nobody is watching us. "We don't have to anymore."

"Don't have to what?" The pull goes out of her hand, but she leaves it there, on the back of my neck. She closes her eyes, and the corners of her mouth turn down in a tense little frown.

"If you don't tell Kandy about Jake, I'm going to."

"No, don't. Pam, don't."

Pam scrambles to her feet and brushes the grass off her T-shirt. She looks at me with broad disgust. "I can't believe you haven't told her. Jesus Christ."

I shrug.

"Are you kidding me?" she says. "You're such a chicken-shit." She stalks off. I think she is going to get something from her car, but then I hear the motor start and the gravel crunch.

Kandy leans in the doorway. "What's her problem?"

"Beats me," I say.

WHEN THE HOUSE is clean—or as clean as it needs to be—we open a bottle of my mother's cabernet, and James makes a toast: "To health-code compliance." Kandy laughs her "haw" donkey laugh. That night, kids tramp through the kitchen and into the living room in twos and threes, refugees from the adult world. They explore the house, locating the beds. The one room we did not clean is the nursery, which was more or less clean already, though changed in what I considered subtle and insidious ways. I duct-tape the door shut and tack a sign on it that says, THIS ROOM CONTAINS AIDS. People know just enough about AIDS to laugh but not enough to go in the room.

James doesn't leave. At first I think he is trying to chaperone me, or spying on me for my mother, but then I see him smoking a joint. He winks at the boys and chats with the girls, and everyone thinks he is strange until he goes out and comes back with a case of vodka, and then he is a hero.

I let people into my basement darkroom, where I have hidden all my expensive stolen chemicals and my prints. Kandy nicked an Oriental carpet from her parents' storage attic, and we threw as many mismatched cushions down the stairs as we could find. It looks like an opium den and quickly becomes the most popular spot in the house. There must be thirty kids down here, watching a stocky boy with the brass nose ring of a bull ink a fairy tattoo onto a girl's wrist. The girl lies with her arm flung out across his lap, trembling and sweaty, and a team of friends pour shots of vodka down her throat.

It is strange to see James down here; nobody else knows this as a private space. My mother has always defended my right to disappear down here without fear of intrusion. For years, James has needled me about what I do down here, and it has been my pleasure to torture him with vagueness. Now he peers into the metal cupboards in the corner and pokes at their contents with pleasure. When he squats to pull out the bins in which I have hidden my prints, I separate myself from the crowd on the floor and walk over to him. He shuffles through the prints, smiling at some. He is careful to hold them at the very edges.

"You're a talent, kiddo," he says. He fixes his gaze on a print of Laura and Courtney on the beach. He smooths his hand over his beard. "Are these they?"

"Who?"

"Your *sisters*. The girls who got you so wound up."

I nod.

James studies me. "I do see a resemblance."

Pam speaks from my side; I didn't know she was there. "I thought your sisters were dead."

I feel caught, though I haven't lied to anyone.

James says, "Did you ever ask them anything?"

"I tried. They kept running away."

Pam says the thing that has been wavering darkly at the edges of my brain all summer, and then there it is, out in the open: "If they're just random strangers, why would they run away from you?"

I shrug, pivot, and charge up the stairs to the kitchen, where I have a particular bottle of tequila in mind. I shout, "Tequila shots!," and kids break off from other groups to follow me. I can't think about my sisters. I throw my head back and let the tequila soak through my tongue to my brain, to soften the edges of all things and cast over me a sweet incandescence.

The night wears on, wild and interminable. Kids leave on strange missions and return in different numbers, with supplies, with stories, with grass stains. Jake shows up late, and we are both too far gone to pretend distance. We are in the kitchen standing and talking with a bunch of kids, and the secret keeping is too much for me, the warmth of his shoulder as it bumps against mine accidentally on purpose, over and over again, his hand on the small of my back as he moves past, muttering, "Excuse me." I fling open the back door and stumble out for some air, some relief.

There by the fire pit is Kandy, and there is James. The

yard is a moonlit gray. Kandy is lying on her side on an in-
flatable pool lounger that someone has laid out as lawn furniture. I can't see her face; her blond hair sheets down on
either side, and her gaze is directed downward, where James
crouches at her side. His back is to me, but I can see his out-
stretched hand cupping the curve of the back of her thigh
a few inches below the hem of her denim skirt, his thumb
dimpling the smooth bronze skin. It is a tableau, a damning
evidentiary photograph. I don't care what just happened or
what will happen next.

I go back inside. I don't know if they've seen me. I need
something. There are so many people in my house. Jake
grabs my hand as I pass back through the kitchen crowd,
and says, "What? What is it?"

I grab a bottle of wine from the table and pull Jake across
the room, rip the duct tape off the door, and yank him into
the nursery. I shut the door behind us and prop a chair beneath the knob. Alone. I breathe. The room spins slowly,
which makes the mobiles above my sisters' cribs appear to
be standing still.

Jake has never been inside the house; there has always
been the chance that my mother might cage him, fatten
him, and bake him in a pie. I watch him take in the nursery and then my mother's shrine. He pulls me in to him and
kisses my forehead. "What happened to you?" he asks, and
I breathe into his neck until I feel calmer. He is sweaty; he's
used to air-conditioning. He smells like warm tea.

"Is it raining?" His voice or mine? We move to the window and put our faces to the glass. It has indeed started to

rain: fuzzy gray verticals as if the world is suffering bad reception. The backyard is empty. How long ago did I see James and Kandy there? Everyone betrays, I think hazily.

Jake puts his mouth over my ear and breathes warmth. "I'm filling you with my air," he says. I picture the air in my body blue and the air in his body red, blending purple from our heads down to our lungs. He slides his fingers down the front of my jeans, and from the way he twitches, almost imperceptibly, I guess that the other girls he's been with shave off their pubic hair. My mother says women do that to please men who wish, in the dark places of their hearts, that they were fucking wide-eyed little eight-year-olds.

We tangle on the nursery floor. Jake holds my head in both his hands. "I love you," he says, and as he says it, I feel something strong and fierce, so I say, "Me, too." He pulls off his T-shirt. A line of dark hair below his navel. His body pale and dimpled, fragile like the body of a dying saint in a religious painting. "I don't have a condom."

"Shit," I say, and find his penis with my hand. He stiffens and grunts. I pretend confidence.

"Um, do you think—" he starts. "Do you think your mom? Might? Somewhere?"

I laugh and laugh and can't stop laughing. I'm sure she does. But the party is still raging out there, and I don't want to leave this room, or for Jake to leave this room, ever again. So I say no, but it's okay, we'll use the rhythm method, even though I'm not really sure what that is.

We are naked, moving, entwined, and then our twining

gains torque and purpose, and my knees splay out and he finds an angle. It is happening, for real. There is a sensitivity in my body like the inside of my mind—as raw-nerved and as subject to wild changes, from ecstatic to unbearable, from yes to no. There, on the floor of my sisters' room, I feel a bright and blinding pain. Jake keeps going; he doesn't notice. After a while, he slumps and we lie in the hazy warmth, breathing, drifting in and out of consciousness. When I shift my weight, I feel myself swollen, a deep interior rug burn. I roll over and bang into the legs of a crib, and I see that I have bled a dark stain on the powder-pink carpet, spreading, saturating, huge. The insides of my thighs are ropy with blood; I have never seen so much blood.

"Oh God."

"Oh my God," echoes Jake, sitting up on his elbows. "You should have told me." And then, touched, feeling himself to be a special and chosen man, more softly, he says, "Oh my God, Olivia." He grabs me around the waist and pulls me down to him, but I can't lie there, I can't roll around in that.

I pull my shorts and shirt back on, and my thought is that maybe I can get to the bathroom before the blood soaks into the cloth and starts to show. I bolt, and Jake is saying, "Jesus, close the door," behind me. I hurry through the party, and everyone is too drunk and too absorbed in their own dramas to notice mine. Two boys are making out in the bathtub, and I have to yell at them to get the hell out. They stare at me, and at the darkening of my shorts, the blood drying on my legs, and they say, "Holy shit, what happened?" I say it was a knife fight and herd them out and lock the door behind them.

I open the toilet tank and scoop out the last of the water with a plastic cup. As I clean myself, a hundred knocks on the door, a hundred what-are-you-doing-in-theres. The blood washes down my legs, circles the drain. I feel a pang of horror—my blood in my sisters' room. I leave my shorts balled in the corner of the tub. My mother's pink bathrobe is hanging on the hook on the bathroom door. I wrap myself in it and go back to the kitchen, clear a path through the crowd to the sink. I get bleach, some bottles of seltzer, and a bucket.

Jake has passed out, sprawled nude on the nursery floor. I kneel beside him and scrub my stain for half an hour with a wooden brush until it fades to nothing and the seltzer water turns to standing blood.

Outside, the rain pounds down. Gardens drown in mud, cats stay inside. The wind tears dead and dying branches from the trees.

IN THE MORNING, things have come apart. Jake is gone. I still feel drunk, like I am swimming through thick air. I move through the sleeping house, kids camped out on the beds and chairs, kids in piles on the ground. Some are awake, and there is a bristling hush to their talk, a darting eye that follows me from room to room. It is only when I have made a full tour of the house and circled back outside and in through the kitchen door that I find my friends. Kandy is standing in the open door to the nursery, staring in. She turns around and her eyes are red-rimmed, little wet dots of mascara smudged below her eyebrows like an angry tribal tattoo. Her hair is mussed to dandelion fluff, her shoulders hunched forward. Pam leans heavily against the kitchen counter.

Kandy draws a deep breath. "You whore." Four or five other kids are in the kitchen looking on, slack-jawed. Some girl I've never seen before puts her arm around Kandy and glares at me. I refuse to believe that Kandy cares more about Jake, who does not love her back, than she does about me. It is outside my experience, such wasted longing, and it seems unworthy of her. I feel disgust, and then the disgust sharpens to a point and becomes anger.

"Who are you?" I shout at the stupid stranger girl. And to my friends, "Who the fuck is this?"

Kandy bears down on me, unembarrassed now of her ugly, blotchy, wet-eyed rage. "I gave you everything," she says, gesturing grandly, squeezing her eyes shut in pain. "And you shat on me. You shat on all of us." I giggle at her grandiosity, and that makes it worse. Kandy's nostrils flare. Pam turns her face away. The thought occurs to me that Pam tried to keep this from happening, that Pam is the one who gave me everything, and I have been careless of her.

"Don't ever talk to me," says Kandy. She turns to go but then, after a moment's consideration, whirls back around and punches me in the stomach. I'm not expecting it, and I fall hard. I can't get my breath. White pulsing heat in my gut. I gasp on the floor, a beached fish. When I have enough breath to sit up, the kitchen is empty.

I have Jake now and little else. I have Blanche. I have ghosts if I want them. I can't help but think how my mother would nod: See how love destroys. I clean the house again, slowly this time. Nobody comes, not even Pam. James pulls up in his rattling green car, and I am gone out the back door as fast as I can run. I don't want to see his face. It seems there is nothing for me in the world, and I cry when I am alone, fat stupid tears, and I hate myself for crying. It is August now. The city-boy lifeguards are as tan as the rest of us. The boardwalk vendors are giving away free corn to get people to buy the sausages.

I have been avoiding Allison Street and that house with its cutesy conch-shell cutout shutters, but now I start walking the street, up and down, up and down. The shutters are closed, the blue car gone from the driveway. The porch is organized in a final way, an until-next-year way. Each year it makes me sad to see summer homes abandoned, as if they have auditioned to contain families and been turned down. I imagine the auburn crown of a girl's head above the privacy fence as she washes off the sand in the outdoor shower. There is nothing to keep my mind from taking me there, into that lingering uncertainty—the redheaded girls, their running forms, the call of their blood.

Jake walks with me one day when I am feeling sad and bold and sorry for myself. I stare at the closed-up house. "Let's go in," I say. Jake kisses my neck and says okay. Since the party, we have spoken less with words and more with our bodies. We have had sex in my house almost every day, though never again in the nursery. Each time is different, but each time since the first, there is a moment when I am vaulted out of myself for a fluttering perfect second. It feels too fragile to be an orgasm, as I've heard them described, but I can understand the French term now, *la petite mort*. It is a tiny death, a momentary reprieve from the world. I am insatiable for this feeling; as soon as the moment collapses, I am waiting for the next one.

We jimmy open the tall wooden gate in the privacy fence and slink around the perimeter of the house until we find a loose lock on a first-floor window in the rear. Inside, the furniture sleeps beneath clear plastic. Gourmet cooking magazines curl in their rack. There are things you wouldn't buy for your real home: white wicker footlockers and dried starfish affixed to Plexiglas and framed. The bookshelves are full of books for show: the complete works of Swift, guides to the flora and fauna of the East Coast. In the bathroom, a model Zen garden has fallen from the top of the toilet tank, sand spilled across the white tile. I step on the tiny sand rake by accident and sit on the ground massaging my heel, and when I get up, I have sand on my butt, and Jake chases me around the house, slapping it off. It feels good to be stupid for a moment.

I scan the tabletops for old mail, something with an address. The drawers of all the end tables and sideboards are locked, which makes me think that these people are a little crazy. I know how to work this kind of lock with a bent fork, but I can't find a fork in the kitchen drawers, so I open the dishwasher, and there the cutlery gleams, all the forks together, tines pointing up, all the knives together, blades down.

Jake comes to the doorway, hefting a wooden statue of a fisherman. "Fucking yuppies."

I try the sideboard drawer with no luck: coasters, place mats, birch-bark napkin rings no doubt made by my ex-sisters at some long-ago Girl Scout camp. In the top of a bedroom closet, at the feet of two twin beds, I find a red nylon gym bag full of damp, balled-up Speedo swimsuits. I imagine Laura and Courtney swimming on their last morning, balling up their suits thoughtlessly to mildew. These are girls who can afford to replace the things they ruin. Printed on the bag is a leaping dolphin and the words: THE FLYING DOLPHINS. 92ND STREET Y.

They are swimmers. No wonder they could vanish beneath the surface of the ocean for so long. And more important, they are from New York City. I search the rest of the house but find no envelopes or letterhead, not even scraps in the garbage that I might tape together. At least now I know where to start.

Jake reclines on a sofa, having peeled back the plastic. I go to him and sit on his chest. He pretends to be crushed to death.

"Jake," I say. "When do you pick up your next package from Max?"

"I don't know. Whenever I want."

"Can it be soon?"

"Why?"

"I need to go on a trip."

"We could go to Philly," he says. "Let's go eat cheese-steaks and watch the Phillies lose."

"No. New York." My heart pumps fast at the thought of it: to end all this. To walk up to these girls, these false sisters, and shake them by the shoulders till they spit out their secrets. To see once and for all if my hand passes through them, to see if they blow away, spiraling up amid the skyscrapers of New York, my mother's city.

C ARRIE, KANDY, AND I retrace our steps. The boardwalk, the beach, the network of alleys behind the
boardwalk shops. It is full night now, and sinister. Only the
bars are open. Ocean Vista has fallen to the bums and burn-
outs, drunks weaving their way past the closed-up snack
shops, collapsing on benches and giving up on getting up.
They gape at me when I approach to ask if they've seen a
little boy, their pores yawning dark, the whites of their eyes
yellow as old milk. Carrie sticks by Kandy, and they trail
behind me as I investigate places where I could hardly expect to find my son: second-story fire escapes, locked-gate
backyards. I feel brittle and explosive, the two of them
thinking what I know they're thinking.

I turn to see Kandy with her elbows on the boardwalk
fence, tucking her head down and sideways to speak to my
daughter over the wind, and I see her in that denim jumpsuit, sixteen years old, sticking her ass out, tossing her hair.
She asked me once what even *happened* between us that summer, exactly? Which dumbfounded me. Kandy recalls her

adolescence frequently and with a removed fascination, as if she is now another species, as if she is no longer responsible for the decisions she made then. *I was a hellion,* she tells her kids, and they don't believe her. I've heard that each time you remember something, the memory is rewritten by the neurons in your brain; that the memories you summon frequently are molded and smoothed—clay on the potter's wheel of your mind—while memories you leave buried can bubble up with photographic precision. This is what I think of Kandy's ability to blur the events of that summer: She thinks back casually. Whereas my memories of that summer attack only on days like today, when I am too weak to keep them out, and then they come at me with a ruthless precision.

I will never ask her the question about James. I'd rather not know. The last time I saw him was at my mother's funeral. He sat in no special seat, just somewhere in the middle of the block of folding chairs at the funeral parlor, wearing a dingy navy suit and looking like an old man, his hair gone entirely white, his legs showing their spindly shape through his suit pants. I know that toward the end, he checked on her daily, he took her on picnics. I didn't talk to him; I went out the back door to smoke after the service and stayed there until I saw his car pull out of the lot. He knew us too well. I didn't want to hear anything true that day.

AFTER COLLEGE, I moved to Chicago. Life unfurled, never simply, but fast. Once I dried out in that cold pl?
I followed a boy to Austin. Though I lost interest in
quickly, I found a new world in Texas, a Martian lan?

with customs comfortingly different from my own. I couldn't imagine my mother there, couldn't phrase my guilt. I loved the long drives on parched roads, the endless land, the clouds of grackles in the trees. I hiked into the woods to swim in natural pools, so small that you were never far from shore. People there were hungry, and I admired that, too. Hot meat on butcher paper, pickles, cold beer. Roosters scratching in the road. Time slowed down, people danced steps that didn't exist in other states.

I lived in an apartment on stilts in what was once a carriage house for a rich estate. I kept it very clean and decorated it minimally. I worked in the basement of a library, where I had to wear gloves to file ancient documents written in languages I couldn't read. When I brought Sam home for the first time, he asked me where was all my stuff? I rested my chin on his chest, and he lifted the hair from my eyes. This is it, I told him. This is all of it. This is me.

That was a lie, of course. I was no blank slate. But by letting Sam generate the objects and patterns of my life, I felt, again, transformed. We had such good years. He brought me a glass of water every night before bed. He was fascinated by the natural world and would read passages from *National Geographic* aloud at the breakfast table with an awe that bordered on the religious. He took us camping and knew every tree, could make incredible meals with nothing but tinfoil and matches. In Austin, I liked running into him unexpectedly when we were out on separate errands, this dark, slim, graceful man with his crisp gray pants, his leather watch, his soft, quiet mouth—and thinking, *That one's mine.* I loved to embarrass him, to bite his neck at concerts or slide my toes up his leg beneath the table at brunch and watch him get that half-pleased, admonishing look.

When Carrie was born, Sam gave up his culinary career and took a job in online marketing for a credit union. When he was younger, his parents had insisted that he earn an MBA as backup, they said, in case cooking didn't work out. He said he enjoyed his work, though he didn't talk about it much. At home, he made us four-course meals. It gave him a reason to resent his parents, to call them infrequently, and I should have realized that he would also find reasons to resent me, the bearer of expensive, dream-deferring children, the carrier of the gene that would make his son a burden. Not that I didn't give him other reasons, too.

MY CELL PHONE rings, and it is the police. "We haven't found him," the officer says right away. "But we wanted you to know we've got everyone out looking. Are you at your friend's house?"

"Yes," I lie.

"We're doing our best. We've got everyone out there."

I tell him that he said that already, and I hang up. I do not miss the look that passes between Carrie and Kandy. I don't care. When my son is found, I will get the police department a gift basket or something. It crosses my mind that I am thinking *when* instead of *if.* I am excluding the possibility of real tragedy. That is probably good for me, to stay positive. Or is it a bad thing, evidence of callousness or delusion?

When all this started, two years ago, Daniel was seven.

First they diagnosed him with ADHD, like half the boys in his class, but the Ritalin multiplied everything by ten. He threw a chair at his teacher. During gym class, while pretending to be a fish as directed in some game, he went piranha and bit a little girl's arm hard enough to draw blood. She bore bruises in the shape of his teeth. Temper tantrums were nothing new, but their causes grew stranger. He began to throw hours-long bargaining fits at bedtime; he said that the floor of his bedroom was rising, and if he went to sleep, he would be squished. He lined the hens up in a row and kicked them into the back fence, but later wept and called himself an asshole over and over, and slapped his arm with a metal spoon. I had to physically lift him out of bed in the mornings and put his toothbrush in his hand before he'd move a muscle, but later in the day, he would run around the house in his Batman cape, singing, knocking picture frames off the walls.

Then he started to have the dreams. At first they sounded to me like normal anxiety dreams. We've all dreamed of being chased, tripping, falling, sitting unprepared for tests, teeth crumbling in the mouth. Daniel would appear in our bed, elbow-crawling up the middle beneath the duvet, slipping beneath Sam's heavy arm. His small pale face inches from mine, the whites of his eyes blue in the moonlight, he would incant his night's horrors. He had taken to heart the idea of exorcism—shaking his sillies out, getting things *out of his system*, and so on. It was a hopeful practice, and I miss it; now he dreams and will not tell.

He used to dream of two lions with saddles but no riders

that would come tearing around corners at him, slavering. Sometimes he was at school, sometimes in a stony place he called the "castle house," sometimes in the old red velvet Austin theater where we took him to see classic movies in the summer. The lions would bound toward him, and he would run sticky-slow, and always they would overtake him. But where my dreams always end with this, the terrible sureness of death, his would go on. He felt the teeth closing through the flesh of his arm, the snap of bone, the pop of lung, and the hot let of blood. He felt agony that he had no words to express—that I could only read in his panicked breathing as he recounted the dreams, and in his surprised look—a look of discovering too early and too viscerally what pain is possible. Whenever he dreamed of falling, he hit the ground jaw-first. Whenever he dreamed he was in a car, he knew to dread the crash, the needling shower of glass, the impact, the sight of his leg hinging bloody from the bone. Sometimes he felt a crack along the nape of his neck and curling up over his skull; he put his fingers inside and he could feel his bad thoughts, little veined knobs on his brain that he couldn't snap off without pulling up the whole veiny net, without ruining himself utterly.

Three psychiatrists in, we got the diagnosis that I already knew in my gut. His terrible visions and his spinouts, though out of proportion with my own experience, were damningly familiar. Before we got married, Sam and I had discussed the likelihood that our kids would inherit bipolar disorder. Sam said it could never matter to him. Come what may. In the hypothetical, it flattered him to be broad-minded. Anyway, to worry that our kids would be bipolar would have been to worry that they'd turn out like me, and I never would have married a man who thought of me as a worst-case scenario.

The diagnosis came ten months ago, and since then Daniel has been stuffed with antipsychotics, mood stabilizers, and a parade of complementary drugs. A drug for each side effect, and for each side effect of each side effect. Nothing has worked; what doesn't knock him out winds him up. We have rules and exercises and therapy sessions, which help, but the underlying problem is chemical, and so, too, will be the solution. Always, I hope: the next pill will bring my boy back.

KANDY PUTS HER arm around me and rubs my shoulders. "I don't think we're going to find him this way," she says. "Do you think he might have gotten on a bus or a train somehow? Trying to get back to Texas?"

Carrie nods vigorously. "He's done weirder stuff than that."

"Did he have any money with him?"

I shrug. Not to my knowledge, but who knows what his father gave him in private at their parting? I can't picture Daniel buying a bus ticket, sitting alone on a bus. Even in his wildest rages, he clings to me or pushes against me. But at least it is something to do, somewhere to look.

We drive to the bus depot and wander through the little convenience store, the dark dumpstery corners of the parking lot, the bus shelter strewn with trampled pamphlets for Ocean Vista's beaches and rides. A fat man sleeps on the ground, a briefcase under his head. An announcement blares through the loudspeaker for the incoming twelve-fifteen bus from Philadelphia.

By the street lamp light I can see a pink cast to Carrie's cheeks and nose. I didn't see her apply sunblock; maybe she thinks she got away with something. As a teenager, I believed that burns would always heal, my skin always return to a pale and perfect smoothness. My shoulders now are a dark and crinkly tan, like balled paper stretched flat. That faith in regeneration and return, that childhood blindness— that was the same faith that made me careless of my mother. I thought she would always be there.

And what if Daniel *has* left me? Not secreted himself away to evaluate the length and intensity of my search but simply gotten on a bus? Again my mother looms above the skyline with her marionette crossbar and strings. It's true, I lost patience with Daniel sometimes this year. There were times when I left the house with nowhere to go, just to get clear of him, to not care for a few hours. I screamed at him, I held down his arms and legs, once I shut him in a closet when I didn't know what else to do. I tried my best, but that's not what he is thinking if he is out there somewhere on a southbound bus. He is remembering how it feels to be pinned down, to be poked and prodded and shoveled full of pills, to be told he is not the same boy he was last year but worse. Today, to have built a dragon and seen it slip into the sea—to have experienced a miracle and tried to share it with me—and to have been disbelieved.

12

· · · · ·

I LEAVE FOR NEW YORK on a still morning with a gym
bag full of supplies: apples, a loaf of bread, tissue packets,
a can opener, a few emergency cans of chickpeas, tampons,
a fifth of gin, my camera. I leash Blanche and wear dark
glasses so I can pretend she is my Seeing Eye dog if anyone gives us trouble. I swipe my mother's expired driver's
license from the kitchen junk drawer. I look old enough that
if I dress right, I can pass for my mother. As I walk away
from the house, I feel the shiver of eyes on my back, though
no life stirs behind those dark windows.

Jake and I take commuter rail up the seaboard, pushing
through towns and wildernesses and lots full of burnt tire.
Jake keeps his knees apart so I can use him like a recliner,
and with his head on the aisle armrest and mine on his chest,
we can both watch the power lines snake blurry with the
speed of the train. Blanche sleeps. At Metuchen, we make
dirty jokes. The ground races invisibly beneath us.

The ticket guy walks past and leans over us so that we
see his face upside down. "Rock and a roll, thump and a

bump," he says as the train lurches, and chuckles to himself. Trees outside the window again, trees and fences and trackside backyards full of men sitting in lawn chairs and tending to charcoal grills, children playing unrecognizable running games, rusting cars, hoods yawning open like the jaws of animals. Taller and taller buildings as we draw near the city.

JAKE DROPS OUR bag in front of the Sunset Park brownstone where Max lives with four pit bulls and a baby girl. The falling bag makes a *whoomp* sound, and the fabric ripples with impact, and the exact and slowed-down way in which I see this makes me realize how tired I am. Jake slept on the train, but I couldn't. We find Max's name on the buzzer panel and push the buzzer for the first floor. Dogs bark. I blink at the hot intersection. A Gulf station with a tire store, a nameless bodega, lines of solid housing, the fronts pink and brown and gray, dotted with fire escapes, plastic lawn furniture in fenced-in areas of concrete, air conditioners jutting from windows. Twenty feet from Max's corner rises the Brooklyn-Queens Expressway, a green metal monster on which anonymous traffic moves in the sky. Smash-fendered cars are parked in gridlock under the highway, and ten boys about our age stand watching us in T-shirts and sneakers that gleam white from the shade. The small buttresses at the top of Max's three-story brownstone shy away from the hot sun like curled toes.

The door swings inward and Max steps up to the screen. He is a white guy, short, with buzzed hair and biceps you can see through his T-shirt. His shirt has a Ziggy cartoon on it:

Ziggy has just walked in the front door and seen his bird in the fishbowl and his fish on the bird perch, and he is saying, "I really DON'T want to hear about it right now." Max is barefoot, and his hands are covered in white powder. Ideas flash through my head of the drug carnival that lies behind him in the house; I picture the baby daughter splashing in a kiddie pool full of cocaine, cocaine spraying in arcs from the ceiling fans, heaping dog bowls full of cocaine. I smirk, and Max takes it for friendliness. "Oh, shit! Yeah yeah yeah, Jake, come in! Who's your lady?" He pushes open the screen with his elbow and ushers us through an unlit hallway into the kitchen, holding up his powdery hands. Boxes of cereal and pasta sit on the floor and table, milk crates stand in for chairs, high cabinets full of cookies and peanut butter are open to the flies. An open jar of stewed cherries, a wooden spoon planted in a bowl of dough. Turns out he was baking a pie.

Blanche is on edge as Max's dogs leap and smack into the sliding glass door to the backyard. She whines and snaps her jaws. "This is Blanche," I tell Max, since he hasn't acknowledged her at all. His attention seems strikingly selective. "Are your dogs okay with other dogs?"

"Oh yeah, no worries, they're trained as shit," he says, and slides open the door. The four of them bound in, all slobber and muscle, and knock me back against the wall asking for scratches, rolling on my feet. There is a sandy-colored female red-nose, two old males, one blue and one brown, and a tawny-and-white-spotted puppy. Blanche does a low squirming dance of submission. They don't pay

any attention to her or to Jake, either. For [...]
they want is me.

THE FIRST DAY we stay with Max, I am lef[t]
Max take off in the morning, a slam of the front door and
a be-back-soon note scrawled on the back of today's page
from Max's daily factoid tear-off calendar and placed next
to my face on the pillow. Today's factoid: *There is a city
called Rome on every continent.* I fix myself cereal. The sad-
eyed missing boy on the milk carton stares at me. His age,
his height, his weight. *Last seen with . . .* I envy him a little.
Somebody is looking for him.

I use Max's old rotary phone to call up the 92nd Street Y,
pretending to be the parent of a Flying Dolphin, though I
could probably ask my questions directly.

"Swim season is over," says the lady on the phone. "We
start up again in the fall."

"Then how is it that my daughter," I say, exaggerating
the vowels in "daughter" almost too much to sound plausi-
bly adult, "tells me she has been swimming at your club?"

"Well, there is free swim. Evenings six to nine."

"Thank you. I'm so relieved to hear that. I thought she
was sneaking out."

"Okay," murmurs the lady, bored.

It is no use heading up to the Y until evening, so I explore.
As I walk the streets of Brooklyn, I wonder how people put
up barbed wire. Does it come in a roll, like a Slinky, that
you stretch from end to end? Or do you wear inch-thick
gloves and unwind it like a ball of yarn? I photograph men

d women wearing Prada and do-rags, women with boots up to their thighs and men with oiled hair, oiled mustaches, oiled shoes. I can catch only a sidelong sense of who these people are, holding my head as I do, high and purposeful, my neck tight-arched, trying to be a New Yorker. I buy a slice of pizza and sit beneath the Brooklyn Bridge, watching tourists mill around the piers. Tourists are the same everywhere, it seems to me, and that lends a sense of home.

Jake left me money, and I fill my pockets with subway tokens. As the 5 train screeches north beneath Manhattan, two kids perform a break-dance routine, spinning off the ceiling, their sneakers printing *Nike* in dust on the tops of the metal poles. I clutch Blanche's leash and wear my dark glasses. People are very polite to me, letting me on first, offering me their seats. When I emerge at Ninety-sixth Street, I pocket the sunglasses. Here is a different world—waifs in sundresses with French bulldogs, and tired businessmen sitting at small round sidewalk café tables with their feet neatly crossed beneath their chairs, trying not to touch knees with other businessmen.

Outside the broad facade of the 92nd Street Y, I wait at a bus stop, feeding Blanche beef jerky from my pocket. I scrutinize each girl who passes through those heavy Y doors, waiting for Laura and Courtney.

FOR THE FIRST few days, New York is like a honeymoon. Jake and I put the baby down for a nap and have sex on the sofa whenever Max is out of the house. We go to the Met and wander through the galleries, sometimes pretending to be part of tour groups so we can listen to the docents. We are not dumb; we know when it is good to listen. I came here once with my mother, but I remember it only as pain in my feet and a little girl's love of Degas. This time it is staggering.

We buy sweet sausages on Orchard Street, and Jake asks me midbite, "Do you think you could live here?" I watch a woman on the fourth floor of an apartment building pull her laundry in from a bowed clothesline strung across the street. I have seen photographs of these streets when the buildings were all tenements and the laundry lines crisscrossed the sky. I picture time as transparencies, see myself lifting one layer after another away from that picture until there is this one clothesline left, this one woman stretching out her window from the waist to tug her children's socks back inside her apartment. This is how time works: a simplification of things, a peeling away of layers of confusion until the present is a clean and simple refinement of history's clutter.

"Olivia?"

"Yeah," I say. "Sure." The woman's clothesline makes me hopeful. I snap a photograph.

ALL MY CONVENTIONAL wisdoms come from my mother. You can't shake your common sense. You can't even resent it. I think of this especially as I keep house for Jake in the city, shocked at his ignorance of simple things: what a steamer is, how to kill a flea. You must drape wet coats on chairs because they will mildew in the closet. Don't eat the outsides of onions. The attic is always hotter than the basement. When you walk through a city, always look like you have a destination and you're in a hurry, and you will be left alone.

I DEVELOP A routine. In the evenings I sit at the bus stop, staked out, and each night at ten I descend once more into the oven of the subways to wander, to brood, to eventually drift back to Max's, where I find Jake sleeping, stoned, or waiting up. In the daytime we play together, but by evening I shake him off. When my stakeouts end, I take the train down to Coney Island and Sheepshead Bay, out to Canarsie or Corona, up to Pelham Bay Park in the Bronx. The subways are an abandoned city in the very early morning— pits of iron and rat poison where you can walk for miles in the dark and sometimes catch the sound of faint, sourceless music. Men and women sleep curled into buildings and cradled by benches. The city above wheezes and whirs. In dim rooms, strangers meet and part. Babies open their eyes to the blinking lights of the night city and, comforted, drift back to sleep. One night I see, through a third-floor window in an ancient warehouse, a man stark naked with his back to the street, painting a portrait. I can't see the woman he is painting from my vantage point, but I can see her image, pornographic, oversize, red and white, reclining with her hands above her head. I take a photograph, but all I get is the hot glare of a streetlight on a window.

I find a place in Sunset Park not far from Max's apartment where, in the morning, grave Chinese men appear in their front window to string up roasted ducks and pigs. The animals' bodies are crimson, like fat sunburned beachgoers.

I wonder what kind of searching my mother will do. I picture bloodhounds and trench-coated detectives fanning out through a pine forest. Or just my mother on our increasingly stained sofa, passed out drunk in a pile of overdue poetry collections from the library.

When I cook and shop, when I brush my hair, when I speak or sleep, I see her habits pushing up through mine. I see my hand holding a knife as hers does to chop an onion, left thumb weighing down the blade, and my voice taking on her lilt when I call to Jake from another room: a two-note slide, *Ja-aake*.

WHEN THEY FINALLY appear, Courtney holding open the door of the Y for Laura, I am calm. I am glad that I left Blanche at Max's today. They look even more corporeal here in New York, away from the dizzy light of the beach. I wait at the bus stop, unmoved by the ebb and flow of commuters. An hour and a half later, they come back out with wet hair, laughing. Laura with a friend, Courtney half a step behind. I follow them at a short distance, keeping them in sight through the sidewalk throng. Then Laura dashes into the street and throws her arm up for a slowing cab.

My ex-sisters and their friend clamber into the back of the cab and start rolling down Lexington. I run to keep up. I try to make it look like I am jogging for exercise, but nobody cares. We turn onto East Eighty-eighth, and soon, right onto Second Avenue. Luckily for me, it is eight-fifteen on a Tuesday, and Second Avenue is a clogged artery (the poor bloodless heart of Manhattan). I have little trouble until the cab makes a left onto Seventy-fourth; not to lose the trail, I make a mad dash through the traffic. A bumper touches my leg with such gentle pressure that the screech of brakes seems unrelated. A sour man curses out the window of his car, but I am through and jogging down Seventy-fourth while the girls spill out of their cab. They could have so easily walked. Spoiled girls.

Laura and Courtney wave to their friend and part ways. It's amazing how people fail to sense they are being fol-lowed. I think I would sense it in a flash. The quick glance of a stranger, that one camel coat seen and seen again through gaps in a crowd. I follow them at a more discreet distance along these quieter streets, until they vanish into a brown-stone on Seventy-third Street with empty window boxes and two stone lions guarding its weathered oak door. Inside, a light flicks on.

I straighten my clothes: jean shorts and a gray Buzzcocks T-shirt. How lost I must look, an orphan, a stray piece of Jersey flotsam. I walk across the street and up those granite steps, and I face the door and its semicircular cut-glass win-dow through which I can see movement, distorted shapes and colors. They are in there. They have led me, finally, to their home.

I knock.

This is as far as I have planned. I should have taken a longer pause; I have run for blocks, and I cannot catch my breath. I feel like I am running, still. I almost turn around, but then there are quick footsteps and the click of a deadbolt sliding free, the brass tongue of a door handle depressed. The door swings open in that interminable way that all important doors do, and there, looking at me in the sober city light, is the grocery-store woman.

Her forehead furrows, and her jaw sets square as she takes me in. Behind her I see expensiveness even before I can interpret and define the objects themselves.

"Olivia," she says. "Come in." She knows my name. She steps aside and I take the step up into the house. Under the warm electric light of a chandelier, the woman looks less pale. Sideboards draped with raw silk line the wood-paneled foyer. Keys rest in a large half-shell. Laura's laugh drifts from upstairs. The woman takes me by the shoulders and looks at my face. People rarely grab each other by both shoulders. It is deeply unsettling. "I'm so happy you've come," she says in a formal way that confuses me and so gives me a jolt of anger.

"Who *are* you?"

She lets out her breath in a choking sound—a tired, terrible laugh. "Oh my gosh," she says. "I'm Christie. I'm your aunt."

SHE WAS MAKING dinner, she says. Can I stay? The question seems ridiculous. I have stumbled into the home of my secret family, can I stay for dinner? She leads me down the hallway to the kitchen at the back of the house, where she sits me down firmly on a stool at a breakfast bar made of dark, textured stone, and gets me a glass of water. She buys frozen meatballs and canned spinach, I notice: cans on the counter, ripped plastic in the trash. Artificial food. A lidless trash can.

"Are you all right?" she asks me, her hand flitting to my forehead to feel my temperature. That flitting motion—so jerky, nothing like the way my mother moves. "Olivia?"

"Yes."

"What are you doing here?" She looks embarrassed at how this came out. "Of course you're welcome, but—" My aunt, I will learn, is not a socially graceful woman. "Did your mother tell you about us?"

I realize my strategy all at once. "Yes. She sent me to visit."

Her disbelief reads on her face, but she has no idea how to proceed. Maybe Laura and Courtney never lie to her, or maybe they are better at it. She busies herself heating meatballs in a pan.

I ask, "So, how come you've never visited *us*?"

"We didn't know where you were."

Christie eyes me, and I think she is trying to plumb the extent of my knowledge. I scramble for cover. "I mean, this summer, in Jersey."

"Your mother would have blown a gasket. You know."

I ask her what a gasket is, and she tells me it's like a plug used in car engines. She smiles at me. A question she can answer. This woman, *Aunt Christie*, leans forward on the bar seriously, and I see the wispy hair around her temples, her hairline curving there like mine.

She tells me that she and the girls usually vacation in Lavallette, and it was a fluke that they rented a house in Ocean Vista this summer, a fluke that they found us. They find the Jersey Shore more fun and more relaxing than their friends' vacation spots in the Hamptons or Cape Cod, and besides, she says, they like going somewhere where they won't see anyone they know. "And then I saw her there, wearing that purple apron, standing at the register. Looking just the same."

"At the grocery store," I say, understanding.

"She didn't tell you."

I am quiet. Caught.

"Would you like a soda?"

Christie gets me the soda, and I think the task makes it easier for her to talk, navigating through the kitchen, cracking ice cubes out of the tray. If we keep talking, I may end up with four or five beverages. She and the girls happened through my mother's checkout line, she says. "Your mother didn't want us to talk to you. She said she'd move you somewhere else. I didn't want to put you through that. I was still deciding what to do." There is a guilty twinge to her tone that makes me suspect that is not entirely true. She was going to let things be, as my mother ordered. My mother is persuasive.

It occurs to me: that shift when Laura and Courtney started running from me. They had been told to stay away. They *did* know me. None of it was in my head. I feel anger more viscerally than relief: My mother knew that I had seen my cousins in the flesh, and rather than tell me the truth, she let me think I was going crazy. *I haven't had a break today*, she said in the grocery store. *Do you think you had an experience?*

Christie paints a portrait in brief phrases, watching me for signs of upset: "The last time I saw your mother before this summer, she was pregnant with you. We tried to find her for a long time. It was so odd just running into her. *Fifteen* years." She pours my soda at an angle to the glass, so there is almost no foam. "I spoke to her several times this summer about meeting you. About wanting to meet you." She searches me for permission to speak frankly about my mother. Whose side am I on? "She made a scene."

There is a hiss as water from the overheating pasta finds the gas flame beneath the pot. Aunt Christie turns down the burner and gets out a strainer. Normal things to do on a normal night.

"Would you like me to call the girls down?"

"No."

"Okay." She shakes the water out of the pasta.

"It's just the three of you?"

She glances at me as she adds the meat. "The girls' father is on a business trip."

I take in the kitchen: polished, uncluttered surfaces, a lazy Susan on a circular wooden table stocked with lemon pepper and gourmet spreads, a purple stained-glass sconce casting cool light over the room, so that I feel vaguely underwater.

"Weird light," I say, and my aunt explains that it was Laura's idea, because she has read that cool colors make you eat less.

"She's trying to lose some weight before track season. She's a sprinter."

"Is she good?" I ask.

"She's very good."

There is the squeak of sneakers on hardwood, and there they are in the doorway, unsummoned, Laura and Courtney, their familiarity laid bare. They stare at me with their large eyes, and then at Christie.

"Cat's out of the bag," says Christie, and the girls move into the room.

"Hi," Laura says, but Courtney swoops forward and hugs me, her long slender arms around my back and my face in her red hair, her chin snug to my shoulder. I go dizzy with the speed of change. When she pulls back, her eyes are watery pink.

We eat dinner at the round table. Silverware clinks. Napkins wipe. Laura and Courtney sit closer together than most people do, and I wonder if, like puppies, they huddle for protection without knowing it. I am a strange, unknown force, potentially threatening to the order of things.

"How long will you be in the city?" Courtney asks. It is so easy to like Courtney—her impulsiveness, her little-girl politeness here at the table, and the memory of her raucous laughter, her head tilted back to rest on a strange boy's shoulder that first night as she watched Jake climb the cross-bracing of the Ocean Spirit.

"I don't know."

Christie tucks her chin down, twirls her pasta. "Your mother doesn't know you're here, does she?"

"Oh, sure."

"Really?"

I can see I won't be able to convince her. "No. She's on a trip."

Christie sets her fork down. "She left you alone?"

"I'm fifteen." I see this is big news for Christie, and my lie generator whirs into action. "She's at this funeral for this film director. This documentarian. They were really old friends."

"Has she left you alone before?"

"No," I lie.

"Well, you're safe here," says Christie, as if I have escaped from a prison camp or a cruel orphanage. "I'll make up the guest room."

Laura picks at her food, eyes averted. "Will she go to Chapin?"

"We'll see."

"I have a place," I tell them. "In Brooklyn."

"Brooklyn!" says Laura.

"Olivia, I'd like you to stay here," says Christie, drawing herself up tall in her chair—another familiar gesture. "Until I'm able to get in touch with your mother. What's the director's name who died?"

"Oh, I don't know."

"How did she know him?"

I think quickly. "He was a client of hers at Debbie's."

"What's that?"

"The brothel she worked at. Before I was born."

They all look at one another, and Courtney laughs, a musical little hiccup.

"*Before* you were born?" asks Christie. She looks at me for a long time and then shakes her head. "Sweetie, no. That can't be true."

Tiny hairs prickle on my arms. "Except it is."

Nobody speaks for a clock-ticking moment, and then Christie tries to take my hand and I retract it. She speaks softly, firmly, carefully. "I think you know this, but your mom doesn't always know what's real and what's not real."

I realize what feels so wrong about the air: There are no pets in this house. These people don't care for animals. Kids who grow up without animals turn into cold people. They turn into bankers. Suddenly, I hate these people and this house and the dark expensive countertops and the raw silk and the way they are all looking at me and waiting to see what I'll do. Who is this bitch to tell me about my own mother? My mother wouldn't have kept me away from them if they were good people. The room warps and blinks, and I am smothered by the clean air of this house where they keep no animals.

Something I do makes everyone stand up. I go. I move down the hallway toward the front door. There is the dark street on the other side of the cut glass. I won't run, I think. I won't let on how hot and muffled and terrible my thinking is, how something is whispering in my ear to *run run run run run!*

Christie follows me into the hallway, but I shake her

hand off my shoulder. My momentum takes me out the door, between the stone lions, down down down the stairs and out, running after all, onto the streets of Manhattan. I run for many blocks so I can focus on the running, on a pain in my lung, and let that fill my thoughts. Lung. Lung. Lung.

On the subway rattling back toward Brooklyn, I watch a woman rip chunks from a Big Mac and feed them to her toddler, who strains against the straps of her stroller open-mouthed like a baby bird. I want my mother in a way I have rarely felt, a physical yearning. I feel like a baby, like that ugly subway baby. I feel stupid and ashamed. *Come back*, I whisper inside my head, and I cross my arms tight across my stomach to hold in the tears that are coming. *Come back for me.*

"ROYAL FLUSH." MAX splays his hand across the rickety card table, and the whole thing lurches, tipping my beer into my lap. I jump up, holding my skirt away from my legs as the beer soaks through. It is dusk. Though I have told Jake nothing of what happened on Seventy-third Street yesterday, there was some relief in morning coffee and morning sex and the smell of his warm neck. We spent the afternoon watching movies on Max's futon, and I am managing, mostly, not to think.

Bees hover and dive around the honeysuckle bushes that grow on the fence around Max's backyard. Jake gets up and, pretending to wring out my skirt, sticks the cotton in his mouth and sucks the beer from it. Max grunts with laughter, and his friend Elena, a Spanish girl with short tight-curled hair, smiles lazily, stirring a pink drink in a tall glass with her fingernail. The dogs muscle over to lap beer from the grass, all but Blanche, who lies serene by the far fence, surveying. I am grateful for the dogs: their trust, their musk, their questionlessness.

Jake has lost a couple hundred dollars to Max at poker, which is most of the cash we brought, aside from the two thousand for the package. I try to explain to Jake that this is a problem. He lays his head on my shoulder and tells me I shouldn't think so much about money. The sky turns violet and then navy, and the cars pass out front with honks and whining brakes, hip-hop and reggae.

Max and Elena go inside, and Jake throws sticks for the dogs. Blanche bounds over to join in. The dogs hurtle across the small yard, smacking up against the fence, things of pure tireless muscle. It is the red-nose getting to the stick first every time. Her wide face is all joy as she trots the stick back to Jake. I sit in the grass, reaching for the dogs when they come near, rubbing their thick necks. They sputter and lick and roll on their backs.

"Let's take them for a walk," says Jake. He has that look of excitement on his face that means he thinks he's found something to do to please Max. He's been getting that look the last few days: bringing back sausage to grill, cleaning the kitchen, gathering the park wildflowers that Max's baby likes to pick apart with her fat, tiny hands. I've never seen him so helpful.

"All of them?" I ask.

"You're right. Let's just take two."

I snap Blanche's leash on her collar. I am very careful not to deprioritize her. The red-nose seems to understand and wriggles up to Jake, wagging her stump of a tail. We find some leashes inside and take Blanche and the red-nose out into the dusk.

The thing happens under the BQE. There are boys under the highway again, in that dark swath of shadow snaking north-south. They could be the same or different boys, but it doesn't matter. They have dogs, too. Jake is talking about Max's supplier upstate, who grows in great greenhouses and deals with only one dealer per city, and only dealers willing to drive up and back. That's power, says Jake feverishly. Controlling the supply.

"Nice dog," a kid in a white T-shirt calls out, pointing at the red-nose on the end of Jake's leash. "You want to sell that dog?"

"Not mine." We walk a little faster, feeling suspicious but not sure yet that they are closing in around us, shuffling to invisible tactical marks all around the underpass.

"She'd fuck your shit up," the kid says to another kid holding on to a white dog, and they start yelling back and forth, kind of friendly. Then they are laughing, and it seems like one of those moments that just passes away. But then the laughing T-shirt kid breaks out of the group and lunges at our red-nosed dog, pointing at the other kid's mangy white dog. He shouts, "Kill!" My understanding lags. The T-shirt kid leaps backward and claps his hands to his face, goes, "Oh shit!," delighted as the red-nose breaks free of Jake's grip like he is a little girl holding on to that leash and surges across the pavement toward the white dog, who comes forward to meet her with the tragic energy of the clear loser.

The red-nose sinks her eager teeth into the fur of the white dog's neck and hangs bloodily to the wound, the white dog screaming and twisting from the tear, where the red-nose holds her off-kilter, so that every twist of her wiry body deepens the wound. Jake is yelling and waving his arms like an idiot, trying to get Max's dog back. I am still holding on to Blanche's leash. Blanche watches the fight with watery eyes, her muscles twitching as though she is asleep and only dreaming of a fight. Does this recall her savage puppyhood? I have no idea; I realize I hardly know her at all. I tug on her leash, turning to run away.

There isn't time to unloop the leash from my wrist before I am on the ground, skinning my legs on the asphalt, dragged into the fray of teeth and blood-wet fur and the brown intent eyes of dogs. I hear Jake scream, the higher pitch of real fear. I am vaguely aware of human movement around me as the boys come toward the dogs, and of the tightness of the nylon leash binding my wrist, Blanche's jerking pulling it tighter and tighter. My skirt is twisted up to my hips, and I feel a flare of anger at these boys looking at my bare thighs, *all these boys*. The red-nose looks huge above me as she raises her head to slam the white dog's body against the pavement. My sinus fills with the stink of blood and dog and fear.

The white dog takes advantage of the shift to get loose and lock his jaws into our red's sandy shoulder. I am thinking of the red-nose, and of how angry Max will be when he finds out, when I feel it: a cold stabbing pain in my thigh. Things go dark and delirious, and I imagine myself bound by the wrists to a giant dartboard, squirming to avoid the rain of dagger-sharp icicles thrown by shadow giants too distant to see.

I am aware of being carried by Jake and someone else, and then the warm staleness of Max's apartment. Somebody gives me something to swallow, and for a while things run clear, like a movie without sound. Where is Blanche? I want to ask.

Jake comes in through the door, the red-nose limping behind him with a huge tear running from her shoulder to her belly, the fur thick and sticky with blood, the edge of the wound discolored where the white dog's teeth penetrated deeper muscle. Blood oozes down her front leg. She looks at me panting, her tongue lolling from her wide smile. Max lifts her huge weight and lays her on the rug. He curses up at Jake. Jake goes to him, and the two of them gesture and yell until Elena comes out half-dressed, in a floral bra, scream-ing, "Oh! Oh!," and kneels over the torn dog, patting the wound with her hands as if that will help.

I see Jake running around the house, picking up our few things and stuffing them back into the duffel. He picks me up last. I feel like a coat left draped over a chair. Then we are out in the sticky night. My leg feels gone. I will find out later that Jake and Max were arguing because Max wouldn't let Jake call an ambulance from his phone line. There was a warrant out for Max, and he refused to risk his safety for mine. Jake is crushed. He imagined a brother in Max; that we would go on living here, a wild, lawless family. But to Max, we are just some stupid kids. The door slams in our faces, and inside we can hear Max keening for his girl dog, and the thinner sound from a distant room of his baby daughter wailing, too, without knowing what for.

IT DOESN'T TAKE long for someone to notice us: a frantic boy carrying a girl in a bloody skirt. The woman who calls us a cab thinks I am giving birth. "Breathe!" she keeps saying to me. "Just breathe!"

I remember nothing of my arrival at the Maimonides emergency room. I do remember surfacing, though, in a two-bed room next to a heavy sleeping woman with a wash of ripe yellow bruising under her eyes. White ceilings, blue curtains on curving tracks. A muted television, a fire on the news.

I have an IV. I feel an impulse to yank it out like people do in movies when they know the killer is still after them. I wince, picturing the thick needle splitting the flesh of my wrist, the twist-tied bouquet of clear tubes torn and gushing fluid onto the floor. Anyway, where would I go? My leg is bandaged and hot. I clench my thigh muscle tentatively, and pain flares from deep bone.

I sit up carefully and catch sight, through the open door, of Jake asleep on a sofa in a carpeted alcove in the hallway, next to a tall potted plant that bends over to shelter him with its leafy arms. He looks very young, curled there on his side. His dark hair falls across his pale face, his elegant cheekbones. My view is suddenly obscured by blue cotton: teddy bears and stars. The thick torso of a nurse shifts into focus, and a face looms down. Hands rearrange me to a lying position. *Honey, how are you feeling? Can you understand me?* A clipboard in her hands and then questions.

What's your name?

Olivia.

How old are you?

Fifteen.

Where do you live?

Far away.

Far away where?

Far, far away.

My leg hurts, and it hurts to think. Jake will wake up and we will have to go home. His parents will come get him, lecture him, make sure he is okay. They'll bring sandwiches for the car ride. But me, I will go home to the same old questions. The empty house or the raving mother. The same old ghosts. To go home now would be to have gained nothing.

I need an address, honey. I need a parent or guardian. She is calling me honey. She is calling me honey, baby, sweetie. *A parent or guardian,* she says. Jake looks so young sleeping on that bench, like a little boy. I think, We are both very young.

"Six-oh-six East Seventy-third Street," I say. "Christie Mader." And then I sleep.

I DREAM OF dogs: dogs who unzip themselves to let other dogs step out, dogs who eat each other cleanly, bite by bite, as if they are made of marzipan.

THE NEXT TIME I wake up, Christie is there. She lays her cold hand on my wrist. She says, "They gave you eighteen stitches."

I ask her if they are the dissolving kind because I don't know what else to ask. No, she says, and we sit in silence. A nurse brings me a tray of mashed potatoes and chicken and a plastic spoon. I see my gym bag on a chair; Jake must have put it there. He is still asleep out on the couch. The way he sleeps, he could be out for twenty hours. The nurses coo over him from their station. Such a handsome kid. I wait for Christie to say that we are family now, or that she is glad I called her *because* we are family now, or something along these maudlin lines, but she sits tight-lipped and careful on the edge of the visitor's chair.

"You can have the guest room," she says at last. I impale my chicken on my spoon and work the mashed potatoes into little balls between my palms. I don't say no.

I am supposed to keep my leg up for a week. They will wheel me downstairs in a hospital chair; off hospital grounds, I am to make do, to lean and lounge. Christie has brought me clean clothes. I recognize the green T-shirt as one of Laura's. A nurse reels in the privacy curtain on its rounded track before throwing back the sheets and helping me step into an elastic-waist skirt. My right thigh is pink at the edges of the bandaging. I am wearing hospital under-wear, baggy and stiff like a cotton sheet. Someone must have changed me. Christie sees me embarrassed and turns away.

Christie has taken care of my bill, my paperwork, the invisible orchestrations behind my quick release. She gives me the same adult-concern smile the nurses do: How did this child come to such harm? Who let this happen? No one knows how to read my shrinking shoulders and my darting gaze as they wheel me into the elevator, because no one recalls that I did not come in alone, that the pretty boy sleeping on the couch carried me in, frantic, before he fell into this deathlike public sleep.

I don't even leave him a note. I watch him sleeping there looking like a disguised prince or a shipwrecked boy god, dark curls on pale brow, and the thought of his waking exhausts me. He will be concerned and heroic; he will make plans. As I am wheeled backward and away from him, into the elevator, I see those filaments that connected us cobwebbing away. I think of his house and his mother and her seven shades of white and his Roman candles and Kandy laying her blond head on his shoulder, dancing, and none of it has anything to do with me. I have been a tourist in his life, and in Ocean Vista, and in my own life, and I feel that I am finished with everyone and everything I know; that my real life has been here in New York, wrapped up like a present, waiting for me to come find it.

13

. . . . .

O CEAN VISTA'S ONLY hospital is called Mercy. The emergency room waiting area is empty, clusters of seats upholstered in a stain-camouflaging navy plaid. I walk to one side of the room and Kandy walks to the other, checking behind things. Carrie stands, hood drawn around her face, arms pretzeled, on the tiled runway that leads from the great sliding doors straight to triage. I imagine a gurney shooting across the linoleum, sparks flying from the wheels, my concussed son lifting his head weakly, asking strangers, *What happened? Where am I?*

Carrie's voice rings out and seems to carry the hard blue quality of the lighting. "We would already know if he was here."

"If he *were* here," I say, and I approach the little desk station by the triage doors, looking for a bell to ring. Where else in the world is an emergency room unmanned? "Hello?" I call out. "Help, please. I'm dying, come help me."

"The police would know, Mom. They keep records. It's

a hospital." Carrie is adhering to a too-strict logic. What of amnesia, what of clerical error?

A short, rosy, piggish woman pushes through the triage doors with both hands to stand behind the desk. Her thin black hair is plastered tight to her head, and she is wearing patchwork blue jeans. Her oddness takes my breath away. Is this the woman who will tell me that my son is dead? And then: these terrible thoughts, these hard, bright, almost funny thoughts that are springing to my mind—are these the thoughts a mother should have?

"Can I help you?" the woman asks, as if she is bored of emergencies.

"Has a nine-year-old boy come in tonight?"

"No. Did you just say you were dying?"

"No."

She hoists herself onto a stool behind the desk and glares at me. Kandy is sitting on one of the plaid sofas, and I join her.

"I bet he'll turn up with some story he'll tell forever," she says. She smiles faintly. The evenness of her breathing calms me down.

"Who *are* you?" I ask her. "When we were kids, you were the last person I thought I'd still know at forty."

"I didn't think I'd make it to forty. Sex, drugs, and rock and roll, baby." She makes a little headbanging gesture and flicks her tongue out. "I remember when we met, the night you climbed the roller coaster. Jesus Christ, that was dangerous. I thought you were so cool." She sighs and rests her head on the back of the sofa. "I wanted to be you."

"You're kidding."

"I was a whole production, you know, and you walked in and you were just effortless."

"Effortlessly what?"

"Lovable." She eyes me.

"That's not true."

"Yes, it is. You were like a magnet. You don't know that?"

The sliding glass doors whoosh open, and two old men enter, one hunching to prop up the other, a bearded man in a Hawaiian shirt who grits his teeth and moves heavily. We stop talking to regard their progress toward the triage station. The taller man readjusts his arm low around the other man's back, to take more weight, and the gesture is so tender and so intimate that I have to look away.

IT IS NOT only through the grace and goodwill of my family that I am about to take up residence in the Seventy-third Street house; half of it belongs to me. It has been vacant for eight months, since Christie left on a fellowship to Oxford, to lecture. She isn't sure when she'll come back. The last time I spoke to her, she said that she has made connections at Oxford that she never expected to make. She sounded robust on the phone; I don't think she was talking about professional connections. I'm happy for her. She deserves whatever happiness she can find. If she comes back, we'll decide which half of the house is mine. We have joked about the possibilities: every other room, basement and attic and a fireman's pole between, each room from waist-level to ceiling. Though they never formally separated, Tom hasn't slept in the house in years.

Laura lives in San Diego, where she runs marketing for a design firm. Her home is full of furniture reupholstered in vintage fabrics, blown-glass sculptures, iPod docks made to look like little tree stumps. She married a journalist and had two sons, and they are a California family. They eat on a porch shaded by palm trees and visited by green Pacific tree frogs who suicide in the kidney-shaped pool. Daniel likes it there, likes diving down to touch the robotic pool vacuum. It is too glossy a world for me; I clunk through it. I never know what to say.

Courtney is still in New York, vanished into the world of theater. She lives downtown with a longtime boyfriend. She is a stage manager. I go to her plays when I can and wait for her in the lobby afterward until she emerges, red-lipsticked and tired and flocked around by interns. She offered to help us move into the house, though she is as unreliable as I am, and I expect her not at ten A.M. with the movers but at ten P.M. with a pizza and apologies. If we make it up to New York at all, if we survive this day, if Daniel is found.

Here is what I hoped for: We move to the Seventy-third Street house and it becomes a new environment, in no way comparable to the ranch in Austin, an environment in which I am mother enough to fill the gap where Sam used to be. We get a puppy. Two puppies. We go to plays. Carrie discovers literature, or chemistry, or tuba, or *something*. Daniel is stimulated but not overstimulated. The new psychiatrist figures him out in three visits. The kids help me chop onions and shell peas before dinner and tell me about their days at their high-scoring magnet schools. Everything knits itself up neatly.

The psychiatrist whom Daniel is going to see in New York is an authority on early-onset bipolar disorder. He has published a book in which he rails against other psychiatrists who refuse to acknowledge the diagnosis, and who refuse to prescribe mood stabilizers for children because of the side effects with which we are now so intimately familiar, and against all the psychiatrists of the past, all the Freud fanatics, who didn't want to diagnose and medicate kids too soon, until their symptoms coalesced into clearly recognizable patterns. I would have had reservations if we had gone to this man first, but now I want anyone with a plan.

And what about me? I ask myself. Where am I in my own hopes? I will have to get a job. My last several in Austin were in dismal academic offices: making copies at a private school, making copies at a university, making copies at a law library. My retinas will burn away, so often do I find myself staring at the moving bar of light beneath the glass plate. People tell me I should be doing more, and I know it. As a teenager, I thought I would become a photographer because I took pictures. In college, I thought I would be a writer because I wrote poems, or an anthropologist because I studied people. I suppose that anyone who does anything is a doer of that thing. But it is a mystery to me how people choose one thing to be and then feel comfortable being that thing forever. It does not serve me well to be so baffled; I have become, by inaction, a professional copier. Like the Xerox machine itself. I guess I hope I figure out what to hope for.

SAM AND I sat together in the child psychiatrist's office but always emerged having heard different things.

"She said not to give in," Sam said, wrestling a bowl of ice cream away from Daniel. "She said to pick our battles," I said, trying to fend him off. Daniel banshee-screaming. Sam tried to do the right things for Daniel at home but was easily discouraged by failure. A reward system failed to make Daniel do his chores, so Sam gave up on all reward systems.

At least at home Sam tried. It was in public that he failed us, not occasionally but every time. At the public pool, Daniel dunked another boy too vigorously and refused to come out of the water. The boy coughed, clinging to the lip of the pool and to his mother's bronzed ankle. Daniel swam toward another kid.

"Control your son!" the mother shrieked at us, as if Sam and I were not already yelling for him to get out of the pool, threatening no more swim time, no more TV, no more dessert. The sun beat down on us, and sunbathing women flipped on their towels for a better view. Sam, agitated to shaking, backed away from me, toward the angry mother, and said *to me*, "Well?"

So I jumped in, fully dressed, and wrestled my boy to safety. As I toweled him off, the angry mother approached us for a redundant browbeating, and it was me that she glared at. Only me. As if by failing to help, Sam had excused himself from fatherhood altogether.

When I wasn't there, things were even worse. Sam's usual tactic was flight—cram Daniel in the car out of sight, roll up the windows, and beeline home to dump him on me. I'd like to know what it is in Sam that made his embarrassment so acute. What backbone-forming experience did his parents deny him? When I think of him shushing Daniel in a restaurant, shaking him by the shoulders, gripped by that selfish fear, I feel no love at all.

Once he made an effort. It was a few weeks after we got Daniel's diagnosis, and Sam was still excited, as if by having a word for Daniel's disorder, we had it cornered. At two-fifty the bus dropped the other kids in front of our house. Carrie slumped up the porch steps and into the living room, where she rested her head on the door frame, formulating some request. I asked her why Daniel wasn't with her, and she raised her eyebrows. "Dad didn't call you?"

I left three messages on Sam's cell before he picked up. "It's hard to hear you," he said through a roaring wind.

"What?"

"It's hard to hear you."

"Where are you?"

"Enchanted Rock," he shouted. "Hiking. Boys' day."

"The doctor said routine is really important right now."

"What?"

"Routine. Is important."

"So's this."

When they got home, it was dark. Daniel went straight to his room and slammed the door, then opened it again momentarily to throw his sandy socks out into the hallway. Sam looked exhausted, which pleased me. See how hard it is. I had taken my job at the university down to part-time so I could watch Daniel in the afternoons after his rages became too much for the babysitter. Sam rarely spent time alone with him.

Sam's T-shirt showed pale wavy lines of dried sweat. I followed him to our bedroom, passing Carrie's room, where she lay on her zebra-striped bedspread with her face in her social studies textbook and pretended she hadn't heard Sam come home. Carrie loves to hike with her dad. Left behind again.

Once we were behind closed doors, I questioned him. "What were you doing? Why didn't you call me?"

"I was going to get a pizza on the way back, but . . ." He shook pebbles out of his shoes right onto the carpet. "It was a sudden thing. I just thought it might help."

"And?"

"I don't know. We climbed to the top and threw the bad parts of ourselves off the edge. Something I read about." I couldn't see Sam doing this imaginary thing. At a party once, I saw him forced to play a theater game where you throw an invisible ball from person to person. He almost couldn't do it, he was so embarrassed.

"What bad parts?" I ask.

"What do you think."

"What are the bad parts? Bad like evil or bad like fruit goes bad?"

He eyed me. "Please be nice to me right now," he said. "He cried the whole way home. Two hours, nonstop."

"About what?"

Sam blew out air. "I don't even fucking know."

Later I found the browser search history on Sam's laptop full of exorcism videos. Monks chanting over a cancerous woman, dancers in hideous masks circling a little boy holding a bound pigeon. An article about the curative power of intention, about a doctor who cured a man's skin condition because he thought he could, but lost the ability once he found out the condition was incurable.

WHEN SOMETHING BROKE in our house, a lamp or a glass, I would take it to my workbench and try to glue it back together. But if Sam found it before I did, he would drop it in the trash without a thought. This is why I left him in the end.

KANDY AND I stand outside the emergency room under the concrete ambulance-port and blink for a moment. It is almost one in the morning. The fireflies have gone out, and traffic has dwindled such that I can hear the surf clearly.

"Where did Carrie go?" Kandy asks. "I thought she was out here." I look around and see empty benches, two EMTs with cups of coffee leaning against a hospital van. *Oh, come on, universe*, I think. *You've got to be kidding.*

"Carrie?" Kandy calls, but I hush her, because I catch the sound of my daughter's whispering. That sleepover sound, drifting from the family room up to my bedroom through the air vents and always with such urgency, such a rush of breath. What is so important? I would wonder as Sam slept on. What is such a secret?

I round the corner of the emergency wing and find Carrie, sitting all folded up behind an empty concrete planter, sweatshirt stretched over her knees, her feet in their flip-flops protruding beneath, cell phone to her ear. She looks up at me, and I see the graphite bleed of her eye makeup below her lower lashes. Poor Carrie. In New York they will make her say "y'all" and "pecan" for them and laugh. They will do their hair differently.

"Don't do that to me," I say.

She drops her chin to her chest and lets out a little hiccupping sob. "Mm-hmm," she says into the phone.

"Who are you talking to?"

She doesn't look up. Ah. She is telling on me. If it's one-something here, it's twelve-something in Texas. I know the chair he will be sitting in and the level of bourbon in his glass. The TV will be tuned to Comedy Central on mute.

"Does he say hi?" I ask. Carrie listens for a second and then holds the phone out to me. I cross over to her and sit as near as I dare. Kandy is sitting on a bench across the emergency driveway, reading a book under a street lamp. She must have had the book in her purse. So prepared.

"Sam," I say into Carrie's phone, and before he speaks, I think I can feel his breath on my cheek, coming through the tiny holes in the purple plastic. I'm trying so hard to focus on the ways he failed us, but I can't help it—his breath makes me think of his lips on my skin, and of the rise of his chest when he sleeps, and of his white toes poking through the threadbare socks that I wanted him to replace. He is probably wearing those socks right now. I don't know when I will stop thinking these thoughts. I had hoped divorce would be a cliff off of which our love would fall and shatter into a million pieces. It turns out divorce is just a piece of paper, and I miss my husband more than I will say out loud, despite everything.

"I don't know what to say to you about all this," he says.

"Nothing is fine."

"Are you okay? Handling it okay, I mean? Carrie says the police are on it, not much else you can do till they find him, right? Olivia? You there?"

"Mm."

"Let me know as soon as you know anything, okay? Will you do that?"

"Yes," I say. Now that he has been invited into the crisis of the custodial parent, I will not be cruel. I snap the phone shut.

Carrie blows out a mouthful of air and pillows her head on the stretched sweatshirt between her knees. I put a hand on her back, but she shivers me off.

"We'll find him," I say.

"Whatever."

"Probably. Odds-wise."

"Probably." She squeezes her eyes shut. "The really bad thing is . . ." she starts. I am silent, afraid to discourage her honesty with my voice or my breath or my touch. "If we didn't find him, it might be . . . Things might be . . ." She inhales sharply, coughs.

"Sweetness," I say.

She picks her head up and fixes me with a tortured look, and I understand: It's Carrie versus Carrie in there. She's battling for her soul. "Does that make me a bad person?"

"No."

"I mean, obviously I hope he's okay. Obviously I, like, love him."

"It's been a bad year for us all." When I think of myself as a teenager, raging through that dire summer, and then I think of the kind of girl that Carrie is, I am ashamed. There is no parallel. Carrie has been betrayed, overshadowed, and overlooked, and here she is, wandering the night streets on my whim, crying not out of self-pity but from her own struggle to be good.

We stand up without speaking, pressed shoulder to shoulder. Kandy drifts to meet us as we make our way back to the parking lot. As we walk, Carrie twines her wrist around the crook of my elbow and hangs on. It's the middle of the night, and nobody is looking. I know I haven't earned the right to comfort her tonight. She is giving me this.

Sometimes I wonder if I would be selfish in a clutch situation; if some black-robed inquisitor stood over my family and said, *Which one shall I take?*, if I wouldn't just close my eyes and wait and see. Or worse, if I wouldn't leave, as I left my mother. But right now I know that I don't need to worry about this, that truly, as he reached for one of my kids, I would yell, *No, take me!* For Carrie and Daniel, I would throw myself in front of a bus. I would eat lava. I would photocopy forever.

14

· · · · ·

THE FIRST FEW days at the Seventy-third Street house are tentative. Clearly, there has been much talk about me since my first visit. Laura and Courtney sit at the foot of my bed, asking me what TV shows I like and what drugs I've done and if I am a virgin. I lie because I don't know yet if I have to. It's hard to think of them as real girls, as cousins. I keep expecting them to run away. I feel more stable in my mind, but also farther from home than I have ever been. They lend me clothing and walk nervously past my open door, asking is there anything I need?

In this household, strong emotion doesn't make sense, and there is an even pace to the passage of time that I have never known. I accidentally lock myself in the bathroom and have to yell until Laura comes to show me how to jiggle the handle. I limp from chair to chair and read magazines with my bandaged right leg propped up on pillows. We go to a movie matinee, and I sit in the aisle seat with a special footstool that the ushers let us drag in. When I turn and look down the row, it's like looking in two facing mirrors, their faces familiar iterations of one face. Nobody forecasts the length of my stay, at least not out loud. It must seem to Laura and Courtney that I have no choice but Christie's guardianship. But I can see an unease in Christie sometimes, a flicker of a glance toward the front door, a twitch at the ringing of the phone, that tells me she knows my mother will come for me; that sooner or later, there will be a reckoning.

I lie on a chaise in the backyard while Christie jabs at her rosebushes with a huge pair of scissors. Abruptly, she says, "Your mother and I made a koi pond when we were in high school, right there," pointing to the green rosebush in the corner, up against the fence. "And now that bush won't flower."

My mother still owns half of this house, Christie tells me. She grew up here. Christie drops these bits of information on me as she passes through rooms, as she brings me glasses of fancy juice: black-currant nectar with seltzer, peach-orange-carrot infusions. Christie has taken time off work to monitor my convalescence, so she is always around the house, angling at me. She is a molecular biologist at NYU. She says it is fascinating work, but when she tries to explain it to me, it puts me off. It sounds too familiar: faith in what cannot be seen.

Christie drives me around to all the animal shelters in Brooklyn, and we walk past kennel after kennel full of dogs who are not Blanche. Despondent mastiffs with lazy, iridescent eyes, fearful gnashing mutts, beagles frenzying against the chain link in their eagerness for the man in work pants to take them into the back room for the best walk in the world.

Endless litters of orphaned puppies. I wonder if they really are orphaned. People just take baby animals; they don't wait long enough to see if the mother is coming back. I imagine the mother dog loping stupidly around, thinking, *I could swear this was the place*. I cannot beat the lump in my throat. Poor Blanche. I crave her rusty smell and the feel of her sleeping bulk against my back. I resolve not to stop looking, but I don't know where else to look.

MIDDLE OF THE night. The front door opens and shuts. I am eating yogurt in the kitchen, reading one of Laura's detective novels with my leg propped up on a chair. The regularity of sleep schedules in this house is something I can't get used to. No lights come on, but the approaching footsteps are sure. A man materializes in the kitchen doorway from the darkness of the hall, and I can see that he is Laura and Courtney's father. They take after him physically: broad shoulders and lean muscle. His forehead, beneath a youthful shag of light brown hair, is deeply lined. He wears square-framed glasses, and there is something hopelessly sad in the architecture of his face in that moment before he realizes I am there.

"Excuse me," he says. "You're Olivia?"

I nod.

"Tom." He shakes my hand like a business acquaintance. "Are you enjoying New York?"

"Yes," I say, reduced to a child's dumb interview answers by the suddenness with which I have been torn from the world of my book. "Thank you."

Tom opens the fridge and stares at its contents, bathed in fluorescence. He selects a Tupperware container and pops the lid. "Shrimp?" he asks, holding it toward me.

"No, thanks."

Tom wanders back into the dark hallway, eating from his Tupperware, and I hear him go upstairs very slowly, hesitating over each heavy step.

TOM'S RETURN OCCASIONS a family outing. I claim that I can walk okay; Christie puts me through a battery of tests in the living room. I wince silently when I come down on my right foot, and the pain blushes out through my thigh, duller and rosier now. I am a good liar, though, and Christie says okay. We go to a fancy Asian fusion restaurant and eat a three-course lunch, my first such. I order duck and it comes whole, its neck twisted in an attitude of shame beneath its breast, its head startlingly attached. I thought they would lop it off before putting it on the plate. It looks like the duck tried to shelter its poor duck face from the heat of the oven. I can't eat it, but I pull the meat apart some to make it seem eaten. I see Tom and Christie glance at each other, I see Laura and Courtney's clean white plates. The silver credit card tucked in the leather folder.

Christie flashes a family membership card at the concierge in the Natural History Museum. We wander apart and come together, ogling displays on puffer-fish anatomy and listening to a gray old man wax passionate in the planetarium about the birth and death of stars. I have to leave my camera in the cloakroom. Christie and Tom share a love of the inner workings of things, and the girls are instinctively curious. I just look at things without reading the placards. I run my thumb along the smooth edge of a meteor when the guards aren't looking, and I see Christie alarmed, fighting the impulse to chastise me.

"Olivia, come take a look at this," says Tom, beckoning me over to a case of prehistoric fossils. "Fantastic!"

I am not sure what he finds so fantastic about these rocks, but he is clearly and forcefully trying to draw my enthusiasm, so I say, "Wow." One minute he puts on a show of enthusiasm like this, and the next I can say something right to his face and he'll barely acknowledge me. Courtney and Laura adore him. They fight for his attention. Sometimes one of them will hang back to talk with him alone and I'll see them walking in step, slouching the same slouch, laughing into their hands.

The museum becomes for me another kind of museum, a Museum of Own Family, in which I can study the rituals and habits of this rare species. I observe my aunt and uncle in front of the dioramas of Early Man. Christie is explaining something to Tom, gesturing with her hands. She looks at the hairy little Homo sapiens behind the glass as she talks, and not at her husband. Tom nods again and again, his hands clasped behind his back. He is wearing a blue polo shirt, khaki shorts, and dopey white folded-down tube socks. They talk without touching and then they drift apart. Laura and Courtney come to get me whenever they find anything particularly interesting. We browse the skeletons of extinct creatures, joking about what they must have looked like. Courtney says to Laura that they are something that sounds like *wumpus-bumpuses*. They squeal with laughter. "Oh, sorry," says Laura, realizing my exclusion. "It's hard to explain."

I find myself alone in a long rectangular room devoted to genetics. Colorful double-helix statues spiral toward the ceiling, and a video about Gregor Mendel plays on a loop. There is a blown-up photograph of a family, two parents and two children. Red circles are printed over their hereditary characteristics: bent little fingers, cleft chins, tiny hairs between the second and third knuckle. The little boy in the picture is holding his mother's hand, and the father has the little girl on his shoulders, and they are all smiling toothpaste smiles. I want to draw red circles around the smiles, around the happiness itself.

We convene on a bench in the grand museum lobby, while Tom slips out to make a phone call on his enormous Motorola cell phone. Christie's aspect changes—the muscles in her face relax, and her hands drop to her purse to fumble for hard candies. "Did you see the extinct-creatures exhibit on the fourth floor?"

We nod.

"Did you take notes, Courtney? You could use that for one of your makeups." Courtney has failed biology and must start this year with a makeup course so that she can mend her permanent record for college admissions. It's the worst thing she could have failed. Courtney sighs. Through the rotating glass doors, I can see Tom gesturing on the phone.

"It's so nice to have you, Olivia," Christie says, drawing my attention back. "It's just such a treat."

This statement works us over like a camera panning out, and we are awkwardly silent, thinking about my presence here. I blurt my question: "So why did my mother leave?" It's the wrong time and place to ask it, and it feels heavier now, having waited in my mouth for days and days.

"To have you," Christie says carefully.

"Why not have me here?"

"She wasn't thinking straight. She had only been diagnosed a year or so before."

"With what?" I ask.

Christie holds out a palm full of hard candies, and Laura and Courtney take theirs automatically. They look at me. "Bipolar disorder. Is that— Have you heard of that before?"

This is, in fact, the first time I have heard the words "bipolar disorder," but that doesn't mean it's news. The term describes my mother perfectly—having two poles, riding the sine wave between them, leaving behind her a wake of disorder. I think of the divine-energies chart. "Oh, sure," I say. "Yeah." They look relieved. "So what happened?" I ask. My toes curl in my shoes.

"She was manic. She thought we wanted to hurt her. What did she tell you about us, growing up? Anything?"

"Just that my grandparents are dead and that she was an only child."

"Yes, your grandparents are dead," Christie says, stung.

Tom comes in, slightly sweaty. "Are my girls having fun?" he says, and everyone smiles mechanically.

"Why would she think you were going to hurt her?" I ask.

"Cab's waiting," Tom says, and everyone jumps up. My question is stranded, unanswered, in the museum lobby as I follow my new family down the great concrete steps and out into the street.

JAKE IS HOME by now, I imagine. Summer is still summer, and maybe they've gotten back into the Emerald, found a suite on another floor. Kids are skinny-dipping and sunbathing and skateboarding and making out. There are backyard parties with kegs of PBR, and long nights of talk, confessions of love. When I think of this exquisite summer going on without me, I feel derailed. But I can't go back to that. I betrayed all the best people. It hurts less to imagine that they hate me than to imagine that they don't. If I go home, it will have to be different. Everything will have to be different.

If my mother has returned, I imagine that the empty house is teaching her lessons. In my absence, she can see that she has been wrong to treat me like a child, to lie to me, to make me doubt my own mind. She is praying—not talking to God but praying, like a penitent—for my safe return. I imagine her tidying everything, readying everything. Collecting her hair in a tight, neat ponytail, trimming her jagged toenails. She puts her tarot decks in a shoe box and slides them under the bed. She balls up the divine-energies chart. She goes to a doctor and takes whatever is prescribed for her; she'd rather be a good mother than a good psychic. She chooses me over everything else.

COURTNEY AND LAURA have their own secret life. Theirs is a muted rebellion, the threat of failure dangling over their heads. Still, they tell Christie they are sleeping over at a friend's house and sneak across town to Columbia dorm parties, where cute, stubbly journalism majors fill their plastic cups with mysterious punch.

They take me along to one of these on a Friday night when Manhattan seems apt to boil over: the screeching traffic, the anxious sidewalk crowds, the city swelter. We meet some of their girlfriends from Chapin, girls in black tank tops and tight tapered jeans, and hail a cab. "This is our estranged cousin," they say to their friends, and we giggle because it is true.

The dorm is a high-rise with a view of the Hudson River. In the elevator, older boys look me up and down. I think I'd better be wild tonight; I could use a thrill to get out of my head after all the illuminations of the week. I study Courtney's warped reflection in the elevator's chrome wall and see not the flesh-and-bone girl I know she is, but the ghost staring back at me, and this gives me a little push, a little reignition. When the elevator stops and we get out, we are mortal again, and I feel the loss and need a drink.

"You're probably used to crazier parties than this," says Laura as we shoulder through the crowded dorm hallway. Cheesy pop music plays from a stereo that someone has dragged into the hall. My friends would roll their eyes and pull all the tape out of the cassettes.

A skinny college boy beckons us into a dorm room, to a table stocked with Boone's Farm wine coolers in pastel colors. I drain mine quickly. We find a room where everyone is dancing, the bunk bed and all the blond college furniture pushed to the walls. *I made it through the wilderness* . . . Strobe lights flash. The alcohol numbs the pain in my leg, and I find I can stand and dance a little if I move from the hips and not the feet. Laura and Courtney's friends are pulling out some ridiculous moves, throwing their arms out horizontally and then vertically, their faces turned to the ceiling, taking themselves very seriously. Courtney catches my eye and we laugh. One by one, they are danced out of our company by pink-cheeked boys with stumbling rhythm. I scan the boys in the room and I've gone around twice before I realize that I'm looking for Jake. I try to shake these thoughts: his soft mouth, his hand on my hip. Laura is leaned up in a corner, talking to a guy in a porkpie hat, gesturing, her eyes wide. Like my mother, I think, watching his rapt expression and her easy body language. She has him completely.

Courtney and I find the bathroom and stand in a line of girls combing their bangs in the mirror, waiting for the two stalls to free up. The bright fluorescent lighting is a relief.

"I should cut my hair," she says.

"Your hair is amazing." I run a hand through it.

She lifts it up at the roots and mimes scissors with her fingers. "I'd cut a second off my fifty-yard fly."

There is something sad and sweet in her look as she

appraises herself—that kind of honesty that bubbles up through heavy drinking, or hours of stargazing, or staring out the window of a car. Girls chatter behind us, girls say, *Ohmygod I have to go so bad.*

"You're lucky you're an only child," says Courtney, and I laugh out loud, which makes her laugh, too, though she doesn't know why it is funny.

"I'll cut it for you," I say.

"Yeah?" We traipse from room to slovenly room, scavenging for scissors, and find some in a desk drawer, next to a skull key chain and a strip of condoms. We set up a chair in the bathroom, and some of the party follows us in: Something is happening! *Some girl's going to shave her head!* They sit on the counters around us or against the wall as I wet down Courtney's hair and brandish the scissors dramatically. I am in my element. I am the girl who makes *something happen*.

"How short do you want it?" I ask Courtney.

She squints solemnly at her reflection. "Short."

I start working the scissors, gnawing off huge chunks of her thick, gorgeous auburn hair. When the first chunk falls, everyone gasps softly, and then the party is rejuvenated, conversations rising over conversations. First I cut it chin-length and give her severe bangs, which makes her look like a librarian, and she makes a *shhh* face and gets somebody to take a picture.

"Definitely still shorter," she says, and I grip it at the roots and shear it close to her scalp.

"Jesus Christ!" Laura pushes her way into the bathroom

to stand behind us. "What are you doing? Mom is going to murder you!"

"I know!" Courtney smiles joyfully. "I know!" Laura reaches out to touch the fuzzy stubble of her sister's head, purses her lips, and walks back out into the hallway.

When I am finished, Courtney has soft little bangs that stand up on their own and spike out over her short forehead. The roots of her hair are darker red, almost purple, so her whole head looks darker, the hair about an inch long, laying flat and glossy like seal fur. She looks like a new person.

She wiggles her shoulders, delighted. "It's so light!" We find boys to dance with, and all night people want to touch Courtney's hair. We finally trip out of the dorm, the lights of Manhattan blurry and moving. We laugh and clutch one another in the street. Laura acts the big sister, making sure we both drink water and spritzing us with fabric deodorizer so Christie won't sniff out what kind of a night we've had. We sleep at one of their friends' apartments on a crowded futon, and in the morning, bleary, wearing borrowed clothes, we walk up the steps to the Seventy-third Street house.

In daylight, Courtney is even more dramatically transformed. She takes a deep breath as we key open the door.

"Hi," calls Laura as we walk down the hallway. "Mom?" I pass through the kitchen doorway behind my cousins and stop short. There, sitting at that round wooden table with a coffee cup in her hands, her eyes red-rimmed and her hair a nest of tangles, is *my* mother.

My body's instinct is to run to her and bury my face in her neck, to cling like a koala. But that would be to concede.

I stand rooted and swaying, speechless. Christie appears in the pantry doorway, holding a box of crackers, bashful in her own house.

My mother tightens her grip around the coffee mug, her knuckles and the tendons of her hand looking oddly skeletal, her nails filed down to pink nubs. "How did you get here?" she hisses.

SHE WANTS TO talk to me alone. Once we are out in the backyard, she looks from side to side. We are in enemy country. We sit in lawn chairs. Christie stands for a second at the glass door with her arms crossed and then ushers the girls out of the kitchen, out of view.

Again, my mother asks, "How did you get here?"

"The train," I say. She throws me a shrewd, sidelong look. "I'm not a baby, I can take the train."

Her hair hangs in greasy clumps, and I want to shear it off clean like Courtney's. She is wearing black pants and a belted red tunic, and her earrings are big dangling brass dandelions.

"I missed you terribly, bunny rabbit," she says.

"Where were you?"

"Visiting a friend."

"No, you weren't."

"You're right." She sighs long.

"You lie to me. You lie to me all the time, and then you yell at *me* for lying."

"I was in the hospital." And there it is at last. She disappears to a hospital, not to some glamorous tryst or secret second family. I don't know if this is good news or bad.

"Christie says you're a fucking nutjob."

"I bet she does." My mother moves her face closer to mine and grips my knees with her hands. She says, the smolder edging back into her voice, "You know, don't you, that there is nothing you can say to make me love you any less."

"What hospital?"

"Creedmoor. Whenever I get outside myself, James drives me to Creedmoor, in Queens. They know me there."

"What do you mean, outside yourself?" I ask, thinking of my own moments, seeing my body from above or behind, feeling myself floating free of gravity.

"I mean when I want to do things I know I don't want to do."

"Like when the voices say to burn shit?"

"Don't be mean."

"What about the talk underneath talk?"

"What about it?" she snaps. "Can't we be figurative anymore?"

"So, what happens at Creedmoor?"

She runs her fingers slowly along the curling hem of her tunic. "They give me medicine and I sleep. I play checkers. I read."

"Medicine that makes you sleep?"

"No, medicine that brings me back to myself."

"So why do you sleep?"

"Because I am so tired."

"What's so tiring about checkers?"

"Oh, Olivia." She throws herself back in her chair, and

her eyes are hooded and raw. "Has Christie been feeding you? You look terrible."

"*You* look terrible."

She chuckles joylessly in her throat.

I stand up. "Is that it?" I walk into the house without waiting for an answer, letting the glass door snap shut behind me on its metal track. Seeing my mother here is horrifying. There is none of our familiar furniture to justify her strangeness: no future-seekers, no cluttered roof garden, no roiling mysterious ocean to make us seem small and sturdy, our faults diminished by closeness to such a deep unknown.

She will assume her right to take me home, I know. I know, too, that Christie and my cousins will assume that I want to stay here. I have a choice, but this is not the Myla I imagined might arrive, cleanly laundered and apologetic, to whisk me away to an improved life. I think she has told me the truth, but it has not redeemed her; she seems more deceitful than before, and shamefully unmasked, perhaps because it was squeezed out of her by circumstance rather than volunteered. I tell myself that she is just a sad, crazy person from a life I no longer have to live. I have been rescued. I tell myself that it will get easier once she leaves.

SHE STAYS FOR lunch. Laura and Courtney treat her with politeness, as they treated me in those first days, and I feel blithely comfortable sitting close to them, across the table from my mother, showing her what I have gained here in New York. She looks at them with unreadable distance. I feel I am declaring allegiance to Christie simply by being a brunette in a roomful of auburn. Christie spreads out cold cuts on china platters, and my mother takes hers with her fingers. Tom does not appear. He must have an escape hatch. A pod into which he leaps when conflict raps on the front door.

When we finish eating, my mother announces abruptly, "I'm going to walk around." We follow her from room to room awkwardly, like a tour group. She touches things: the grandfather clock in the hall, the hardwood highboy and her father's model planes resting on its dusty top. She climbs the stairs, sliding her hand up the banister as if she does it every day. A few times she stops to glower at artwork that Christie has hung on the walls, bland impressionist mush. As she walks down the dim upstairs hallway, I can feel the process of her remembering. I glance around at Christie and my cousins to see if they are getting this shock of empathy, too, but they seem distracted, contained. They are seeing my mother move through the house, while I am seeing the house move through my mother. There is a sense of brokenness and insufficiency and then a sense of crushing loneliness. My mother turns around to look me in the eye and smiles a grim smile. She knows I'm receiving her.

My mother's bedroom belongs now to Laura, and it is hung with athletic medals and magazine pictures of movie-star heartthrobs. I cluster with my cousins in the doorway. "I had the bed over here," says my mother, gesturing toward the far corner, and Laura nods. She peers at a photo of

Laura sprinting, breaking the tape of a finish line. "Strong legs," she mutters. Laura looks embarrassed.

My mother goes to the bay window, pats the window seat cushions, and stares out at the bright city. "Remember the moon man?" she asks impulsively, and Christie moves past us to join her at the window.

"The moon man and his green moon suit." Christie turns to us. "Your grandfather."

My mother, gazing out, recites, " 'The moon man goes where the moon only knows, and he carries a shovel and pick. And he digs into Mars to find chocolate bars that he feeds to the moon when she's sick.' "

"Grandpa wrote that?" asks Courtney. I would have had a grandpa.

Christie says, "Well, I don't know if he ever actually wrote his stories down. Myla, you remember so well."

Laura says into the silence, "A story that rhymes is a poem," and Christie shoots her a dark look.

My mother turns her attention back to us, stony now. "I have a good memory."

"Why haven't I ever heard that?" I ask her.

"Because I never felt like saying it."

"But now you do?"

"I did for a moment," my mother says haughtily. Laura and Courtney share a look. They are only getting to see my mother in a low time. I wish they could see her on a better day. But it doesn't matter.

A door slams downstairs, and Tom's whistling drifts up

from the foyer. Christie holds up a spread-fingered warning hand to my mother. "Let me tell him you're here," she says, and goes out. Low mutterings rise.

A thought moves across my mother's face. We stand waiting until Christie pokes her head back into Laura's room, asking if we'd mind giving the grown-ups some privacy. Laura and Courtney seem to know the drill. My mother follows Christie out of the room, and Christie closes the door behind her. We hear them go downstairs and into Tom's study.

Laura peels back her blue paisley rug, and the three of us press our ears flush to the damp wood floor. We look at one another's sideways faces as we listen. What will happen now that our parents are alone together? It is like a chemistry experiment, the bonding of volatile substances.

Sound travels in this old brownstone; the floors rest right on top of the ceilings. Still, our parents speak quietly, and most of the time, we can hear only the shape and tone of their voices. I can't make out my mother's voice at all, but Christie's spikes a few times in "so long" and one anguished "Myla" and one "you think" that sounds like part of "what did you think would happen." Tom's voice rises and clips. Hearing this, Laura and Courtney's eyebrows lift. Tom does not raise his voice often. At one point I hear him say, loud and clear, "I'd get her." Then there is quiet and we sit up to rub our sore necks.

"God," says Courtney. "I bet Mom's messing it up."

"Messing what up?" I ask.

"She wants you to stay here."

"Here I am."

"I mean permanently. She doesn't think your mom is, you know. Fit." My first thought is of the three of us arm in arm on the street, wearing school uniforms, watching TV, cleaning the house. Though Laura and Courtney aren't the ones who have to clean this house. There is a weekly maid service.

Laura adds, "She means that our mom thinks your mom should be on lithium all the time if she's going to keep living with you. Am I supposed to say Aunt Myla?"

"What's lithium?"

"It's a mood stabilizer." Laura inclines her head in disbelief at my blank look. "Like, a pill."

"How do you know this stuff?"

"God, Olivia, how do you not?" she says, and Courtney elbows her.

"So what if she doesn't want to be stabilized?"

Laura screws up her face distastefully. "That would be unfortunate, right? That would be masochistic."

I don't know what "masochistic" means, but I can see that they don't understand about divine energies. If a pill would make her better, it would also make her someone else. That idea rankles: She could have been steady all through my childhood—no disappearances, no spinouts, no weeks passed out on the sofa—and she chose to be otherwise. She was selfish, though she would never see it that way. But how much do we really choose these things? I think. How can I blame her for her gift of sight?

"She can tell the future. Sometimes she can tell what you're thinking. She knew all about Jim Jones."

They look at me dubiously.

"She has a chart with tides and constellations, and her psychic energy follows these patterns, like, she gets really, really psychic for a while, and then she has to wait to get psychic again and get her energy back."

"So," says Laura slowly, "is she psychic right now?"

"No, now she's just tired." I get up. "I gotta pee."

I slip into the hallway, closing the door soundlessly behind me. The floorboards creak gently beneath my socked feet. I can hear clanking in the kitchen, and as I take the three steps down to the landing at the top of the stairs, I see my mother and Tom in the foyer below. I insinuate myself into the low shadows. I watch them through the banister posts.

My mother is standing in the middle of the foyer, facing away from me in an unusual attitude of rigidity, her hands clutched together in front of her. A foot away from her, Tom leans against the long wooden mail table with his ankles crossed, looking anywhere but at her. My mother is speaking too quietly to hear. She turns her head to the side to push her hair behind her ear, and her face is full of misery. Then she steps forward, closing the gap between them, and takes hold of Tom's arm at the elbow, her thumb in the crook and her fingers wrapped around, her freckled, slender forearm laid on top of his muscular one, his tawny arm hair, his gold watch. Her body follows her arm forward, and she arches her back to look up at him in a gesture of pleading, of submission. Her voice quavers. I am horrified.

This is when I know, although maybe I knew when I first met Tom, or even earlier, in Christie's oblique attentions.

I have seen this gesture before, this reaching plea. I can't piece together the specifics, but I understand: my mother and Tom. A big red circle around his brown hair, my brown hair. His attached earlobes, mine.

Tom shakes her off and, rattled, blusters through the door to his office and closes it. This office was once my grandfather's, and I imagine my mother as a little girl, doing puzzles on the floor while he typed on an old clacking typewriter. Now it is my father's, and she is not welcome.

As I creep back along the hallway, I probe my interior for some filial emotion and come up dry. Shouldn't I feel something? Nobody knows that I know, so I don't have to fake my way through some kind of tearful reunion, and that is a relief. What I do feel, more strongly than anything I will ever feel for Tom, is vindication. Laura and Courtney are my sisters. I was never mistaken at all.

WHEN WE ARE allowed to come downstairs, Christie and my mother are sitting in the living room. All the furniture here is complementary-colored: soft blues and oranges. A bowl of wasabi peas on the table. Tom is gone.

The afternoon passes in stilted efforts at conversation. I see my mother retreat inward as the minutes tick by: She hunches her shoulders, sinks into Christie's expensive sofa, and unfocuses her eyes. We go out for pizza at a place Christie thinks my mother will remember. "Stand up straight," my mother snaps at me on the walk over. She doesn't know that my leg pains me, and she can't sense it, or maybe she just isn't trying.

I stand with Laura in line, choosing toppings. As Christie pays, I see Courtney and my mother talking at a table. My mother is holding Courtney's right hand cupped in her left, tracing lines across it with a bitten fingernail. I've always found palm reading too intimate for public places. Your hand spread and splayed, all its secret rumples stretched raw, and a stranger touching those secret places, learning things about your heart that you don't know, yourself.

I smack my tray down hard on the table next to Courtney. Courtney, who is once again my sister.

"I'm going to have four kids," she says.

"I thought you were at half strength or something," says Laura to my mother.

"That's true. But palm reading doesn't require any ability. It's just like reading a book."

My mother tells Courtney that her lifeline splits in the middle, which means she will reinvent herself. She will travel a great deal, but her travels will bring her sorrow. I can see the effort of speaking and moving and eating in the lines of my mother's forehead, the heavy pauses between her words. Every now and again she fixes me with a pleading look, a *get me out of here* look. Christie eats primly, wiping orange grease from the corners of her thin lips.

UNDER THE TALL Manhattan streetlights, I stand with my mother by her car. Empty iced-tea bottles litter the backseat, and a paper bag from Wendy's is balled up in the drink holder.

"Do you need to gather your things from the house?" she asks me.

"No," I mumble.

My mother's face collapses as she registers my unwillingness. She buckles against the car and strains there as if against a wind. She cries. Her gulping breaths ring excruciatingly loud and wet in the quiet street. She reaches out to me, and I let her put her arms around me and lay her cheek on my shoulder.

"Why did you leave here?" I ask her. She breathes on my shoulder. "Why did you say my sisters were dead?"

"They *are* dead."

"Did you *love* Tom?"

"Yes."

"If I came home, would it be any different?"

I wait for a long time, and then she says, "No."

She doesn't loosen her arms when I pull away, and that makes it worse, so I shove backward. As I turn away, I catch a glimpse of my mother that I will never shake: the lines of the car lit yellow by the streetlight, all those horizontals interrupted by the dark bedraggled mass of my mother, her wilted posture, the dandelion earrings oxidizing in the jungle of her hair, greasy to the color of rum. Her look heavy and blank like a sky full of rain, and her hands trembling half-raised, caught somewhere between reaching out for me and dropping slack to her sides.

15

·   ·   ·   ·   ·

WHEN WE GET back to Kandy's, Carrie goes right to the hall bathroom. I hear the water running and know she is sticking her face under the tap, washing away the mascara tear smear. It's two o'clock. We find the electrician asleep on the sunroom couch, a long-haired dachshund curled behind his knees. How did I completely fail to notice earlier that Kandy has a dog?

A television audience stops clapping, and Ricky emerges into the kitchen, up the steps from the sunken den. "No calls," he says.

"Thanks for being our man on the ground," says Kandy.

Ricky pours a mug of coffee from a half-drunk pot and slugs it black. He gestures at me with the pot.

"No, thank you," I say. He is trying so hard to be responsible. Maybe that's all it takes. Trying.

Carrie brushes by me. "I'll have some." Ricky pours coffee into a tall blue hand-thrown mug for her, and she holds it without drinking just long enough that he understands and starts rooting through the cabinets for sugar.

Kandy flats her palms on my back and leans forward, tucking her chin over my shoulder. "Are you going to sleep? The kids can stand watch."

Carrie follows Ricky back down the three carpeted steps into the den, slow, so as not to spill her coffee. Through the doorway, I can see them sitting side by side on the leather sofa, their backs to me, watching a late-night talk show. Their slender necks and the hoods of their sweatshirts. The dark wispy hair at the nape: baby hair.

My daughter looks at me over her shoulder. She must expect me to snap out of it any second now, to dump out her coffee and send her to bed. Her lips are bright from wind chap, and her cheeks are flushed, and now that she has washed away her eye makeup, she looks more than ever like my family, like Courtney especially, and like my mother.

"She'll be fine," Kandy says. I don't know which one of us she is talking to. I think of Jake and of all the boys who came after. I remember them angrily, as if they hurt me, though it was almost always the other way around. I wonder which way it will be for Carrie. I think of my grandmother, who took a bottle of painkillers ten days after my grandfather died. Christie is angry with her— with her ghost—that she didn't want to go on living for her children and her grandchildren. That she was so singly devoted. I picture my grandparents as I know them from the family photos, always together, always collaborators. I picture them at a table in a restaurant, alone together, though there are other people in the shot. Then I picture him disappearing and her still there, unsure of where to put her hands, unsure of the reason she's come to dinner or what the point of dinner is anymore, without him, unsure of how to get home and what will be the point of going home, since he will not be there.

Imagine what that love must have been like. Fifty years of that love. In the end, I am jealous of my heartsick grandmother, because the joining of herself with her lover gave her a joy so large that its absence felt to her like the absence of the world.

THE LAST PERFECT day I can remember was the day the chicks came in the mail. Carrie was eleven and Daniel seven. She was still my muddy girl, barefoot and earnest, stealing berries from the colander, standing behind the sofa to braid and unbraid my hair. And Daniel was still Daniel. His rages had started, but it would be a year of escalation before his diagnosis. We waited in the cool morning for the P.O. to open its doors, all four of us, and Sam opened the chirping box right there on the counter to make sure I hadn't been swindled. Our four chicks wobbled together in a squalling fuzzy mass. Carrie reached in and stroked them with the tips of her fingers.

In the car we listened to *Abbey Road*. We stopped to pick up breakfast tacos, and I remember Daniel on Sam's shoulders, jiggling up and down, asking for extra bacon, and the gloss of Sam's black hair in the sun. We put the chicks in the cat-proof brooder box in the spare bedroom and dipped each of their beaks into the waterer, as we'd seen in online tutorials, and then we all sat Indian-style on the floor and watched them dart and huddle and collide. We spent the whole day together in that room, watching, talking, paging through chicken-keeping books. We had rarely been so quiet together, so unprogrammed. We were stewards of new life. I lay on the floor, resting my head on Sam's slim thigh, and Carrie read out a list of parasites to watch for. Daniel positioned the chicks face-to-face, each pair in succession, and introduced them to each other. *Chicken, this is chicken.* We went for a bike ride around Town Lake in the twilight, and then my kids fell asleep together in the hammock. This was back when Daniel could fall asleep anywhere, without fear or fuss.

It wasn't that Daniel's disorder came on suddenly, but that there was an end to the possibility of perfect days. Where before there had been good and bad days, after the chicks arrived, it became good and bad hours. I don't see how this could have been causal, but the hens suffered for the implication. The pre-chicken years, a golden time. When we woke up on Sunday morning, the black Australorp chick was dead. It might have been that the heat lamp was set too low, or it might have been failure to thrive, which is as inclusive a term as I know. Daniel came into the kitchen with the bird in his sweaty palm.

"Oh my God," screeched Carrie, flying toward him. "What did you do?"

"It's okay, it's okay," said Daniel, and I was about to tell him gently that the chick might not prove to be okay, when he said, "It's just dead, it's okay."

See how like my mother.

TONIGHT, PUTTING ON pajamas seems like giving up. I pull the drawstring too tight around my hips and leave it that way. I lie on the bed in Kandy's guest room. I have struggled to be good for my kids. I have been secretive, it's true, and selfish. Sometimes I am Christie, remote and functional, and sometimes I am my mother, a shower of sparks. I want to live in the space between them. I want to be everything my mother was that was good and none of the bad. I know this is impossible, the yin without the yang.

If Daniel is delivered to me this night, I swear I will try harder. I will be better. I close my eyes, and there is Daniel in a boat, Daniel with a suitcase at his father's door, police officers laughing, gullible written on the ceiling. I keep thinking I hear my cell phone ringing, but I surface to silence again and again. At last fatigue takes me over, lets me sink and drift. Daniel broken, Daniel dying, Daniel dead. My mother as James found her, sitting at the kitchen table in her black sundress with the gold buttons and her black high heels, her hair curled with an iron, her head fallen back, her throat arched impossibly. Her mouth wide open, her hands dangling and swollen purple. My thoughts unspool, and I am stolen down into the dark.

. . . . .

16

I WAIT UNTIL EVENING, when Tom is still at work and my sisters are out swimming, and I ask Christie for the rest of the story. She gets us tall glasses of iced tea, and we sit on the sofa in the living room. I can almost see the wheels turning in her head as she calculates what she can say and what she can't.

"Is there stuff you haven't told my sisters?" I ask her.

"You mean your cousins."

"My sisters."

She looks at me in horror, and for a moment I think I'm wrong about Tom. Then she breathes, "Are you angry?" I shake my head. She takes a long pull on her tea and sets it down firmly, nods once to herself, and starts to talk. She bumbles at first, repeating herself. These are memories rarely summoned. As she relaxes, her diction grows sharper, as she must have talked when she was a younger woman, furious with a sister who couldn't help but leave a trail of disaster through the years of her growing up.

I listen closely, putting together images of my mother

as Christie describes her and images of the mother I know in order to form a composite Myla. I remember everything Christie told me that evening and on into the night, in low tones, after we moved to retired old armchairs in the sticky attic so as not to be heard. As I have grown older, Christie's version of events has become part of my own, tempered with my own imaginations and improved by the million small revisions of memory.

THE SECOND FLOOR hallway of the Seventy-third Street house is a dim interior artery, light escaping the door cracks of the northeast-facing rooms and gleaming, pooled in the grooves in the floorboards. When I imagine my mother's childhood, this is where I start. I conjure the hallway as it is now, and I think myself back through time until I am standing in the hallway of my mother's childhood, and it is the same hallway, but now I see posters tacked to two of the doors: Bob Dylan holding up the "Subterranean Homesick Blues" card reading "basement," and Klimt's *The Kiss*. Now there is a white cat shadowing along the baseboards.

This is the theater of selective memory, where imaginary versions of my mother, my grandparents, Aunt Christie, and Tom play out scenes from the time before me. I blink and the story changes. I blink and the sympathetic version scrolls out before me, where my mother is a persecuted lover, weeping into her pillow as my grandmother stands in the doorway, shaking her grave head. I blink again, and

Christie's version flares up, and my mother is unbearable, breaking plates against the wall, cajoling, deceiving, sliding her toes up Tom's leg beneath the lace tablecloth as Christie passes a platter of meat to her father.

Here, I am a glint in my mother's eye, a ghost from a future she hasn't begun to imagine. It is 1970, and she is nineteen. She ties her hair back with thick bright ribbons, she smokes on the stoop, paging through *Les Fleurs du Mal* for her course in the French Romantics at Marymount. She goes to Marymount because it is only blocks from the house; her parents can keep her safe here. Everyone understands safety differently.

She holds the cigarette with a certain arch to her wrist, a certain absorption in her young face. Her skin is perfect. When she walks down the sidewalk, men turn to watch until she is gone. She pretends she doesn't notice, but she does. She checks her reflection in the windows of parked cars.

MYLA ASCENDS INTO the heights of her mania, winging easy on the rush, ideas coming quickly, the poems she read last week opening up and splaying themselves out for her like willing autopsies singing yes yes *yes*. She asks to be excused from dinner, her red hair loose, her left hand fingering chords on the stem of her wineglass, and my grandparents glance at each other. My grandmother is a small, collected woman. After a glass or two, she will tell stories that knock you out, stories from her days of running clubs for U.S. servicemen in Australia, India, Romania. She is a member of the Junior League; she knows every ballroom dance. She tells her friends that her youngest has a nervous condition, and they nod understandingly, as if it is not 1970 but 1870, and Myla bound for an asylum for hysterics.

The psychiatrist at Columbia Presbyterian has told them that Myla is manic-depressive, but they are hoping she will grow out of it. It is not the lows that shake my grandmother. Myla lies princess-still in her canopied bed, her flesh a dead weight on her bones, the passage of time a dull march toward nothing. My grandmother brings her strong coffee and strokes her hair and tells her that she is too pure for this world. Depression is something she can understand; after all, the world can be for her, too, a dull and killing place. It is when Myla hits the highest highs that my grandmother frantically rushes her to Columbia, where she sits stiff-necked and prim in the waiting room, as if this posture will signal to passersby that here is a woman of proud stock, here is a mother whose daughter has not just been found sucking off a stranger in a Central Park grotto or trying to borrow a four-hundred-dollar gown from Bergdorf's or painting all the interior walls of her home different shades of green while everyone was out, drops of paint hardened like mossy coins on the oak veneer of the sideboards, the end tables, the carved Indian chests.

I OPEN THE Bob Dylan door and I'm in Christie's room. Christie's room is orderly. Her intelligence is everywhere. Records in milk crates, framed photographs of friends on the walls, a writing desk pushed flush to the window, where she labors over formulas and proofs. A fish tank.

Here loop all the stories of the sisters. They age from little silken-haired girls racing pet mice in wooden-block mazes, playing house, pulling hair, to lanky preteens sprawled on the rug reading Jane Austen and sharing school secrets, to teenagers, and here they split. Christie in an army-surplus jacket, her chestnut hair darkening, her face growing long and thoughtful, her time spent already on serious things: chemistry and math, the perfect natural logic of the world. She trusts implicitly that, as she ages, more and more doors will unlock for her, and she will never lose the easy facility of her mind. She trusts the world to make sense. She is right. She is lucky.

I get carried away in this room.

My mother, two years younger than Christie and, as a child, easier to love, breaks everyone's fragile hearts when she starts acting out (as my grandmother calls it). Here she cries her secrets out to Christie late at night. They both test into Hunter; my grandfather believes in the quality of American public schools. Christie, budding genius, listens with concern to the tragic epics of Myla's school days. Christie quietly wins a national science fair while my mother's quest for a choir part in *Our Town* has her parents wrapped up for weeks. Myla shoves a police officer at a peace rally and spends a night in jail. Myla brings home four stray dogs a month. Myla gets ragingly drunk at a college party, Christie rescues her. Myla tells everyone about Christie's secret crush and then weeps for a week before she can apologize. By then, it's Christie comforting Myla rather than the other way around. Christie accepts these frequent apologies. This is how her sister is. She only has one sister.

ON THE RIGHT side of the hallway, my grandparents' door is always closed. Their bed is navy-sheeted and made with hospital corners. Flowers on a nightstand are freshened twice a week by the part-time maid. Large windows look out over the patio and the garden, the traffic noise fainter at the back of the house. My grandparents sleep in S shapes, facing each other. My grandmother makes the rules and runs this family, but at night in this room, she is silly with love for her beau. My grandparents read to each other: Hemingway, Faulkner, Fitzgerald. If there is one thing my grandmother is sure of, it is the strength of her marriage. She hopes the same for her girls: husbands of wit and integrity. A deep and certain bond.

She dislikes Tom from the moment Christie introduces him; my grandmother has some prescience in her, too.

WHEN CHRISTIE BRINGS Tom home from college, Myla wants him immediately. She feels like she knows him from somewhere, she feels like he's part of her future. Tom wears a brown corduroy jacket and knows about macroeconomics. He nods as people talk. He rests his hand around Christie's waist when they walk up the stairs.

My grandfather approves of him, and Christie is suffused with pleasure. After lunch, she helps my grandmother with the clearing up. Tom mills around the living room, picking up objects and setting them down. He reaches for a book from the top shelf, and his sweater lifts above his weathered belt, his abdomen soft and taut. Myla sits in an armchair by the fireplace and looks. "I can get you a ladder," she says.

Tom takes the book down and smiles at her, buoyed by a sense of accomplishment at having wanted something and gotten it. Myla crosses her legs in front of her on the footstool, yawns, arches her long back. Tom loves Christie, but he lives in a city of women—women yawning like cats, women in lipstick and blazers running for cabs, goddesses diving into the city pools with strong thighs and shining hair. In the moment of seeing, he loves them all.

Tom is a man my mother loved who did not deserve it. He has no more claim to me than a test tube would have. Yet there he will always be, claim or no claim, in my thoughtless patterns of speech, on the medical history forms I fill out in doctor's offices, in expressions on my children's faces, on my own face. I have his mouth, this Cupid's bow, this slender lower lip.

I OPEN THE Klimt door and I'm in my mother's room. Here is the furniture of my childhood but younger, innocent and just-bought: the ceramic swans, the brass library lamp with its green shade like a banker's visor, the pink and gold saris dripping their tassels across these New York windows. Scattered animal figurines from boxes of Lipton tea. Books stacked in towers by the bed. Mugs on the books, flowers wilting from the mugs.

I was conceived here.

There they are, my parents, Myla and Tom, rutting sweaty, rolling together on my mother's childhood sheets— white with little pink flowers—the duvet kicked to the floor, the white cat watching sleepily from the cupola window seat. A little girl's canopy bed, lace curtains trying their translucent hardest to conceal the act underway. She is off her lithium. This is the first time. Tom gasps, breathless with the thrill of doing the wrong thing, and Myla gasps, breathless with love. Tom is fascinated with the way he can feel the bare outline of Christie beneath Myla's voluptuous movement; this wild thing is inside his fiancée, too, but buried deep, while in Myla it trembles raw on the surface. She bites his lip, she grins. She felt that if she never had him, she would waste away, as if under a spell. (She would cry for rampion, she would promise her firstborn!) Now that she has him, she is a million times strong, she is the happiest girl in the world. She does not even think of Christie. Christie belongs to another story.

Inside my mother, two eggs have traveled a long blue corridor. They cling to the wall of her uterus and they wait.

THROUGHOUT, MY GRANDFATHER is absent. He works in accounts at an aeronautical engineering firm. He drinks brandy in his study with men from Pan Am who wave at Myla as she passes through the foyer with Marymount friends, a blur of bright colors and swishing hair. He goes on business trips that he does not like to explain. He says it's dull stuff, dull as bones. Christie meets him for lunch in midtown, and he orders her roast beef every time. Some-times Myla sits in the backyard to watch him work on his models, gluing tiny plastic pieces and clamping them to set. At times like these, he doesn't hear a word spoken to him. He works with complete focus. He does not acknowledge sandwiches left on the patio table.

He has been unfair to Myla since she hit fourteen and de-veloped her moods. She reminds him of his father, of whom he does not speak. He is deeply ashamed of the gene swim-ming in his code that he has passed to his daughter. Nobody knows the sort of memories that rise when he is made to think of his father: a purple-faced drunk bearing down on him for a hiding, the belt slithering from its loops, the devil in his eye. The outlandish claims of injury, the threatening letters unfurling from the clackety typewriter, the plate-breaking, the neighbors afraid. Then the apologies. The fits of crying, the lost jobs, the hard times. The shame.

It could have helped Myla to know, he thinks later. There could have been a vitamin to take, or a set of exercises to keep the mind strong. It could be his fault, all his fault. His thoughts die with him at sixty-eight, of adrenal failure, in a wing of Columbia Presbyterian not far from the room where Myla used to lie on a couch and tell the psychiatrist what it felt like to feel nothing at all.

MY SISTERS ARE born into the toilet, not into the hands of mournful nurses, as my mother always told me. They are a bloody spurt, they are a stomach cramp. They are unex-pected and then they are gone.

When she feels the first pangs, Myla skips Classics and walks home slowly from Marymount, clutching *The Symposium* to her chest. On her way home, she sees a group of friends and accepts a party invitation. It is spring, and her mother is growing dwarf azaleas in the window boxes. They have put her on enormous doses of lithium and thorazine, and everything is hidden under muffling blankets and tinged sadly yellow. It is only spring because the calendar says so. Her mother and Christie and the psychiatrist are a cruel little coven, meeting at secret locations to calibrate Myla's mind. She feels that they have murdered her senses, but she doesn't have enough in her to stay angry.

The living room is strewn with silver and white boxes, ribbons shredded by the cat, wedding detritus. Christie and Tom have flown to Brazil, where they are eating seviche on some sunbaked balcony, fingering the new gold rings on their fingers. Myla can't imagine that they are making love. Not Christie. She staggers up the stairs and makes it to the toilet.

She grips her knees and bears out the cramp. The sun slants through the high window in the shower, casting trembling squares of light on the bath mat. She wonders if the lithium dulls pain, too, if this pain in her belly is really much worse than she can tell, and she is going to die here, alone on the toilet.

Then she heaves. A weight drops. She parts her legs and sees blood. She gets down on her hands and knees and understands that there, rising to the top of the watery pink pulp in the toilet bowl, are two dolls. No, not dolls. She blinks. They came out knotted together, but they float apart.

She reaches into the mess and lifts them. They have tiny curled fists with grain-of-sand fingernails. Their bodies are like wrung-out washcloths, and the pale globes of their heads have pressed shallow dents each into the other. They are slick with her blood.

Myla sits on her bathroom floor, holding her girls. She hates the sadness she feels because it is a lithium sadness, with measure. This is the moment for her wailing heart, for the leaping feelings of her natural self. She imagines silver dollars tiny enough for their eyes. The heads of pins. She would like to cry. It will haunt her forever that she didn't cry.

She stares at them for a long time, waiting in case there is magic at work, in case they will stir, stretch, awaken. Eventually she holds the girls out over the toilet bowl in her palm and slowly inclines her wrist, so that it might seem to some observant God that they simply fell—oops—back into the murk. They float for a few minutes and then they slip from view. She looks at the clock and learns that hours have passed. She flushes the toilet.

She takes a shower and an aspirin. She hears a door slam downstairs. She puts on a pair of linen pants and a pearl-throat blouse and she goes to the party, where she dances and laughs, though her voice seems to come from a place outside her body. The lithium does that. She feels a strange new hollowness in her abdomen, a yearning to restore a thing she didn't know she had. She drinks a bottle of wine and passes out on her friend's couch. She wakes up to a stern phone call from her mother: *Young lady* . . .

She stops taking the pills.

CHRISTIE ANNOUNCES HER pregnancy in July. Manhattan is tropical; the girls take turns standing before the open refrigerator and bathing in ice water in the claw-foot tub. Nobody will install air-conditioning units here until the nineties. My grandfather gave Christie and Tom the down payment for an apartment in Chelsea, but they were burgled after a month, and they are staying at the Seventy-third Street house until they can find a new place.

Christie does it at dinner. She uses trite language, and it makes Myla angry. "We're expecting a new addition," she says, as if they are planning a new wing of a building. She looks radiant, and this, too, makes Myla angry. My grandparents raise their glasses; my grandmother springs from her seat to hug and gush. The salad warms.

Myla watches Tom, the sweat stains at the armpits of his shirt, his handsome, blank smile as he shakes my grandfather's hand. He doesn't know he's been here before. He thinks he is a first-time father. Of course Tom and Christie will have children. Christie will raise them while Tom wins bread. Myla understands that. Her attraction to Tom has lost all its subtlety and become a biological imperative. All she can feel is her hollow interior, all she can think of are those girls in her bloody palm and how to get them back.

MY MOTHER PURSUES Tom. She seduces, she covets. She slides into months of rapid joy, the lithium pills flushed, dissolving in the same septic water beneath New York City where the bodies of the twins disintegrate. They begin to coalesce as I will know them, fat baby legs, ghostly baby cries. She feels their hunger, their pleasure, the patterns of their sleep. Her attention span allows her to read nothing but poetry. She goes weeks without sleep. She knows the future, she hears the talk beneath talk.

Tom yields easily. Christie is fat, Myla is thin. Christie needs backrubs and space. Christie needs quiet togetherness. Myla is a Bond girl, glittering-eyed and breathless, bolting wildly toward climax. She beguiles him. Tom lies that he is going to a meeting. Myla lies that she is on birth control. They tangle in the empty house once, twice, five times before they conceive me.

It is unglamorous. My father doesn't want me, and my mother thinks I am someone else. Two people. She sends Tom away grinning foolishly, and she rocks on her back on the bed. She stares at herself in the mirror for a long time. She is so grateful for her extraordinary senses: She can feel a burgeoning in her gut like fast-motion footage of plants flowering. This is what her body wants, this is her destiny. She feels that God has given her back her girls and that their guardianship will be the glory and purpose of her life.

I know the kind of mad driving joy that makes my mother's decisions for her. I know how sure she must have felt and how beautiful the future must have looked to her. Though she would never admit it, especially not to me, I know that she must have had moments of regret and shame, too, moments when she came back down to earth and caught glimpses of the tightly sprung trap she had set for herself, and bore it out regardless.

CHRISTIE SAYS SHE didn't know about the affair until Myla started to show, but I don't understand how she could have missed it. She who knew my mother better than anyone, who could tell from her posture and tone of voice if she was up or down or level, couldn't see the flush of wrongdoing on my mother's cheeks. On the other hand, it's easy to believe that Tom didn't let on. In photos, his smile is always the same.

January 1971 now. Christie is eight months along with her twins, Myla three months along with me. Christie's belly is enormous. My mother has been wearing loose, concealing clothing, and it's not until she escorts her sister to balloon around in the pool at the 92nd Street Y that she is given away. She sits in a T-shirt, dangling her legs in the water, as Christie rolls and moans. Myla feels the cosmic rightness of sharing pregnancy with her sister, and she sometimes wishes she could tell Christie. Other times she feels fiercely protective of her secret. Her family and her shrink won't let her live in a dormitory or go on a trip with her girlfriends. They would never let her bear a child. She will be an old-maid librarian if they have their way. So she is waiting them out. She's feeling healthy, even-keeled, this month. She thinks, hopefully, that she has shaken the illness; the gravity of pregnancy has washed it away. She has thought such things before. Each calm period seems like the one that will last forever. Off the lithium, the world has regained its colors and its brilliant associations—the character of things.

Christie puts her hands together to squirt water at Myla, as she has done countless times before in this pool. Myla squeals. In the moment before Myla is found out, they are little-girl sisters, playing old games. Christie grabs her sister's legs and pulls, and Myla splashes into the pool bottom-first. When she comes up, she is laughing, she has forgotten herself, but Christie sees it: the swelling of Myla's breasts under the translucent cotton, the low roundness of her belly. She would never have noticed if she hadn't just watched her own similar body swell and round in the same places. Christie's hand shoots out to feel Myla's belly, and there is the tight skin, the hard bump.

"Oh no," says Christie. "Oh no." She understands without running through the alternatives; she has known, or suspected and not let herself know. In one horrible torrent of thought, Christie sees that she has picked the wrong husband, and that her family is about to supernova, and that she will never want to divorce if she doesn't right now, and she thinks of Tom and she just doesn't.

"I'm sorry," says my mother, and who knows if she means it.

Christie says nothing but grits her teeth and looks at Myla, blood coloring her face. This is how her sister is. She only has one sister.

MY MOTHER'S ROOM. She has turned her overstuffed blue armchair to face the door, and she sits queenlike, awaiting the storming of her defenses. She knows they are coming. She hears their thoughts humming in the walls of the house. And they do come: her mother, her father, Christie, the family doctor. Everyone but Tom.

I picture it as an ambush: my grandparents advancing on her with forceps, a maniacal abortionist ready with knives to cut me out right there in the armchair. Christie says it was civil, and that sounds more likely, but there is no less threat in civility. They file up the stairs and knock on her door, they sit on the edge of her bed, lean against the tall posts. The psychiatrist has told them to put her at ease. Christie tries to sit on the bed but can't and lies back against the pillows, rubbing circles across her enormous belly.

My grandmother moves close and flutters her hand across my mother's arm, trying to squeeze reassuringly but unused to touching her daughters. "We all make mistakes," she says. "It's not the end of the world."

But it is, and Myla knows it. She could never have me here, the bastard daughter of the crazy daughter of the president of the Junior League. How would it *look*? When my grandparents discuss Myla's future, at night, curled together in their navy bed, they wonder what strings they can pull to set her up in a steady low-profile job and who will ever want to marry her. They discuss the costs of hospitalization, how best to word that delicate clause in their wills.

My mother has already chosen me, and she listens to them from a remove because she knows she is leaving. She has begun to detach. She becomes minutely aware of her heartbeat, her breath inflating tiny alveoli in the depths of her lungs, the feeding warmth of my body inside hers. Reality turns inward. Myla watches as the people she loves lose their substance, become transparent. My grandmother is a brisk ghost, gesturing, rings bright on her ghostly hands. Her heart is a black boot. My grandfather is shot through with hot white veins, like photographs of frantic highways taken from great height. And then she sees her sister. There, on the inside of Christie, twisting in the weightless dark, are two baby girls. Not one. Twins. She stares at them until she understands, or thinks she does, and then she feels betrayed: Tom gave them away. He gave her girls away to Christie. She shakes her head to clear it, and the filmy doctor looks concerned. Myla looks down at her own slight swell, and she can't see me, but this is the moment when she knows I am a new girl, not a rebirth at all but a deathless daughter, a never flushed thing.

My grandmother looks to my grandfather, who coughs and says something about a surgeon. Christie looks at Myla, wet-eyed and unable to speak. Myla sits still until they back out of the room. She hears the key turn in the latch; they long ago installed a lock on the outside of her door, and she long ago learned how to pick it. For a few days she allows them to keep her under surveillance and lockdown. She thinks hard about all these people and all the different things they want. And she thinks about me. A few times Christie comes in to sit with her, trying to understand how she could have done what she has done. Myla tells her about losing the twins and about the terrible hollowness that followed. The urgency she felt.

Christie goes into labor late at night. Myla listens to her family rushing around outside her door, packing a bag, voices quick with excitement. She hears Tom say, "Careful," as Christie walks down the front steps. It is the last word she will hear from any of them for fifteen years.

When they are gone, she goes out into the night and buys a junker from a classmate's brother. She loads it with boxes: everything in her parents' house that she can call her own. When you're twenty, it's not running away. It's just leaving.

She kisses the white cat and puts her forehead to his. He is the only one who wishes her well. She drives south. On the New Jersey Turnpike, she feels me kick at the inside of her ribs, and she listens to her old things rattling around in cardboard boxes in the back, and she thinks of Christie screaming in a hospital bed, Tom's hand smoothing the hair from her sweaty forehead. She thinks of her twins crowning between her sister's thighs, her tiny washcloth girls grown fat and pink, gasping that cold hospital air and screaming, screaming, screaming their way into the world she has left behind.

IN THE DREAM, I am back in our house in Austin, dou-
bled over the gray Formica kitchen table, a knifing pain
in my belly. Sam is holding my right hand in both of his,
asking, *What's wrong?* He seems to want to comfort, but I
feel a panicked need to have my hands free, for what I don't
know. His grip on my wrist looks gentle but is not. I kick
the table from beneath, and it shatters upward as if made of
glass. Sam's hands fly up to shield his face, and I sprint to the
bathroom before the shards can rain back down.

I pull my pants down and kick them off, collapse on the
toilet. The pain. My stomach heaves. A weight drops. I part
my legs and see blood. I get down on my hands and knees
and see, rising to the top of the watery pink pulp in the toilet
bowl, three plucked chickens.

Sam? I yell. *Sam?*

I open the door and find the hallway changed. The walls
and floor are made of stone and lit moon blue. The hallway
extends into darkness. I know to be afraid. I see their eyes
first, four gleaming disks, and by then they are already upon

me: two lions with great empty red and gold saddles, stirrups flung back with the speed of their approach. Their mouths are great toothy caverns, incisors yellow and crusted with plaque. Their matted golden fur ripples with contracting muscle, their manes are full of things I have lost: watches, safety pins, bus tickets. They close the distance between us in two bounds, and one enfolds me in its enormous paws and jerks me close, my head back and my throat prone. The moment the teeth touch my skin, I am gone.

The sky above me is a flat blue plate. Shells carve into my back through my towel. Laura lies on one side of me, Courtney on the other. We are all wearing black one-piece bathing suits and no sunblock. Our thighs are bright white. I can feel the top layer of skin crisping, curling away. I feel so tired, like a bag of sand.

Daniel enters my field of vision, looming above me. His face is shadowy, and beyond him it is blindingly bright. *Mom*, he says, *I want to show you something.* Courtney scuttles her hand across the sand and grabs his leg playfully. He shakes free of her. *Mom, come on.* I roll onto my stomach to tan my back. Daniel walks to the bottom of my towel, reaches down for my hands, and hoists me to my feet with a strength he does not have. He points down the beach, where a long, scaly golden dragon is crawling toward the surf. We watch her little legs flail as the tide lifts her from the beach, as she learns to swim.

IT IS NIGHT, and raining. A plastic bag scurries around the poured concrete beneath the Ocean Spirit. The red cars sleep in their tunnel at the end of the track. The white cross-bracing stretches skyward, creaking with the gusts of warm wet air. I can see Daniel's bare feet above me, blinking in and out of view as he climbs.

My camera bounces against my back in the wind, and the foam strap presses into my throat. The wind is a terrific whisper all around me, louder and louder as I climb. I am afraid for Daniel; I must stop him, I must catch him and take him home. The horizontal beams and the joints come down at me one and then the next and then the next. I slow down to rub the rain out of my eyes, and this is when I see my sisters on the beach, walking side by side toward the water in their black bathing suits. Their gait is quick, their legs strong, their arms swinging at their sides. I call out to them, and they turn and wave, and then they walk into the ocean, deeper and deeper, until they are gone.

I look up and see Daniel clinging to a splintered strut, flapping in the gusts. The wind seems to be the darkness itself, knitting itself up and snapping taut like a black cloth, wrapping him up and yanking him out toward the void. I am able, now, to scuttle vertically up the structure toward my son, like a spider. But he is ripped free before I can reach him.

He seems to fall within a spotlight. I can see every pore of his skin, the roundness of each strand of hair, the yellow dandelion fibers contracting in his brown eyes. He is smiling a little, and his look is alert as it sweeps past me to focus on the ground. I think, Oh no, he will land jaw-first, he will not wake up. But then I remember that this isn't his dream.

Now there are hundreds of people on the ground. They hold their arms up and move in small circles. As Daniel plummets, they surge together, so many hands straining up to catch. And then he is among them and they disperse and I can see the one who has caught him, her auburn hair, the glinting buttons on her black sundress, her freckled shoulders. I call out to her, *Wait, wait for me!* She doesn't hear me; I am too high up and the wind steals my breath away. She takes Daniel's hand in hers, and they walk past the Jamaican Bobsled and the Haunted Ruins and the Whirling Teacups and around a corner out of view.

DANIEL SITS IN my seat in the cluttered blue kitchen. My mother sets down three bowls of Cream of Wheat. I can see my sisters in their high chairs and they are, as she always said, the most beautiful babies. Their skin is pearly, their curls fine and blond, their mouths like the tiniest strawberries. Their little fingers curl and uncurl. A game of Monopoly is in progress, Daniel's money tucked in his customary neat piles beneath his side of the board, organized according to bill. My mother's money spills from both pockets of her black sundress. She has lost a five hundred to the floor, but I can't tell her; I realize that I am outside. I am looking through the window above the sink.

My mother spoons Cream of Wheat into my sisters' mouths, taking bites herself whenever she finds a lump. She always loved the lumps; she hardly stirred at all. Daniel is chattering happily, but I can't hear him through the window glass. He says something funny and my mother says something back and they laugh. Even the babies laugh.

I walk around to the front of the house. The tomato plants are heavy with overripe fruit. I pick the ripest and hold them in my T-shirt. I don't want to come home empty-handed.

I knock. I hear her approaching footsteps, I see her shadow grow through the window glass. I feel the weight of her hand on the door pull. I thrill like a feverish child. Any minute now I'll be inside.

S CHOOL IS STARTING. New green Chapin uniforms for Laura and Courtney come in the mail. I skulk around the Seventy-third Street house, mostly healed but feeling wretched. Since my mother's visit, things have continued as before, in a state of suspension, when I thought they would ease back down to earth. Courtney wakes me up with her saltwater gargling across the hall at six A.M. I eat the last ice-cream sandwich, I hog the comfy chair, I kick off my shoes in the wrong places and people trip on them. I am forgiven.

Eventually Christie forces the issue and registers me to start tenth grade at Chapin. She puts a rush on my uniform order, but even so, I will have to start the year in Laura's old blazer, which is too short in the arms. I know there is a tuition deposit, but she won't say how much.

"We need to get your things from the house," she says, "at least." Christie is afraid, and legitimately so, that my mother will return some night, maybe with reinforcements. She needs me to tell my mother that the choice I've made is final. On the drive down the coast, Christie plays the Beach

Boys and wears sunglasses and tries to be fun. I look out the window and think. What if everything is different? What if my absence has cured her, like a sharp blow to the head?

I watch the back of my house flicker by through the trees, and then we are past, headed for the highway exit to loop back around to the front. The parkway is broad and leafy, and the rubber-tire smell goes straight to my brain. The traffic noise, the particular whirring call of a bird, the roadside restaurants and their missing-letter billboards.

We pull into the driveway. The house stands yet, the windows taped and boarded. A blue tarp has been tacked over the hole in my room, but the bottom has come undone, and it billows outward in the breeze. Wild rabbits freeze and stare at me from the lawn. The door stands open. From inside, the roar of a studio audience. Electricity's back on. Christie unsnaps her seat belt and I grab her arm. "Let me go in first." She nods.

As I walk the flagstone path to my front door, I feel a sudden spine-straightening attack of adultness. Even if my absence hasn't reformed her, maybe it has sunk her to a depth of woe such that she would do anything to have me back. Maybe I could state my terms. I would clear out the nursery—that would be the first thing. Somebody would come and trash-pick the high chairs from the side of the highway. I would take her not to her old wallowing ground, Creedmoor, but to the very best psychiatrist, the foremost expert on whatever would help the most. I'd tell her we were going on a picnic. Men in white jackets would wrestle her through the clinic doors, and I'd wait in the car, eating grapes and summer sausage from a picnic basket, and when she came back out, she would be calm and smiling and permanently reasonable and she would say, *Thank you. I didn't know it, but that was just what I needed.*

She is not on the couch. The TV is tuned to *Wheel of Fortune*, the coffee table cluttered with crusty dishes and fast-food wrappers. I go from room to room. The Christmas lights on the wooden cross blink. I pause over the crib, an image flashing before my eyes of Laura and Courtney scrunching up their long teenage bodies to fit in there, pulling the pink frilly blanket up to their chins, laughing their heads off.

She's not in the backyard. The fire pit is a mess of ash. The tomato and pepper plants ringing the house have not died but are heavy with rotting fruit. A few at the corner of the house are crushed and bleed sap and tomato guts around the edges of terra-cotta shards. As I round the corner, I see more and more of these shards, concentrated at the base of the ladder that rises to the roof.

I climb. With each rung, my dread increases, and I make it more inevitable that this will be what I see: She has shot herself. She has slit her wrists. The roof a shining pool of blood. When my vision clears the tar-paper eave of our flat roof, I almost fall. My mother is lying on her back and she is naked. What I think is clotted blood turns, when I look longer, into dirt. Dirt everywhere, scattered around her and over her, and the curling pulled roots of strawberries and basil. A sweet, rotten smell. Dirt on her white stomach and matted to her black triangle of pubic hair. Dirt on her face. Her eyes are closed and she holds a trowel to her chest.

I scramble up, banging my knees. She would think of dirt in this way: ashes to ashes, dust to dust. My first response is not sadness, as I am acutely aware that it should be, but a towering wave of fury that she would do it here, in such a way that I might find her. Christie's voice from the ground: "Everything okay?" My hands fist at my sides. I kick the dirt as hard as I can. The wind picks it up and rains it down on her.

She opens her eyes. Dirt slides from her eyelids and the lines of her face. She looks at me and yelps. Her body, which an instant ago seemed overwhelmingly *dead,* now seems overwhelmingly *naked.*

"Why are you naked?" I scream. Christie's head appears at the top of the ladder.

"Thank you," my mother breathes, but she is talking to the sky, not to me. And I understand: This is some kind of ritual. She thinks she conjured me. She won't even let me own my return.

Christie and I gather my things from the house. We put my clothing in trash bags and heave them into the trunk of Christie's car. I pack up what is left of my darkroom, but I leave my prints behind—boardwalk portraits, gulls in the sky, my friends laughing, my sisters walking in the dark. The pictures feel like dangerous contaminants. To take them to New York would be to invite my old life into my new life, to grant a power and a proof to memories that, right now, I'd rather erase completely.

In the bathroom trash, I see the pill bottles from the hospital, which my mother has not bothered to dispose of secretly

now that I am gone. Thorazine, Tegretol. I pick the orange
and pink pills from among the balled Kleenex and dental
floss. I put them back in the bottles, fifty-fifty chance I've
got the colors right, and put the bottles back in the medicine
cabinet. My mother appears eventually. She slumps on the living room sofa in her pink robe, her legs crossed on the coffee
table looking like somebody else's legs, skinny and showing
patches of a mean sunburn. She watches us carry objects out
of the house. Her face droops as if she's had a stroke.

When the car is packed, we walk back into the living
room and stand waiting. I can hear the kitchen clock slow-
ticking. I tilt my foot out of my sandal and dig my pinkie toe
through the carpet loops. Finally, my mother says to Christie, "You win, I guess."

"No, Myla."

My mother jolts to life. She screams, "I have a lawyer
who will have her back here in days. Days!"

"A lawyer's not going to change Olivia's mind," Christie
says in a level tone that I know she means as gentle but that
my mother will take as condescending.

My mother laughs. "You shouldn't fuck with me, you
of all people should know not to fuck with me. I know the
method and the minute of your death." She rests her face in
her hands, elbows on the table, and sighs long. She raises
her eyes to Christie and talks through her spread fingers.
"She doesn't even look like me. She looks like you. You put
her in me as a trick. You're like one of those birds that lays
its eggs in other birds' nests. So I would feed her the most,
so the others would get nothing."

Christie looks at me. I can't speak. A tiny demon in my mouth is hanging on to my top and bottom teeth, clamping my jaw shut. My mother lolls her head sideways on the sofa pillow and closes her eyes. "You want to go with her?"

I nod, but her eyes are closed, so she can't see it. I wait for her to open them, and she waits for me to speak, and neither of us will concede. She doesn't move for the longest time. So I leave.

And that's it.

I ADOLESCE. I become a Mader, though there is no legal transfer of custody. I always expect her to come for me—I hope for it and I dread it—and I dream out the window during classes at Chapin: my mother swooping in on a broomstick, a man in a hat on the street lifting an elastic mustache and winking at me, taking my hand, a long strand of auburn escaping from a short wig. But she does not come.

Neither do I go to her. At first I think I will be forced to visit—that Christie will drive us all down at Christmastime or next summer. But Christie is as avoidant as I am, and she doesn't bring it up. I am so busy, always, with courses and camps and trips. It is easy not to think about the decision I am making, and besides, I am still so angry. I am angry that my mother does not come, and I would be angry if she came. In the grips of this new normal, I can see every way she slighted me, everything my sisters had that I did not have. I picture myself as a little girl, alone in the house, unbathed, eating cereal out of the box, lying to the neighbor lady when she stuck her head in to ask why the car was gone. I think,

My mother can come to *me* when she's ready to apologize. Only, she never does; she never will. Is it pride that keeps her away, even after six months, a year, two years? Shame? Some psychic intuition of misfortune to come? Or is this the first and only time that she has taken a decision of mine seriously? I do not have the wherewithal to ask her, so I will be left with this bitter puzzle for the rest of my life.

Tom spends less and less time at the Seventy-third Street house, and my sisters don't know why. They stop believing that he works such long hours; they recognize the frailty of his alibis. They conference gravely when he is gone, and when he does appear in the foyer, stamping off snow, they flutter to bring him his Scotch and take his coat. It is not hard for me to keep the secret of my parentage from my sisters; I am a facile secret-keeper. They will learn the whole truth from Christie in a few years, once they're living on their own, and they will be angry. I will be a wedge driven between Tom and his family. For now, though, he doesn't know what to do with me. He worries his hands and reads the paper. He jumps when he finds me in unexpected places. I can't say I don't enjoy making him squirm.

Sometimes I find Christie sitting in the backyard doing nothing, with the watering can or the shears in her lap, and I feel sorry for something I'm not sure I should feel sorry for. At these times I go back inside and pretend not to have seen her.

I wear my camera less and less. I find myself taking photos only when other people might, at parties or on trips. I stop needing to pin everything down. My split with Jake,

Pam, and Kandy is complete, as it must be. I see them in dreams, but in daylight I learn to keep the past out of my thoughts. I do not want anyone to call me crazy, not anymore. I do not want to be a visionary or to be notable in any way at all.

Despite all this, I am not a different girl in New York. I can't stop lying. I smoke, I drink, I make questionable friends. I buy hallucinogenic mushrooms and share them with my sisters. Courtney becomes convinced that she is following a green glowing path below the sidewalk, and Laura and I follow her, snickering, all the way to midtown. None of this has the character of the summer, though, and it is not until a year and a half later, when I am seventeen and have my first documented manic episode, that I understand why. Christie is the one to point it out to me after a few days: my sleeplessness, my darting attention, my flashing temper, my rapid rhyming laughing speech. I will never know if my mother understood what was happening to me all summer and refused to address it, or if she was so deep in herself that she couldn't see it in me.

I sit opposite my first psychiatrist, Dr. Kaiser, a short, glowing man. He describes for me things I thought were mine alone: the glimmering and speed of things, the sense of being chosen, the aching thing that seems like love but isn't. He uses the term "pressured thinking." I am embarrassed, as if he has seen me naked. Dr. Kaiser hands me my diagnosis, my inheritance. I make my own chart, and there is nothing divine about it. My lines spike and plummet randomly, and for long, long stretches they plateau.

My chart looks like an EKG—a strong but irregular heartbeat. Soon I have my own little orange pill canisters full of my mother's poison: lithium. For me, it works. It is not the dull muffling thing it was for her. They prescribe smaller amounts now than they used to, and it doesn't feel like anything to me so much as the absence of a threat. Some small dark thing that used to crouch in the corner of my brain stands up and walks away.

WHEN JAKE MADE it home in August 1987, he went to my mother's house looking for me. I didn't know this until years later, when he looked me up at Penn State and we sat drinking thin coffee in the student union. I apologized, but by then it didn't matter. He had a Mohawk and a graduate fellowship in economics at the University of Oregon. I was a bitter story he told each new girlfriend, a failed first love. He said he'd driven to my house the morning after his parents collected him from New York. He found my mother asleep in the sunny backyard, burned pink, and she told him I was safe and sound and coming home soon. He said she made him a grilled-cheese sandwich on the fire pit. I asked him what they talked about, and he shrugged, but I don't believe he'd forgotten. I imagined it and felt a guilty solipsistic thrill: two adversaries, my brokenhearted lovers, drawn together to mourn my absence. My mother was still alive then, and I could afford to think that way when I allowed myself to think of her at all.

Kandy found me at the funeral. Her transformation was still fresh. She wore a gray turtleneck, and her hair was bobbed and natural brown. We sat outside the funeral home and smoked cigarettes and talked about movies we'd seen lately, and it was the only thing that got me through. Pam never came after me. I don't blame her. I didn't look for her, either. I hear that she's a math teacher in West Orange. There are those people in your life who matter instantly, on another plane, and you have to marry them or kill them or run the hell away, you can't do it halfway. I hope her house is full of paintings. I hope somebody loves her.

WHEN JAMES FINDS my mother, it's the police who call me. I am twenty-one. I am studying for a final in Renaissance culture. I have never gone back to Ocean Vista, not even for a visit. My roommate watches me take the call. Outside our window, petals blow by, a boy throws a Frisbee for a dog. "I'm so sorry to have to tell you this," says the voice on the phone. The voice asks me if I would like to arrange for a funeral, if I would like to speak to the funeral director, he's right here, and so on, in such a way that by repeating "yes" over and over, I commit to a time and date, to a flight home and an announcement in the paper. In New York the police would not do this. The voice calls James "her companion, Mr. Feldman." In the paper I will find him listed beside myself as her survivor. I am told the facts: a toxic level of lithium in the blood, a painless death at the kitchen table. I wonder who prescribed lithium for her again, or if she asked for it, if she thought it the most fitting poison. I sometimes imagine that it was an accident and that she was trying earnestly to be well. The rest I feel I know.

James unlocks the door with his key, one of so many on his brass key ring. He has a pizza in one hand, or a bag of fish fry. He calls out to my mother, *Hey-o, anybody home?* It is dusk in my imagination, and light pools in the low places of the living room. The air stinks of incense. He moves slowly through our house with his slumping gait, and as he turns in to the kitchen, he drops what he is carrying—the pizza smacks, the fish fry bag spills loose breading across the carpet.

There she is in her black sundress, her head slung back. That arched throat. Her skull heavy in her skin. She has arranged objects of importance on the table: my sisters' sterilized bottles, a little pile of sand, a bird's wing, a rusty trowel. A half-drunk bottle of wine, a glass bearing the pink imprint of her lips. Always there are things I can't make sense of. Worry dolls. Ketchup bottle tops. A strip of condoms. Spanish coins. Sometimes I imagine there is a picture of me on the table, sometimes I don't.

James presses a finger to her neck. He hovers over her, making the phone call, describing what he sees. While he is waiting for them to come, he lifts her bloated hands into her lap and massages them gently. He has never felt so alone. Always before, she has called him. Always before, he has come in time.

Here is what I would say to those people who would judge her, what I say to myself on some days: What if all the transcendent moments of your life, the sound-track moments, the radiant detail, the gleaming thing at the center of life that loves you, that loves beauty—God or whatever you call it—what if all this were part of your illness? Would you seek treatment? I have, and sometimes I wonder if the greatest passions are just out of my reach. And sometimes I am so grateful.

I imagine what she was thinking, where she thought she was going. I imagine she has gone to her twins. She is rocking them, one in each arm, in a new place. Maybe I am the ghost there, my camera to my eye, peering through the windows of their house, a box by a new parkway, the air thick with salt from a new ocean. She tells them, Your sister is a star in the sky and a shadow on the grass, she will follow you through your life, and you will never be alone.

. . . . .

I SWIM UP OUT of sleep. It feels like there is a crust to break through, a pudding-skin membrane between dreaming and not dreaming. The images from my dream hold fast with uncommon vividness: the lunging lions, the chickens in the toilet, the Monopoly money spilling from my mother's pockets. This is not me, I think. This is not how I dream. This is Daniel talking to me.

I swing myself out of bed and grope for my shoes in the dark. I will not stop to think or I will stop altogether. I sling my purse over my shoulder and go. The carpeted stairs absorb my footsteps. I pass the living room doorway and backtrack to look in on Carrie over the back of the sofa. She is sleeping hard, breathing audibly, like a pug. Her left arm is tucked tightly under her head and her eyelids flutter. Ricky is asleep on another chair, his arms crossed over his chest. Outside, I pull the front door gingerly until I hear the click. I cross the dewy grass to where my car slumbers in Kandy's driveway. The dashboard lights cast a pale glow over my striped pajama pants.

I drive north. Stoplights blink red. I wend my way to old familiar routes. A yellow convertible tears around a corner, and someone throws something out the window—a plastic cup, a sparkling spray of soda under a street lamp. I can still feel the heat from my dream. I put my hand to my flushed cheek and trace the web of pillow marks.

I make the turn that should take me home, but the street is different. It used to be straight through, but now it curves out to the highway. They gave us an exit finally. In the crook of that curve, in the place where our house stood, is the Wendy's. They have paved over the grass in some prescribed corporate shape, but there is no curb where the asphalt ends, nothing to shore up against. It is a weird black island in a field. Wendy grins down at me from her neon sign. The windows are aggressively lit but only a few cars are parked in the lot, at the far edge of the asphalt.

I pull in, and it's the angle of the turn that gets me, maybe, or some subconscious neural response to this spot, the precision of longitude and latitude. I feel it with my whole body: to turn up the drive, to swing my feet out of the car, to walk up our crooked path, to watch my mother's ankles in front of me and the hem of her long skirt swishing, revealing flagstone after flagstone. I'm home.

I park across two spots. I run toward the doors, and at first I think I am still dreaming, and this is the kind of dream where clothing is heavy and you can't get where you want to go, but I am proved wrong by my hand on the cool door pull and the waft of hamburger as I pass through. A boy with a shaved head regards me blearily from the registers. I turn and there is Daniel.

He is sitting in a booth facing me. Before him, a mess of silver foil and grease-spotted fry cartons. He says, "Hi, Mom," and scrambles off his seat, and I surge toward him and he is in my arms and crying a deep hiccupping cry into my shirt. I clutch him to my chest. He is safe. He is here. It is over.

When I can bear to, I ease off so we can look at each other. His pale teary face, his wild hair. "Are you okay?" I ask him. He nods. He slides back into the booth and I sit down opposite him. "What happened? Did something happen?" He shakes his head and balls a piece of foil in his palm, smooths it out, balls it again. "How did you get here?"

"I walked." He exhales. He is in his quiet room.

"How did you know where it was?"

"Where what was?"

"This." I wave my arm around the restaurant. I can see it, by the craggy tree line outside the windows and by my gut: We are in my mother's bedroom. We are sitting in the middle of the bed.

"Sorry I got so mad. I got really mad."

"Were you hiding?"

"At the beginning."

I don't want to lecture him on danger. I know he knows. I know he's sorry. "Why didn't you come out when you saw us leaving?"

"I was going to, but it was, like, suddenly you were gone."

"What do you mean? Did you get distracted?"

"No."

"And then what did you do?"

"Nothing."

"Daniel, it's been—" I check my watch. "Seven hours."

He furrows his brow. "I hid and then I walked around for a while and then I came here." I scan him again for damage. He seems whole, or maybe slightly more than whole; he is giving off an energy such as you feel in dancers who have just finished dancing and stand facing the audience, breathing.

"Why did you come *here*?"

"I met this lady." He looks at me steadily. "She had red hair. She knew me."

"You mean on the sign? Wendy?"

"No!" He squawks with laughter and then quiets. "That's silly."

I see it more clearly now, my mother's house enclosing us. The acne-cheeked register boy slumps on our cream chenille sofa, chin in his hand. Blanche shoves her muzzle into the cooling fries. There are my sisters' cribs, on either side of the condiment bar. "Do you know," I ask my son, "where we are?"

He nods.

"Did she say anything to you?"

"Yeah," he says, "she talks a lot." He smiles at the empty table beside our booth and says to it, "You do!"

Where has my son spent this night, in what dimension? I feel myself crumble to pieces, and I trust him. I turn to face the empty table. If I try, I can imagine that the air looks denser there. Daniel rests his head sideways on his small shoulder, studying me. I wish I could see what he sees. I want to put my ear to her singing chest, to wrap her hair around my fingers. I have things I need to ask her. If Daniel is going to see ghosts, I need to know the rules. He goes back to crinkling his foil, but I know he is watching me. Watching us both. Maybe she is looking at me. Maybe she is leaning forward, one arm on the tabletop, her silver bracelet tinkling against the linoleum, her lips parted, almost smiling. Or maybe she is looking at Daniel.

My son looks tired and brilliant, his elbows planted on the greasy table, his skin so thin and fine, the blood beneath pumping boldly and without my help. He seems double to me, both the most and least familiar person in the world. It occurs to me that I will never know what he saw tonight or where he went. I will lose him this way again and again, and find him, just as I have lost and found Carrie tonight, as well. He will open doors that are closed to me; he will hear the talk underneath talk. Though I stand beside him, we will always be in different rooms, and I think this is how it always has been, though I have never seen it so clearly.

Now I imagine my mother reaching to smooth the hair from my forehead. And now, under Daniel's encouraging look, I can imagine her speaking. I can imagine her doing anything. I can make her do handstands or dance with a hat and cane. I can make her happy, I can make her mad. She says, *Olivia, my tiny bunny rabbit, I am home!* She says, *Shall we go swimming, you and I?* She says, *I forgive you.* Only, it doesn't mean anything. In me, there is no conduit to her. In me there is only me. So what I must do, I can do alone, and I do it silently and completely: I forgive us both.

Daniel shudders, and I think he is going into a trance or about to be possessed or something, but then he only vomits a little into a fry carton. I swing around to his side of the booth to hold him. I run my fingernails through his hair. "Poor sickie."

"I ate five bacon cheeseburgers," he says, and smiles sheepishly.

I look for the register boy, thinking only now to be angry, but he is gone; he must be in the back, in what was once my bedroom. I hoist Daniel onto my hip like a toddler and he clings, his forehead to my shoulder, his legs around my waist. I carry him out into the parking lot, into the cool night. The stars above us burn through the smog. The grass around the asphalt island ripples with wind and with the shadows of the swaying trees. Daniel will get heavier, and soon I will not be able to carry him like this. He will turn into a teenager and then into a man. He will struggle with his illness and his gifts. Carrie will keep moving away from me and then, I hope, come back. They will change constantly, and I will let them.

Daniel is asleep before I lower him into the passenger seat of the car. I drive back to Kandy's house flush with calm, and when we get there, the lights are all on. Everyone is inside drinking coffee, waiting for us, hoping that we are safe, that we are together, that we are ready for what comes next.

Acknowledgments

.   .   .   .   .

With thanks to:

Wendy Weil, in memoriam, for taking me on, for finding this book a home, and for all her kindness and wisdom along the way;

Maya Ziv, my champion at Harper, for her vision, her diligence, and her boundless enthusiasm;

Emma Patterson and Emily Forland, for their faith, hard work, and expertise—and Emma, for that first email, which put so many fears to rest;

Everyone who read early sections and drafts of this book, for invaluable criticism, encouragement, and expertise: Jim Magnuson, Stephen Harrigan, Antonya Nelson, Elizabeth McCracken, Paula Smith, Jim Hynes, and Ashley Angert;

The Michener Center for Writers at UT-Austin for the support, the fellowship, the barbecue, and the gift of three incredible years, and to my impossibly talented cohort there, who taught me so much, and especially Jen Graham, a brilliant reader and friend;

The Mid-Atlantic Arts Foundation, the Millay Colony

for the Arts, Norton Island, Interlochen Arts Academy, and Vermont Studio Center for providing me with time, space, and community at several crucial moments that allowed me to finish this book;

My parents, for all their love and encouragement, for never suggesting a more stable career direction, and for filling my childhood with stories;

And most of all Russ, my first reader and my best friend, for every day.

ABOUT THE AUTHOR

SARAH CORNWELL grew up in Narberth, Pennsylvania. Her fiction has appeared in publications including *The 2013 Pushcart Prize Anthology*, *The Missouri Review*, *Mid-American Review*, *Gulf Coast*, and *Hunger Mountain*, and her screenwriting has been honored with a Humanitas Prize. A former James Michener Fellow, Sarah has worked as an investigator of police misconduct, a writer in the schools, an MCAT tutor, a psychological research interviewer, a toy seller, and a screenwriter. She currently lives in Los Angeles.